The Lying Tongue
A Novel

Jesús E. Beltran-Ruiz

ISBN 978-1-7389400-0-4

DEDICATION

To my wife, Kaitlyn, who always believed in me.

CONTENTS

THIS IS A WORK OF FICTION

Names, characters, businesses, organizations, places, events
and incidents either are the product of the author's imagination
or are used fictitiously. Any resemblance to actual persons, living or dead, events or locales, is entirely coincidental. Also, I
can't afford to pay for an editor, so please take it easy on me.
It's my first novel.

"There are six things that the Lord hates, seven that are an abomination to him: haughty eyes, **a lying tongue**, and hands that shed innocent blood, a heart that devises wicked plans, feet that make haste to run to evil, a false witness who breathes out lies, and one who sows discord among brothers."

Proverbs 6: 16 - 19

Part 1: The Coffee Shop

1

My bedroom was dark and cramped. The only light, weak and artificial, was cast by the microwave's digital clock to my left. I had been struggling for the better part of the last hour trying to fall back asleep. I do know, however, when I'm pursuing a lost cause, so at quarter past three I gave up. I took my thick red blanket off my stiff body, got up and turned the light on.

After a few moments of sitting at the end of the bed, blinking and rubbing my eyes to get used to the brightness of the room I took my uniform from the old stereo at the far end of the room— where the tv used to be and which I used as an improvised coat rack–, dusted the flour and powdered sugar off it, and started to get dressed. The thick, cardboard-like brown shirt already had permanent stains from sugar glaze and cooking oil, so patting it did little to improve its appearance. *What's that silly thing middle-aged people say all the time?* I thought after I saw in the mirror how ridiculous I looked with the coffee shop's branded visor wrapped around my head. *Oh yes. Another day, another dollar.* By then I was already wondering multiple times a day how much longer it would take me to snap and quit my job, each unrestful night and early morning start adding a straw to the camel's back.

At the beginning of the summer, however, I actually felt grateful for getting that crappy job, always keeping in mind all the trouble I had gone through to even get interviewed for it. In the end, the only reason why I was even offered that morning baker position was because Jude, my best friend, was already working at the coffee shop and had put in a good word on me when I applied for it. Had it not been for him, I'm sure that the boiled-cabbage-smelling old lady who took my resume would have tossed it in the garbage as soon as she saw the hispanic name at the top.

I went downstairs to the washroom, brushed my teeth, wet my hair and combed it. That was the extent of my morning routine. I had started showering at night, right before going to bed, so that I didn't have to wake up earlier than I already had to in preparation for going to work.

It was mid-June and the mornings were crisp and fresh so I went back upstairs to grab my bike and leave. It was still pitch black except from the street lamps, so I turned on the little portable lights from my bike and rode into the darkness.

I arrived at the coffee shop at four o'clock and started my routine. I went to the walk-in freezer and took out the trays of frozen donuts, bagels and other high on trans-fats baked goods. Then I transferred them one by one into the two ovens, turned the power on and headed to the smaller fridge at the other end of the room and took out the pre-cooked slices of bacon to warm them up in the microwave, because we don't have a grill. That would make what we cook resemble real food a bit too much for head office's taste.

The coffee shop likes to lie to your face and claim that your baked goods are always fresh, when in reality they were made in a factory in Toronto and reheated (by me, in this case) in an industrial oven. Another wonderful thing about my workplace is that management also expects bakers to have everything ready to go in the kitchen–donuts, bagels, croissants, egg patties, sausage patties and so on–by six in the morning but that was never the case. I was lucky to have most things at the front display case at quarter to seven.

The following three hours of my routine were always a blur of angry and underpaid co-workers yelling to each other to get the orders ready for the angry and already-late-for-work customers, with me in between trying to anticipate which items would run out so that I could reheat more of them.

At around ten thirty most customers would be already at work, and the few ones still pestering us with their caffeine and sugar needs were often less confrontational, so I would allow myself to slow down just enough to catch my breath.

The last hour of work was always the one which one could have somehow accurately described as normal. Dull. Fine. Just fine. And I'm sure that, had all my shifts been as inoffensive and boring as that last hour of my work day always was, I would have indeed lasted all summer working at the coffee shop. After all, it was my first job in Canada, and even though I was technically a part-time employee, only making fourteen dollars an hour, it was a lot of money for me if you considered the fact that minimum wage in Mexico was somewhere around two hundred pesos, or fourteen dollars and seventeen cents, Canadian. Per day.

But my days working at the coffee shop were numbered and it wouldn't take too long for another much more exciting "career opportunity"–in appearance only, though–to present itself to me, like an oasis in the middle of a desert of mediocrity. Now, looking back at that dreadful summer, I'm certain that accepting that job offer was the single worst mistake I could have made, because while I didn't pull the trigger on that fateful night, I can't begin to imagine how different our lives would have been this day if I hadn't gotten us involved with Franco D'Amico, or perhaps, I'm just too ashamed to do so.

2

If there is something that I actually liked about working at the coffee shop was the immense feeling of relief, catharsis even, that I had when I'd bike back home after a monotonous and tedious–and somehow still physically demanding at the same time–day of work.

That summer I was obsessed with the hit song of the summer *This Is America,* and also with another gem from a few years prior called *Stolen Dance*, and I'd always listen to both back to back as soon as I jumped on my red bike's wide and plush woman's seat. It was my ritual, oddly comforting. Restorative even. The way back home was downhill and it made my ride quite enjoyable, gentle gusts of wind caressing my face and drying the sweat off my brow.

When I reached the big willow tree on (the rather unoriginally named) Willow Street I turned left and got off the bike and pushed it to the backyard–letting it rest next to one of those expensive pre-made sheds you can buy at Home Depot–of the house where I was staying.

Despite my best attempts at entering the house through various different access points–doors, windows, the entrance to the basement/doomsday bunker–Cliff would always shout a warm greeting at me and guilt me into having a small conversation with him about work, school and my boring and uneventful personal life.

"Marco, my boy! How was work today?" he said. He had perfectly combed graying hair plastered with gel, a bushy yet neat goatee and a very long nose that always reminded me of an eggplant.

"Same old, same old. How's your day so far Cliff?" I replied as usual.

"Amazing! I got up at five in the morning and spent just over an hour doing cardio at the gym and then another hour lifting weights, all of that before I got home to do some office work! Pretty impressive, huh?" I never found out what that "office work" was. He claimed he was a financial advisor from an international financial firm which had no physical offices in Canada–hence his home office–, but whenever I asked him questions about his job, he would suddenly stop being as chatty as he normally was, and I never cared to push him further to tell me any details anyway.

"That's good to hear," I replied. "I'm exhausted from my glamorous job baking donuts so I think I will go have a little nap before I hang out with Stella".

"Okay buddy, but I still think you should get some more exercise, you're starting to look a little jiggly. When you first got here your goal was to lose ten pounds and now I wouldn't be surprised if you weighed fifteen pounds more than you did back then!" Cliff replied, typing something on his laptop without really looking at me.

"I know. I will go back to the gym when school starts again next fall, but for now I will just go to bed. See you later, Cliff."

"You bet!"

I shuffled to Cliff's oldest son's room, which was now mine since he had moved away to Toronto for college a few years before. His name was Mike and up until that point I had never met him, even though he apparently always visited Cliff on Christmas and other holidays, whenever he could.

I opened the door of my bedroom and I didn't even get to walk three steps before I collapsed on the bed. I thought I'd drift away into a deep and restful sleep in no time, but the sun was bright and strong, shining through my curtains as if they were not even there and illuminating the room to a degree that made sleeping almost impossible.

After about forty minutes of tossing and turning on my bed, I gave up, and thought maybe it would be a good thing to skip my nap to let my tiredness accumulate in me like poison and make it easier for me to fall asleep at night. *Maybe I won't need to take three pills of melatonin tonight,* I thought.

3

At 5:30 PM I got out of the house (this time Cliff was not home, so I avoided another one of our classic uncomfortable talks on my way out) and went straight into Stella's car. It was a dark blue Mazda 3 that she had just bought a few weeks ago, with the works: bluetooth, a full-color digital screen, heated seats, remote-start. She was still living with her parents and had a pretty good job working for a fancy daycare–the one which rich stay-at-home-moms who love pilates, book clubs and chai lattes put their kids in for up to ten hours a day despite not needing to–, so she was able to save up more than enough money for the down payment.

I sat on the passenger's seat, closed the door and kissed her. I had been in a constant state of disbelief since the day she decided to date me, not only because she was absolutely gorgeous, but also because she had a kind heart to match. She had long, brown hair with slight waves at the bottom and fine lips that housed the warmest smile I had ever seen, one of those ones that continued all the way to her eyes, providing proof of its sincerity and making her appear as if she were squinting. One day I asked her if she could still see when she smiled. She laughed and said she could.

"I missed you," she asked after making out in the car for a bit. "How was your day?"

"Not too bad," I answered, because even though it had been rough thanks to my lack of sleep, it could have been worse, like the time one of the ovens at work was out of order, so I got yelled at more than usual for a couple of painful and slow hours until the maintenance guy came over and fixed it.

"Did you have supper already?"

"No, I had a big lunch at work because food is dirt cheap now with my employee discount. But I could eat now."

She started driving and said, "Okay, good. I told my mom you'd probably come home with me for supper again today so she saved some food for you, too."

When we got to her parent's place we ate roast pork (not my favorite main dish) with garlic mashed potatoes (my favorite side-dish) and veggies (meh), and after excusing ourselves we went up to her bedroom to *cuddle* and watch a few episodes of *Friends*.

Stella did get the chance to watch *Friends* for a while, but by then my body had reached its limit and I finally fell asleep.

4

I woke up again an hour later, feeling more tired than before and went out for a drive with Stella. We stopped at a McDonald's at my request and I got a medium fry.

"You're obsessed with fries," Stella said, matter-of-factly.

"Yeah, well, my parents never let me have much fast food back in Mexico so now I'm just making up for it."

Stella stole a few fries from me once every few minutes and kept driving until about nine thirty. The sun was down but there was still a bit of light out, which made me feel sad and almost disappointed when she turned around to take me back to Cliff's so that I could go to bed early and get at least five hours of sleep to recover from another day at the coffee shop. That was the bare minimum I needed in order to sort of function properly, and it had been over a week since the last time I had reached it.

Stella stopped the car outside of 117 Willow Street, and I kissed her goodbye, got out of the car and waved at her as she drove back to her house.

There were two cars in the driveway. Cliff's and his girlfriend's. Anna, another immigrant (from Greece) that had moved to Canada in 1985, recently married and very pregnant. She knew almost no English back then, which I'm sure only added to the confusion and existential dread that she had experienced in her first year in the country, but now she was quite fluent with her accent still noticeable but not distracting at all. Although the idea of divorce had been planted in her head early in her toxic marriage, she decided to stay with her abusive husband until their only daughter had gone to college. "That was the worst mistake I ever made," she'd said to me one night while Cliff was playing poker with some of his friends. "There's nothing worse than wasting years of your life sucking your ex's hairy penis because you were too scared of being single again. I don't want you to ever be in that position, okay?" I didn't like dicks, despite what my high school classmates said behind my back.

"Okay," I replied.

She met Cliff six years ago after having brief flings with a few less than spectacular balding middle aged men, or as Anna described them, *a bunch of creepy old guys* that she found on an online dating website. Cliff might be a bit overbearing, but based on what Anna had told me about her past *lovers* (also her words, not mine), he was a knight in shining armor compared to them. "And he's got his life put together," she added, "half of the other people I slept with back then didn't even own a house."

As soon as I stepped through the door a sweet and spicy smell welcomed me, making my mouth water. I suspected Anna was making goulash.

"Hey buddy, how are you?" Cliff said to me from his leather couch in the living room, a can of beer in his right hand and the TV remote in the left.

"Not bad," I said, flatly, not having the energy to start a conversation, so I walked to the kitchen to have a look at Anna's food instead.

"Hey Marco, how are you?" Anna said, stirring a big pot of goulash, just as I thought.

"Not bad, a little tired though. How are you?"

"I'm good, thanks, just making some goulash. Do you want to have some? It's almost re–"

"No! Him and I are on a diet!" Cliff yelled, still from the living room.

"Is that so?" Anna said, and winked at me.

I shrugged. "Apparently."

"He's gaining weight so we're both on a diet now, hon. He can hang out with us but no more food for him. I'm sure he already ate."

"I mean, he's not wrong," I said to Anna.

She ignored my comment and proceeded to pour goulash in a tupperware with a red lid and handed it to me.

"Thank you," I whispered, heading back to my room. Anna gave me a smile that reminded me of my own mom and went back to stir the pot.

I took my clothes off, put my pajamas on and fell asleep as soon as I put my head on my pillow. I had a long and uninterrupted sleep with no dreams.

5

The following weekend could be considered uneventful for most people, but that was the exact thing I needed after a busy week of hard, minimum wage work at the coffee shop.

I was out and about most of Saturday, but that didn't stop Cliff from trying to give me life advice every time I went in and out of the house. At one point I had to go back to my room to change clothes after I accidentally wet myself with a Diet Coke during lunch–because back then I thought that drinking Diet Coke instead of regular Coke would be of much help when my diet consisted of a daily intake of three thousand calories that came straight from ultra-processed foods–so that I looked presentable for supper.

"Oh jeez buddy, you're heading back out already?" Cliff asked as I was walking out the door.

"Yeah, we're going out for supper with some friends"

"Right on, right on," he replied. "Where are you guys eating?"

"We're going to try that new sushi place out," I said, hoping to get the small talk out of the way quickly.

"Oh sushi is great pal, enjoy. Just don't tip them," Cliff said. There was a pause which I took for my cue to ask him to explain to me the reason for that specific piece of advice.

"Oh why?"

"Because," Cliff started, using a wise tone that tried (a bit too hard) to express his years of experience in life, I guess. "I know the owners, they are Chinese, and they employ a lot of their family members who barely know how to speak English. My buddy Al told me that they take advantage of them and keep their tips for themselves, the owners do. Poor waiters, but anyway, just don't tip because if you do it would just go straight into the owner's pockets."

I just stared at him for a moment, trying to decide if he was being serious or not. When he furrowed his brow and lowered his glasses, I knew he wasn't joking. "Oh shit, that's awful. I guess I won't tip then," I said.

"Good. I'll let you go now, little buddy, so you're not late. Say hi to Stella for me, and don't forget to wear a condom."

He never missed the chance to give me unsolicited advice, especially of the sexual kind, and it always made me think of just how awkward and humiliating it must have been to have "the talk" with his son. But to be fair, even though I had an almost endless supply of complaints about Cliff, I honestly think he did care about me in his own *special* way. He was just a bit too much, in my opinion, but he had been a successful man his whole life–according to himself, and to his big and to his beautiful house, too–which I'm sure gave him (at least in his mind) reason to act as if he knew more than, well, everyone, and therefore found it his duty to give me guidance whenever he could.

***

Sunday was a beautiful sunny day in Northern Ontario (so naturally, Stella and I spent it inside, watching TV and reading), but even the promise of being able to spend one more relaxing day without doing anything productive wasn't enough to stop me from dreading going back to work.

There were plenty of reasons for me to start considering quitting my job at the coffee shop–which I didn't shy away from sharing with Stella and my poor friends who were too polite to shut me up after complaining about the dubious foods I reheated–, such as horrible work hours, horrible customers, horrible coworkers, my increasingly horrible sleeping schedule, but the main reason was because of how it made it almost impossible for me to enjoy all of my time off without feeling anxiety creeping up on me, like my own personal demon feasting on my stress and always barely visible from the corner of my eye, where he'd loom and whisper his evil countdown of the hours I had left before my next shift. The sense of anxiety that I felt before going back to work not only intensified as the weeks went by, but it also expanded.

After what should have been a good weekend spent with my girlfriend, she drove me back to my place, I kissed her goodnight and watched her drive away.

When I turned around and started walking up the driveway I saw through the big living room bay window that the TV was on. Anna's car also hadn't moved all weekend and judging by the hour I assumed that she and Cliff were watching the British talent show they liked. I did not have the patience nor the required energy to engage in another meaningless conversation with them–or specifically, with Cliff–this time, so I headed to the side of the house, my bedroom window (which I had left unlocked in case of situations such as this one were to present themselves) and crawled in.

It took me close to an hour to fall asleep, but I was rewarded with a night of sleep which was uninterrupted by my usual urge to pee at 2 AM (which is a byproduct of having a rather small bladder, even for a small man such as myself).

Then, after enjoying a total of five hours drifting in complete blackness, my alarm woke me up. I lay awake in my bed for a few minutes, not thinking about anything in particular while at the same time coming to terms with the fact that yet another day at the coffee shop was about to begin.

I got out of bed and prepared myself to go to work while my neighbors–and almost everyone else living in the city–were fortunate enough to still have a few more hours of rest before their own crappy day started.

6

The only thing that happened that day which might be considered out of the ordinary was that my boss, Darlene, was sick and stayed home, so I had one less person yelling at me. "Count your blessings," my mom always said, but even Darlene's absence wasn't enough to make my day pleasurable, not by a long shot. *Not until I get the fuck out of this place,* I thought to myself as I cleaned grease off my counters.

At noon, when the evening baker came to relieve me, I put my headphones on and biked towards the library, listening to the raspy vocals of *Stolen Dance.*

***

The public library was the architectural embodiment of the 90's, a time capsule. The carpet in particular seemed to have been last cleaned back then. Irregular shapes–mostly stylized triangles–painted with bright neon colors rested on top of dotted patterns and adorned the walls and carpets. The air smelled strongly of mildew, and was pungent enough to remind you of your uncle's rec room with dim lighting which had been flooded a few years ago. Outdated posters stating that *Drugs Are Gay* inhabited the tall–and also halfway-up carpeted–pillars that bisected the main hall. Light beige computer monitors the size of a small guitar amplifier were placed atop flimsy tables at the far left corner of the library.

I picked the computer with the mouse and keyboard that looked the most functional and logged myself in. It took the archaic machine a couple of minutes to decide that my credentials were correct, and when it did, I proceeded to open the internet browser. I had to wait another five minutes before it could load Google, and by then when the computer's fan was full blast.

I opened my email and downloaded a Word document that I had sent to myself a month and a half before containing my resume. I updated it with my current work experience and saved it.

I saved the new copy of my resume on Google Drive and then I went on to print twenty copies. When the printer finished spitting out sheets of paper with my resume (along with a pale blue line from top to bottom, on the left corner of the page) I took them, sighed and put them in my backpack, not before noticing that the last person who had used the printer had left behind a grainy photocopy of, presumably, their ass, so I tossed it in the garbage.

I walked back to the computer to log out when I heard a raspy, ancient voice say, "Excuse me young man, could you please explain this?" I turned around and saw the old librarian judging me with harsh eyes under her Coke-bottle glasses, holding the sheet of paper with the photocopied ass.

"I don't know. Somebody photocopied their butt, I guess," I explained without paying much attention to her.

"Young man, the resources from the library are not to be wasted in vulgar and immature pranks. I'm going to have to ask you for your information to write a report–"

"But it wasn't me," I interrupted.

"Then who was it?" the old librarian said in an irritated and amused tone, as if she was talking to someone stupid (or a *simpleton*, as I imagined she might call them) trying to convince her that the moon was made of cheese. "Nobody but you has used the printer today."

"Well, then it must have been somebody that came here yesterday who did it."

The old librarian let out a sarcastic chuckle. "Young man, don't try to fool me. I was working here yesterday too, and if somebody had tried to photocopy their *behind* then, I'm positive I would have caught them. The library isn't that big, you know." She was trying to hide a nasty, yellow smile now. This was her favorite part of her job, I'm sure of it. People like her thrive when they have the opportunity to belittle and bully others.

"With all due respect, I'm afraid you're wrong Mrs. ...?"

"Townsend."

"I'm afraid you're wrong, Mrs. Townsend. First of all, did you see me sitting on the printer?"

"Well,"–the old librarian's eyes widened ever so slightly–"no. I suppose I didn't."

"I'm pretty sure that if you compare my *behind* to the one in that copy you'll notice that mine has a birthmark that the other one doesn't." The old librarian started to blush. "But I would rather not expose myself to you, so I suggest you review the security footage–"

"I am not very *tech savvy*–" the old librarian started to say before I cut her off.

"I'm sure there's somebody *tech savvy* that works here who would be happy to help you, and when they help you review the footage you will see that I didn't photocopy my ass." At this, Mrs. Townsend gasped.

"Young man–"

"I'm a bit too busy for this," I lied. "Just check the security footage." I picked up my backpack, and started towards the exit. All my life I had been a quiet and shy guy, but after I moved to a Canada (and once I managed to shake off the culture shock I felt for the first couple of weeks) and started to appreciate the freedom that came with living on your own, I decided I would try to stand up for myself more often, even if the first step was not putting up with an old lady bitching at me.

I had heard stories about that old librarian from some of my friends, who all had been tormented by her at one point in their lives or another. She was a bit of a local celebrity–some said it was because of her uninterrupted dedication to the library since 1979, others because of the astonishing length of the stick she hid up her *behind*–, and after my little exchange I had with her I felt like I had been pretty cool. As lame as that may sound.

7

I took my resumes out of my backpack and placed them on my dresser, next to an empty can of Pringles. I knew that looking for another job in the near future was eventually going to be something I had to do, but I didn't know when.

I was about to lay down and try to have a quick nap before Stella got off work, when my phone began to buzz. I would have ignored the call but I recognized the phone number as Darlene's and answered, with not much excitement, hoping that she wouldn't ask me to come back to work to cover someone else's shift or something like that. But to my surprise, that was not the case.

"Hello, Marco?"

"Yes?" I said, scratching the back of my left hand.

"Is Jude with you by any chance? I know you guys are good friends," Darlene asked.

"Uhh no, why?"

Darlene sighed. "He was supposed to come in to work twenty minutes ago but he didn't and now he's not answering his phone".

I had a pretty good idea of the reason why Jude decided not to show up, but as a good friend, I lied for him. "Oh, I think he said to me last night that he was feeling a little sick."

"Oh great," she said. "Well thanks Marco. I will ask Carly to cover his shift then. Please tell him to call me back whenever he feels better. Have a good day."

"Thanks Darlene."

She hung up the phone.

This wasn't the first time that Jude had decided to quit a job and simply stopped showing up to work, instead of putting in his two weeks notice, and I felt bad for Darlene. She did yell at us a lot, but I don't think she deserved to have so many employees quit as often as they did. But that was the nature of working at the coffee shop, and Jude's unprofessional resignation would not stop me from leaving my job eventually too.

8

Jude lived in an apartment in the west end of town–which is also known as the sketchy end of town, home of drug dealers, drug addicts, industrial-glue-and-paint-remover fanatics, prostitutes, OnlyFans entrepreneurs, con men, NFT aficionados, blockchain-obsessed wannabe influencers, burglars who kept their loot on their front lawn to display it for potential (criminal) customers, suspects of murder who had escaped jail thanks to a loophole in the law or lack of evidence, and many other groups of *special* people–, so I looked for spare change for the bus in the back pockets of the two jeans I wore regularly–none of them clean–, put on some a (clean) shirt and headed out.

Cliff was still watching America's Got Talent, cackling with every lame joke the judges said and praising every shallow and gimmicky performance he saw on the screen, so there was no need for me to leave through the window. He wouldn't have tried to talk to me even if I wanted to. Talent shows were his bread and butter. They were his religion.

I had to run to the bus stop, clumsily and sweating enough to stink up my shirt already, but I made it. Public transport was never my preferred way of travel, but the last time I'd biked to Jude's apartment a crackhead with a snake tattoo on his pimply shaved head had tried to steal my bike, and I barely managed to scare him away (because when you're high on crack, you get braver, apparently) when I took a prop gun I'd bought for one of my short films out of my backpack and waved it at him. "Vete de aqui hijo de puta," I'd yelled at the confused crackhead, trying to sound as Mexican as I could, "o te va a cargar la verga." After that incident I vowed never to bring valuables with me whenever I went over to Jude's to hang out. And I still had the prop gun in my backpack.

The bus was empty except for myself, which made the ride a lot more enjoyable than usual since I didn't have to squeeze in between smelly passengers like a sardine. When I got off the bus situated right in front of Jude's apartment I could see his bare-chested form through the window of his apartment on the third floor. I smiled. He had curtains but liked to keep them open most of the time for some reason.

I walked to the apartment building and buzzed number thirty-three.

9

Jude's apartment was fragrant, as usual. I didn't always know what it smelled like, but again, it was never unpleasant. Some weeks he would go through an Indian cuisine phase, some others it would be an Asian-Fusion phase, and sometimes he'd just try to experiment and come up with new culinary creations. These were always my favorites, except for the time when he tried to make his own rendition of tacos. They were not bad, but having been born and raised in Mexico, I couldn't avoid comparing it to my grandma's authentic cooking, and unfortunately, Jude's Tacos were just not the real deal.

Another thing I really appreciated about my friendship with Jude was that he had his own apartment, small as it was, and he didn't mind it when I decided to stop by unannounced, even when we didn't end up doing anything exciting. It was just nice and comforting having a friend that would always be okay with sharing his *alone time* with me, such as the many times that I spent the evening doing homework at his apartment while he played tunes with his guitar.

He also had a large collection of books of all kinds (mainly philosophy books from his college years—he was 4 years older than me). I never read any of those, but the few fiction novels he had were quite good and I had already borrowed almost all of them by then.

That day, when Jude—a very tall, pale guy with long and curly hair who somehow was able to make you feel like you've been friends with him forever—opened the door to let me in, there was a vague scent of cinnamon and maple syrup. If I had to guess, he was going through another phase of trying to reinvent the American breakfast. A quick look at the kitchen allowed me to confirm my suspicions: there was an empty jar of amber maple syrup in the area of his counter dedicated for recycling. Next to it were two cartons of eggs.

We walked past the kitchen and sat on an old green couch that had seen better years, but which still did the job. Jude grabbed his guitar from the stand next to him and started playing an eclectic mix of original, half-finished compositions, and a wide selection of bits and pieces of songs by The Animals (his favorite one being their cover of *The House of the Rising Sun*), Pink Floyd and The Stooges.

"So, you didn't show up to work today," I said casually after he finished playing the chorus of *Paint It Black.*

"Nope."

"Why?"

Jude started playing another song I didn't recognize, but was sure I'd heard somewhere before. "It's just not for me man," he said.

"So you're giving your two weeks?"

Jude stopped playing his guitar for a moment, then seemed to consider something, and resumed playing the elusive song. "No."

Of course. Now the list of things that gave me anxiety had one more item added to it, and it made me feel guilty for having spent so much time thinking about quitting over the past couple of days. But my job was terrible, and inconveniencing Darlene with my resignation wasn't enough to make me reconsider. I knew I was going to quit. I just had to find another job first.

"I think I'll quit too," I said out loud for the first time, making it feel real. Final. It didn't help me feel less guilt, but it was a start. "The hours are horrible and my sleep schedule is so bizarre and I'm surprised I haven't quit already."

Jude stopped playing his guitar again and put it down. "Yeah, but it's more than just that, my dude. It's, uh, the whole establishment, yes. The owners reward and encourage managers and supervisors for overworking us and making us feel miserable."

"Yeah I guess you're right." I said, scratching the eczema rash behind my left hand, which was flaring up and refused to go away. Maybe because I kept forgetting to buy more Hydrocortisone.

"I'll start looking for another job soon, but first I will probably go to Toronto for a few days in a week or so to visit some friends that moved there for college. Have you ever been there?" Jude said, now fidgeting with his guitar pick.

"Kind of."

Jude looked at me and lifted his eyebrows.

"The only time I've been there was when I stopped at the airport to catch another flight to come here," I explained. That day I had to take three different planes–and I ended up spreading my body like a starfish on an uncomfortable bench in order to get some sleep during a particularly long layover–to travel from Mazatlan, the happy beach town where I was born and raised, to my new home in White Peaks, Ontario.

"Dude, you should come with me. It'll be a lot of fun," Jude said, smiling and nodding his head slightly.

It did sound like a lot of fun, but I didn't think it would be a good idea. "I don't know, Jude. I don't have a lot of money and I've heard Toronto is an expensive place."

"Don't worry about money, my dude. I got you. And we'd be staying at my friend's house for free anyway."

"I'll think about it," I said. "Do you think your friend would be okay with having a stranger staying over though?"

"Yeah, of course."

"Could you ask her?"

"Yes, yes I definitely will."

"Okay, I guess I will take a look at my savings and I'll let you know, then." I knew very well that I had enough savings, but they were for emergencies only, and wasting them on a weekend out of town was a stupid idea. *I'll think about it. Maybe I'll ask Stella what she thinks,* I said to myself.

Jude and I left our conversation there, with the possibility of me joining the Toronto trip up in the air, and moved on to play *Mario Kart* on his Wii.

10

I began Tuesday morning by oversleeping. When I finally woke up to pee, I felt suspiciously refreshed. I looked at the clock on my phone and my heart sank. It was already 4:15 AM.

I ran back to my bedroom–after I finished my morning pee, of course–as fast as I could and rushed to put my work clothes on. I must have made a lot of noise, because when I was about to get out, I heard a knock.

"Marco, is everything okay?" Cliff said from the other side of the door, which I opened. The sight of my landlord (and roommate) was not a very pleasant one, especially this early in the morning. His hair was sticking up like a massive cow lick and his eyes looked puffy and smaller than usual.

"Yes, I'm just late for work," I said, already a little out of breath.

"Oh shoot, sorry about that buddy," Cliff said in between yawns. "I guess I should give you a ride, but just this once, and try to be quiet next time you're late for work." He winked at me, unless he was trying to blink an eye booger out. It was too early in the morning for me to tell.

I was surprised, to say the least, by Cliff's offer because he used to complain about gas prices all the time–that was why he drove across the river to gas up in the States–, but I wasn't going to comment on that. Sometimes you just have to shut up and not question it when something good happens to you.

I made it to the coffee shop five minutes early.

Most of the morning staff, including Darlene, started their shifts at 6 AM, which meant that I always got to hear their complaints about how *sleepy* they feel and how *inhuman* it was to have to work so early, all of this after I had already spent the previous two hours reheating dozens upon dozens of mediocre baked goods for ungrateful–caffeine and sugar addicted–customers.

"We have two types of ovens at the coffee shop," Darlene had told me on my first day of work. The biggest one was for breakfast items (sausage patties, "egg" patties, hash browns) and cake -type donuts, and the smaller one was for the yeast-type–gross as it may sound–variety. On top of going into great detail about why it was so important that we never mixed these types of donuts up, they also stressed the importance of not cramming too many items so that they'd have enough time and heat to completely thaw. But that morning I was already half an hour late, and I decided it was better to upset our customers by giving them food that was not reheated quite right (and everything was pre-cooked, so it was safe to eat as it was, with no risk of food poisoning) than to annoy them by not having their precious donuts and breakfast wraps first thing in the morning.

I tossed bagels, muffins and donuts left and right in the ovens, double-stacking the trays of eggs and sausage patties in a reheating frenzy so that by the time Darlene and the rest of my coworkers arrived I'd have things under control. I was *not* in the mood to get yelled at.

I got into a sort of trance. I found a rhythm. And for the first time ever I managed to get all of the food ready and on the shelves and food warmers right on time. Even Darlene, who I thought was only able to notice you when you did something wrong, complimented me for "finally figuring out how to do your job." Thanks to that small form of positive reinforcement even my coworkers whining felt bearable.

After the morning rush subsided at around ten o'clock, the coffee shop got unusually quiet, so I stocked up the donuts that were running low and then I went to the front of the store and just... hung out, because there was nothing else for me to do. Another first. I was on a roll.

Margaret and Lynne, the two sandwich station ladies–both in their late fifties–, were chatting merrily about how back in the day you could buy a large coffee, a dozen donuts and six bagels for two cents or something along those lines, I didn't pay much attention to be honest, and even though I was born decades after those *golden years* had come and gone, I joined them in their conversation.

"You young guys have it so easy nowadays," Margaret explained to me with the condescending tone that was almost exclusive to older people. "You can just come in the drive-thru and get breakfast all day! When I first started working here,"–twenty-two years ago, according to her–"breakfast meant breakfast. If you came into the store at even just one minute after eleven, too bad, you were shit out of luck! No breakfast for you!"

"Yes, yes! I remember that!" Lynne exclaimed, her eyes sparkling. "Those were good days, now we gotta bother poor Marco here to get us eggs and sausages all day," she said in a mock-pity tone and then snorted.

"While it would definitely be nice not to have to cook those weird egg patties past eleven, I see no reason not to have breakfast food available all day. Back home I used to eat eggs,"–this was a lie. I refused to eat eggs back in Mexico–"at night."

"Eggs for *supper*?" Margaret gasped, not bothering to mask the disgust in her tone. "*Beaners* do some weird shit down south, don't they? Eggs for supper–" Over the past couple of weeks, using the word *beaner* was the least racist thing I'd heard Margaret say. She came from a different age, when doctors used to say smoking was safe and asbestos was seen as something inoffensive, so I just started ignoring it when she made these types of comments.

"Yes, nowadays even Canadians do that *breakfast for supper* nonsense. Eating that much sugar not only rotted their teeth but also their minds. They can't focus for more than two minutes anymore, but that is thanks to cell phones and blue light and–"

I tuned out.

After a while of passively participating in their conversation, nodding once in a while, until my bladder reached its full capacity, so I excused myself.

"Mhmm," Margaret said.

I started walking towards the kitchen at the back of the coffee shop, and as soon as I passed the swinging doors I stepped on a small puddle of sugar-glaze that I must have spilled during my morning reheating frenzy. I put my right foot down, felt as if I'd fallen into a hole and smacked my ass on the floor. My bladder relaxed. I didn't even notice I'd wet myself, I just closed my eyes.

After receiving a hearty dose of ill-willed laughter from all of my coworkers, who also weren't busy and had come to see what the hell had happened, Darlene helped me stand up, and when I put pressure on my left foot I let out a pathetic little yelp.

After everyone laughed themselves silly (again), Darlene let me wait in her office for a cab to come pick me up, wet and in pain, and said I could take a few days off.

Well, shit, I thought, *if I knew all it took for me to get off work for a few days without feeling guilty was to sprain my ankle and pee myself, I would have done it weeks ago.*

11

On Thursday evening Darlene called me on the phone and asked me how I was doing. "It hurts a little but I'm feeling a lot better now," I said.

"That's great news, Marco!" The excitement in her tone told me that something bad was coming. "Esther called in sick for tomorrow, and Liz is still out of town so we got no one else that knows how to bake to cover her shift."

Ah, of course.

"Do you think you can come back to work tomorrow morning?"

I swallowed. "Yeah... I guess I can. I mean, my ankle still hurts a bit but–"

And before I could say another word, Darlene interrupted me with a "Thanks, see you in the morning. Bye."

My little impromptu break was sadly over.

12

Going back to work the following day wasn't terrible. It was busy as usual, that was to be expected, and my ankle started throbbing after a few hours of standing up and walking around, but at least busy days at the coffee shop tended to sort of numb my brain, my thoughts, and it made time go by faster than usual.

After my shift was over I biked home and went straight to bed. My body demanded some well deserved rest from me and allowed me to start snoring not too long after I put my head on my pillow.

I had some strange dreams about Chris McCandless again, this time I was cooking some stew for him with hopes of nursing him back to health before his body turned to dust and vanished in the wind. I forgot all about it shortly after I woke up.

What had woken me up that evening was the phone. It was Stella. We talked for a bit about how our days had gone–good for her, dull for me–, and eventually we decided we'd better get something to eat and then go back to her place to *cuddle*. I had no objection to either of those things.

She picked me up from Cliff's fifteen minutes after I hung up, and we headed towards Westside Cafe. It was by no means a great restaurant, but, well, actually it wasn't very good at all either, however the food was always greasy and hot, and the portions were huge. Whenever we made the trip there we liked to order a regular sized poutine when we ate at Westside, because of how massive it was–once we'd asked for a large poutine just to see how much bigger than the regular was, and it indeed was indeed *large*. Humongous, actually. It came served on a stainless steel platter big enough to house a small turkey, and we only managed to eat about two thirds of the poutine before we called it quits. One of the servers had offered us to box the leftovers of our gargantuan meal, but we refused because reheated poutine is soggy and gross. Unless you had an air-fryer, but as a broke college student, I did not have one, and Stella refused to see (or smell) fries for weeks after that day, so they threw the last third of our meal in the garbage.

That day, we weren't in the mood for having another poutine and decided instead to get *breakfast for supper*, because I had planted the idea in Stella's mind when I told her about my conversation with the sandwich station ladies. Stella ordered a *Westside Special*, which included two eggs (sunny side up), three strips of bacon and two slices of marble rye bread, buttered. I, on the other hand, went for a huge omelette with cheddar cheese, mushrooms, onions, green peppers and bacon, with a side of hash browns (the real deal, mind you, not a hash brown patty).

Our waiter Carl was not great at his job, and what he lacked in hair he more than made up for in ear-hair, arm-hair and a big bushy mustache, but he did an okay job that day. He was a major step-up from the waitress that usually worked that shift, Sadie (Westside only ever had one waiter at all times), who tended to get our orders wrong and make inappropriate comments about her customer's personal appearance–she had twice now noted that I was developing a large *beer belly*. We had an idea of why she was absent, because a few weeks prior Stella and I had read in the White Peaks Online– the local newspaper's website–that "a waitress from a fan-favorite restaurant in the west end of town broke into a local electronics store, CJ's Digital Solutions, and stole $2,500 dollars in merchandise before fleeing the county."

"That sounds like the plot of a bad movie," Stella had said, and I agreed.

Living in a small town where news–gossip, to be accurate– traveled faster than the speed of sound, it was easy to connect the dots and assume that the waitress from the article was none other than Sadie. It was common knowledge in the city that she had a criminal record of stealing and breaking and entering. I can't help but wonder where she decided to move after her successful robbery. We never found out. Maybe she'd made enough money from selling her loot to travel to an exotic country, maybe Mexico, but that was very unlikely given how expensive plane tickets were nowadays. Also because Sadie wasn't terribly bright.

Our meals narrowly escaped being sprinkled with Carl's armhair and we were grateful for it, so we started to eat. Vegetable oil or some other unhealthy fat oozing with every bite we took.

"So," I started, "Jude invited me to go with him to Toronto for a few days in a week or so." I had been going over the thought of the trip, almost obsessively, since Jude had suggested it, and I felt like I needed to talk to Stella about it so that she could help me convince myself that it was a bad idea.

"Oh yeah, that sounds fun."

"Really?" I pointed to the left side of my mouth to let her know that a small piece of egg had stuck to her face. Stella removed it with a napkin.

"Yes, why wouldn't it? I'd love to go myself if I had the chance."

That was not the way I expected our conversation to go. "Oh well, I guess I might take his offer then."

"Yes, you should," she paused, and after chewing another bite of bacon, she continued: "As long as you have enough money for it, it should be fine."

There it is, I thought. "I think I do have enough money in my savings, and Jude said we could stay at her friend's house for free. I'd just have to spend money on food and to pitch in for gas."

Stella disregarded my comment, probably because she found her meal more interesting. I couldn't blame her. "We should come here more often, it's so cheap and delicious."

"Yeah, their food's pretty good," I agreed, thinking to myself that indeed, I hated my job–I did print more resumes for a reason, after all–and a week off sounded like a good way to relax despite having already had a break from work after I peed myself. "I'll call Jude tomorrow to tell him I'm on board."

We finished our meals, paid our separate bills and went back to Stella's place to *cuddle* some more.

13

My biological clock, or perhaps my work anxiety, didn't allow me to sleep past five thirty in the morning. I took three pills of melatonin, made myself a cup of chamomile tea, and when none of those things helped me doze again, I gave up. Sometime later, at around noon, I called Jude on the phone. After three muffled rings, a deep and sleepy voice answered the phone.

"Mhmmhmm?"

"Sorry dude, did I wake you up?"

A big and mighty yawn was my answer. "Nah, I woke up a minute ago to take a piss," Jude finally said. "What's up?"

"Oh good, hey I was thinking and I think I will go on that Toronto trip you talked to me about."

"What trip?"

I hesitated for a moment. "Uhh, I thought you said you were planning to visit some friends in Toronto next week or something?"

"Ohhh yeah," Jude said and yawned again. "Right on my dude."

"When will it be? I gotta ask Darlene for those days off."

"We'll leave next Friday and we'll come on Tuesday, I think."

"Okay, sounds good–" I paused for a moment, then said, "Do you need me to transfer you some money for gas and what not?".

"Nah, it's all good, Erin is coming too and she said she'd pitch in for gas. She needs a ride to Newmarket to see some friends so I will just drop her off on our way to Toronto."

Of course. I had introduced Jude to Erin, one of the first friends I made in Canada, a few months before, and had regretted it almost right away. She was a good person, there was no doubt about that, but she was rough around the edges, and sometimes her bluntness could be confused with rudeness. Actually, sometimes it was too hard to tell what her intentions were, which sometimes made me feel a little uneasy around her. That was something I liked about Jude, who (almost) always was straightforward.

"Dude, you still there?" Jude asked.

"Yeah, I am," I said. I hadn't realized that I'd grown quiet. *It'll be a fun trip,* I thought. And how right I was.

"Okay, good," Jude said. "Hey I gotta go to the library to print some resumes,"–none of us had a printer at home–"do you wanna go there with me? We can grab a bite to eat first."

"Yeah sure. Right now?"

"Soon. Let me just shower real quick and then I'll pick you up. Say, half an hour?"

"Sure."

14

Jude's car was a forest green station wagon with thick strips of imitation wood wrapped around the doors, just underneath the windows. *The Mirth* was its name. "The what?" I'd said the first time I saw it.

"The Mirth," he said again, his voice soft and fatherly. "It's like, uh, happiness but stronger. I chose that name because that's what I want people to feel when we go for a ride and all that."

It had a baseball-sized dent next to his left headlight. Its interior was a very sad shade of beige that had seen better days, before it accumulated an eclectic collection of stains, and the radio worked only when it wanted to. The speakers and cassette player did still function, however, and Jude stored his dad's collection of tapes in an old Walmart bag under the driver's seat. He had anything you could think of from the seventies and eighties.

I jumped in *The Mirth* and we drove off. Jude was listening to *The Red Telephone* by Love that day, one of my favorite songs he'd shown me. *One day when I have a good job and enough disposable income I'll buy that album on vinyl,* I said to myself.

"Sorry I was a little late, my dude," Jude said, three hours after our phone call.

"It's fine."

"Do you mind if we go to the A&W before we stop at the library?"

"Yeah for sure, I'm starving."

15

After having a nutritious burger breakfast we made it to the library. Jude headed to the computer area while I went to the reception, looking for Mrs. Townsend's nasty face. She was organizing some checked-in books behind the desk. I cleared my throat.

"Just a moment please," she said.

I was not in a rush and had nothing better to do that day, but I still felt annoyed at Mrs. Townsend's deliberate slowness. It was as if she were savoring every sweet second that she was making me wait, like the last couple of spoonfuls of a bowl of ice cream, which for some reason always were the best.

After scanning and placing the last book on an old cart with small, screechy wheels, the old librarian turned around and looked at me. There was a little pause in which she just stared at me with a blank expression on her face, and then her lips curled up slightly, just a suggestion of an ugly grin.

"Oh. It's *you*," she said in a slow, monotonous tone, punctuating every word. I could tell that she was working hard to hide her hideous smile.

"Yes, it's me. Did you get the chance to see the security–"

"Good," she interrupted, "I was hoping you'd stop by one of these days."

"Oh?"

"Can I see your library card for a second?"

I narrowed my eyes with suspicion for a second.

"Please?" Mrs. Townsend said, stretching her skinny arm towards me.

"Sure."

The old librarian smiled and crouched beneath the desk. I looked towards the computer area, where Jude was now printing his own batch of resumes when I heard something snap. I turned around and saw Mrs. Townsend with scissors on her right hand and my library card, cut in half, in the other.

"What the fuck?"

"Language!" Mrs. Townsend said, her crooked grin vanished.

"*Why would you do that?*" I said, still processing what had just happened. "Did you even look at the security footage?"

Mrs. Townsend ignored my question. "I'm sorry, but like I said I'm not tech savvy," the old bitch replied. "For now, and until someone from I.T. can help me with that, I'm going to have to *politely* ask you to vacate the premises."

I opened my mouth to say something mean and vulgar, took a deep breath, and decided not to. "You can't be serious," was what I said instead.

"I'm afraid I am," she said, sounding very pleased with herself. "I do not make the rules here, I just enforce them. Goodbye now," she said and walked into her office, at the back of the reception. I couldn't see it, but I was sure that her loathsome grin was back on her leathery face.

Two can play this stupid game, I said to myself. *Resentful old bitch.* I got out of the library and got back into The Mirth. I was deep into my own angry thoughts, imagining how happy the old librarian would be feeling for the rest of the week–I probably made her entire *month*–when Jude entered the car.

"Why did you just leave dude?" he asked, feigning irritation and slamming the door shut as if to make a point. "I thought you'd hang around".

"That old bitch banned me from the library," I explained.

Jude's fake exasperation disappeared. "Oh shit, why?"

"Because she thinks I photocopied my ass."

An uncomfortable silence. Then, Jude looked at me, only for a second, before he bursted with hiccuping laughter.

"It's not funny, Jude. It wasn't me but the old bitch didn't even bother to check the security footage or anything. She just decided I was guilty because, I don't know, because she's an ass herself."

Jude ignored my explanation and kept laughing for a good while, his eyes tearing up, his cheeks turning red. It took him some time for him to calm himself, but he eventually managed to do it. "Aw man, that's just hilarious," he said, now just chuckling.

"No it 's not. I gotta do something to–"

"That was my ass, man."

I shook my head and blinked until I found something to say. *"What?"*

"Yeah that was me. Sorry man, I didn't mean to leave one of my ass prints behind."

"Are you fucking serious?"

Jude nodded.

"Dude, you gotta go back and tell that to the librarian," I pleaded.

"Nah man, then she'll ban me," he said and started the car.

"Dude, what the fuck." It was more of a statement than a question. "I need you to fix this."

"It'll be okay man, just go to the library whenever she's not working."

"She's *always* working."

Jude made no reply. He just drove.

"You're unbelievable," I muttered, looking out the window.

"Don't worry about it, my dude. You'll figure this out, you're a smart guy," Jude said after a while. "Just think about the Toronto trip and all the fun we're going to have. We can do all kinds of cool things down there."

"Yeah, I guess I will," I said to him, and the vague form of an idea started to unveil in my head. *Two can play this stupid game,* I thought.

16

The following Monday I was back at the coffee shop, feeling a little less miserable than usual, because of the plan I'd come up with. I had received an email with my work schedule for the week the day before, and to my surprise, I had Saturday and Sunday off. Now I'd just have to talk to Darlene to ask her if she could find someone to take my Friday shift, which so far was the only day that conflicted with my Toronto trip plans. I wanted to have this conversation with her that day during our break, to give her as much notice as possible, but she was off until Wednesday. That was okay though, I had some other important things to do that evening anyway.

I was supposed to be done for the day at noon as usual, but Esther, one of the other bakers, called the store a few minutes before my shift was over, and said she quit. *Of course this would happen today,* I thought. *Now I'm going to have a really hard time asking Darlene to find someone to cover my Friday shift.* I knew that I could just call in, pretending to be sick, but although Darlene used to yell at me as much as she yelled at anyone else, she could be pleasant, and I didn't want to put her in a position in which she'd be forced to bake by herself. It took the assistant manager close to an hour to track Liz down to come to the store to cover Esther's shift. This was not good. Far from it.

By the time Liz came in and I was able to leave work I had barely enough time to get to my appointment with the White Peaks Online staff.

***

I originally meant to bike to the newspaper's offices after work, but by the time I had changed into clean, decent clothes (which I had stored in my backpack just in case I didn't have time to stop home and get dressed there) and cleaned sugar glaze off my hair and face it was way too late for me to ride my bike all the way downtown, so I had to spend twenty dollars in a cab to get to my appointment on time. But despite all the difficulties that I ran into that afternoon, everything else went well.

When I arrived at the White Peaks Online's offices, a smug, young receptionist with short, blonde hair who had dressed himself in business-casual clothes that were far too big for him, rolled his eyes when I greeted him. He put his cell phone away and said, with an annoying nasal voice, "How can I help you, uh, sir?"

"I have an appointment with Rob," I said.

"Rob? Okay, just give me a second." He dialed some numbers on the work phone's pad, and after a quick exchange with (presumably) Rob, the receptionist hung up and returned his reluctant attention to me. "Down the hall and to the left, past the staff room," he said.

I walked in the direction I was told, but most of the rooms I passed had no windows, so I had to peek at every open door to figure out which one was the staff room, which in turn caused me to make uncomfortable eye contact with a lot of skinny, depressed-looking employees, who seemed to be holding onto their coffee cups for dear life. When I finally found the conference room, a tall middle aged man with curly hair and a receding hairline got up from his chair when I walked in. He was wearing a sport jacket over a graphic shirt with the Nasa logo on it.

"Hi, Marco, right?" Rob said in a cheerful, nasal voice too much like the receptionist's, but deeper. "I see you met my son, Tom. He's the receptionist."

Ah! Now I know why they gave a job to such an apathetic guy, I thought. "Yes, nice guy," I lied.

"The best. He *just* started working here this summer and he's already got the hang of things. Like father, like son, as I say. A hard worker, yes sir."

We shook hands and Rob invited me to sit down. The chair was old but comfortable. It had probably been a fancy chair eight years ago, but now some of the paint on the arm rests had rubbed off, and the leather on the top was cracking, but the chair was still sturdy, plush and it did its job. Rob sat in front of me, at the other side of the long oak table, its surface reflecting light like a dirty mirror. We were a good ten feet away from each other. Nice and intimate.

"So tell me, what exactly happened to you at the library?" Rob asked, taking a notepad and pen from his pocket.

I tried to be as polite as possible. "Well, you see, Rob. As I mentioned in my email, last week I went to the library to work on a personal project, a poem collection I was writing for my family abroad." Being polite does not always mean being honest as well. At first I thought Rob would see right through my bullshit, but a guy that convinces himself that his bratty kid is a hard worker can be easily deceived. "That's actually quite nice of you," he said and started writing.

"Thank you. So anyway, when I went to print what I had so far from my collection, I noticed that somebody had umm, made photocopies of their butt. They'd left one behind, and when I saw it I threw it in the garbage. Now, when I was about to leave, the librarian called me over and when then she started scolding me about how I was damaging the library's property and how immature I had been. I tried to explain to her that it wasn't me, and when I suggested that a quick look at their security camera footage would clear things out, she got very angry, lost her temper and kicked me out." I shook my head and looked at Rob out of the corner of my eye. He was smiling and scribbling away.

"Oh no, that's awfully rude and unfair of her," he said.

"Yes it is, but I don't blame her. I've heard she's been working at that library for many, many years, so she was probably just acting on instinct. I'm sure she's had to deal with tons of people that don't respect the library."

"But of course," Rob said, his eyes still stuck to his notepad. His hairy-knuckled hand still writing notes.

"I thought she'd get over it in a day or two, because she really didn't have any proof of me photocopying my butt, but I was wrong. Last Saturday I went back to the library to do some more writing and Mrs. Townsend came to talk to me as soon as she saw me walking through the door and demanded that I give her my library card. When I did, she cut it in half and told me she'd banned me."

"No!" Rob gasped.

"Yes," I said and looked down at the floor.

"This is a very, *very* unfortunate situation, Marco. Would it be okay if we wrote a little story about it? Maybe it'll help her *reconsider* her decision to ban you."

Bingo. "Yes of course, I tried to talk to Mrs. Townsend in a civilized manner, but she refused and asked the security guard to kick me out of the library." There were no security guards at the library, but I had to spice my story up if I wanted people to read it, but it didn't matter if no one did. I just wanted Mrs. Townsend to feel ashamed next time she browsed her precious White Peaks Online, to which she devoted a lot of her time, based on all the times I went to the library and saw her staring numbly at the local news page instead of doing her job.

"Excellent, thank you Marco. We should be able to write something up about your unfortunate situation within the next couple of days. I will send you an email with a link to the story once it's on the website," and with that, Rob showed me the way out.

"Thank you for coming to us, we're always happy to hear anyone that has an important story to tell."

"Thank you for taking the time to listen to it, Rob," I said. "Have a good day."

"You too, buddy." I shook Rob's hand again and nodded to Tom, who was standing next to his father at the door. I could see the similarities between the two of them now: big nose, curly hair, broad shoulders, no brain.

I left the White Peaks Online offices feeling lighter, happy even, like the meeting had been a success, but I never heard back from Rob again.

17

I wouldn't if I found out that Darlene had been hired exclusively for her unnatural skills at finding people willing to work at the coffee shop, because even though her competency at management was questionable, she had already found, interviewed and hired two new bakers before I even started my next shift. She put me in charge of training Bhupinder, who was supposed to cover some of the evening shifts, and after my disastrous first day teaching him the ins and outs of baking at the coffee shop, one would have thought that my chances of taking some time off to go on the Toronto trip were close to inexistent. But that was not the case.

Having to train someone for this miserable job was hard, however. To begin with, the kitchen was tiny and labyrinthic, and hard as it was for me to navigate it on my own, carrying awkward trays of donuts and bagels through the narrow hallways, but having two bakers–and, mind you, I wasn't even experienced enough to be training anyone in the first place–in there at the same time caused us to make physical contact with each other in the most uncomfortable and intimate ways. Our asses rubbed each other more than once that day.

The girls that worked at the front of the coffee shop performing the glamorous tasks of interacting with our customers directly had been all over Bhupinder though, asking him questions about where he was from (India), the reason why he decided to move into the small and almost God forsaken town of White Peaks (he didn't convince us with his 'because it's so beautiful here with so much nature everywhere' explanation) and other surface level inquiries. He was enjoying the attention he was getting until Carly decided to give him the nickname *Boop*.

After acquiring such a memorable title (which was catching on at the coffee shop despite his visible aversion towards it), his mood soured and his willingness to learn went away to a far away and mysterious land. Probably India. He still followed me around half listening to me, but he also spent a good couple hours staring at his phone and not looking up at me, even when I was showing him how to use machines like the ancient industrial dishwasher–about which the owner had said would be replaced "soon" weeks ago but still hadn't been–in the proper way as to avoid getting your fingers smashed and burned with scalding, soapy water. "Yeah, okay, sure," he'd said to me while playing *Crossy Road*.

But by far the worst part of my day was when I took Boop to the walk-in fridge with me to help familiarize him with the location of our frozen baked goods. "We're supposed to be able to unlock the door both from inside and outside, but someone broke the handle before I started working here," I said while I held out the door open for him. When we were both in, I grabbed a little white bucket that we kept on the left side of the door against the wall and shoved it in between his face and the screen of his phone. "Always use this bucket to keep the door ajar when you come in here so that you don't get locked in. The front staff rarely come back here and they won't hear you scream if you get stuck. This freezer is pretty soundproof".

"Uh, yeah sure, sure." Boop said and pushed the bucket towards me. He returned to play *Crossy Road.*

I put the bucket in place and turned around to show him where we stored the potato wedges. I went on a long tangent about how sometimes when no one was paying attention, I'd snack at the wedges because they were tasty and well seasoned, and when I moved to the other side of the freezer to show him where the muffins where located, it appeared like Boop had decided that he had been on his feet for way too long already, and snatched the little white bucket to use as a make-shift chair. I heard the familiar metallic slam of the door and all of the sudden I felt a lot colder, physically and emotionally.

"Boop what the fuck! I told you not to close the stupid door," I yelled at him. The sight of him still playing that stupid game on his phone made my stomach wretch and feel sick with anger.

"Don't call me that, I hate it," he said in a heavily accented voice, ignoring my remarks about the door. "I'm sick of that nickname."

"Well I'm sick of you not listening to me. Now start screaming, because it will be a long time before anyone at the front can hear us and let us out."

Boop got up, dismissed me with the wave of his tan hand, and reached for the door handle. "What are you talking about? We can just—" and the look of surprise and terror in his face when he couldn't open the door almost made being stuck in the freezer with him worth it. He put a foot against the door and pulled on the handle. The handle broke. He paced around the freezer for a few moments, rubbing his face and breathing heavily. "What's the store's phone number?" he said, "I'll just call and they will come open the door"

I was going to explain to him that there was no service within the freezer, but he found out on his own after having a quick look at his phone. He started pounding at the door and said, "Hello! Hello! Help! We're stuck in here!"

"Yeah, keep doing that," I agreed and then took the winter jackets that were hanging on a rusty hook on the wall next to the door. I handed one to Boop and put the other one on. It was too big on me, but that didn't really matter.

The jackets were originally for the cold months of the year, when going to the back of the coffee shop to dispose of garbage bags and receiving shipments of frozen food at minus twenty degrees celsius made those tasks more annoying than usual, but at some point someone had thought that the best place to store them was in the freezer in case someone got locked in. I never thought I'd be in a situation like that, but felt grateful for the warmth that the jacket gave me nonetheless.

After fifteen or twenty minutes of enduring Boop's non-stop crying for help (and hitting and kicking the door), Darlene heard us on her way to her office and let us out. She looked at our cold selves and blushed a little when she realized that my trainee had slushy snot coming from his sharp nose and frozen tears around his eyes and on his cheeks.

"Are you guys, uhh, okay?"

"We are now, thank you." I replied, stepping out of the cold metal box. Boop nodded in silence. He was still shivering, but color was coming back to his face.

I knew my chances of getting the time off I wanted were almost zero, but I still had to ask. "Darlene, can I talk to you for a second?"

"Not now, Marco, but we can chat after your shift," she said and went to her office.

For the rest of the day, Boop kept the winter jacket on and listened to me with care. He even seemed to have grown fond of his nickname, chuckling when people said things like "Hey Boop, what a first day you've had, eh?"

18

When my shift was done, and after I finished my first day training Boop, I went to the washroom. I took my hat off, washed my face and fixed my hair to look a little more presentable for Darlene. "Come in," she said before I could knock on her office door. "How was the rest your day training Bhupinder?"

"Not terrible," I lied. "We had a bit of a rough start as you know, but he really got into it after a while. He's a fast learner."

"Really? That's good to hear." If Darlene thought I was lying, she didn't care. "Keep it up, and please let me know if you think he needs extra days of training before we leave him on his own. Baking is the most important position here, you know?"

"Yeah for sure." I took a deep breath. "So uhm, there was something I wanted to ask you, if you don't mind." I noticed my hands had started to shake a little. It wasn't very noticeable, but I was anxious and in my mind I looked like a crack addict.

"What is it?" Darlene asked, looking at me with narrowing eyes.

"Well, I need to take tomorrow off and–"

"You can't."

I stared at her, bitter disappointment again twisting inside my stomach. I knew I should have asked for the days off with more time in advance, and that it was perhaps wrong for me to get mad after hearing Darlene's firm response, but I insisted, stubbornly, like a child. "I'm sorry, but I wasn't asking you, I was just letting you know. I'm going to be out of town until Tuesday. I can come back to work then," I said, surprised at the lack of emotion with which I had spoken.

"I'm going to pretend you didn't just say that, because you have always been respectful to me," she replied, tensing her mouth,

43

her wrinkly lips. "I need you here tomorrow as planned. And Saturday and Sunday too. I need you to keep training Bhupinder until I can trust him to work all alone, and seeing how today's little accident went, I'd say that it'll be a while until he can. *Certainly* not tomorrow."

I wanted to quit then, to feel the sweet satisfaction that would come from not having to wake up at three in the morning every day, to know that I would never have to step foot in that shitty coffee shop, but something inside me didn't let me. I just stood there staring at my boss.

"You can go now, Marco. See you in the morning," Darlene said before turning to her computer to resume whatever she was doing before I came to talk to her.

I walked to the door, looked back at Darlene for a moment, the words *I quit* feeling like a ball stuck in my throat, and turned around, resigned. I sighed and how rough and extra depressing the next couple of days would be.

I left.

***

I hadn't taken more than five steps when the feeling of the ball stuck in my throat came back to me, stronger and, unfortunately, more real than ever. I felt little droplets of sweat forming on my forehead and the air around me suddenly turned cold. The fine, light brown hairs on my arms stood up, reminding me of an angry cat puffing up.

A bitter, red-hot burning sensation traveled from the top of my belly upwards. I panicked.

I tried to control myself, and closed my eyes for a moment.

"Marco, is everything alright?" Darlene said from her office. I stood there, feeling weak and both warm and cool at the same time.

This can't happen to me, not now, I thought to myself. I tried to pat my belly, hoping it would ease the whirlwind within, but it didn't work. The moment my clammy hand touched my fat stomach I felt it twist and turn. I even heard it doing so. When I could no longer hold it in, I turned around, rushing in the direction of the staff washroom. Every step I took was heavy and unsettling, and when I reached the door, it was locked.

"Occupied," Boop's voice said from the other side of the door.

Then I felt a hand with long, skinny fingers touch my shoulder, making my stomach lurch. Before Darlene even had time to finish asking me what was going on, I turned towards her, looked at her in the eyes for a split second, grimacing, and spewed what a few hours ago had been my lunch on the floor, spattering greenish-brown specks of stomach juices and partly-digested food on her neat, black shoes. It was an amazing feat of human resilience that I'd had enough power within me to yank my head out of the way before me and my breakfast wrap parted ways, avoiding my boss' face altogether.

Darlene stared down at her feet and looked back up to see me for a second. Color had escaped her face entirely, and her lips quivered for a moment. I immediately got out of her way. She retched.

I am one of those people who, when they hear others vomit, can't physically help themselves from partaking in the activity. After a second round of throwing up–presumably the cereal I'd had before coming in to work–, I crawled on the floor, putting as much distance between me and the acidic reek from the puddles of puke.

I stopped in my kitchen, resting my back on the walk-in freezer's door, my stomach feeling at peace. A minute later, John, the chubby, bald cleaner with an impressive red beard made his way into the staff room with a bucket and mop in hand to clean our mess.

19

That evening I managed to have a long and well deserved nap after I got back home. When I woke up again the day was over and the night's cool and dark blanket was already resting over White

Peaks. The puffy white smoke emanating from the steel plant's ancient chimneys slowly tried to reach the sky.

I got up to turn the light on and when I returned to my bed I had a revelation. There was no way for Darlene to know that the reason why I had thrown up at work was because of a bad breakfast wrap, so for all she knew I could be having a bad stomach flu. I sat in silence for a moment. *This is my chance,* I said to myself. I looked around me and found my phone laying on the floor. I looked for Darlene's number and started typing.

> Sorry about today, I think I caught a bug or something. I've been sick all evening.

> It 's fine. Just don't come back until you're back to normal. Take all week if you have to.

> Okay, thanks. See you next week.

Part 2: The Mirth

1

After my brief text exchange with Darlene, I gave Jude a call. The phone rang seven times before it decided it was time to forward me to the automatic answering machine. A moderately disorientated sounding Jude said, *"Uh, this is Jacob's phone. Sorry I, uhh... can't make it, I must be busy, so uhh... please leave a message at the tone. Or not. Thanks."*

I opted for the second option. Jude knew it was me. He'd call me back later, so I decided it was time to pack. We were supposed to leave the following day, Friday, and come back on Monday, so I only needed to pack enough clothes for four days.

I went to my small closet and grabbed five shirts, two pairs of dark blue jeans (one closer to black than the other), a black lightweight bomber jacket in case it got windy in Toronto, and eight pairs of underwear. Yes, just the bare essentials for a short trip to the big city.

I lay my clothes on my bed and tried to fold them as best as I could, with below average results. Once I had them sorted out in two small piles, I grabbed the book I was reading (*Catcher in the Rye*–which had been a bit of a disappointment so far, given that I was already a third into the novel and there were no catchers nor any rye yet) from my dresser, my eczema cream, a roll of toilet paper –experience had taught me that you really *never* know when you'll need it, especially when you go on a hike–, and a small Polaroid picture of Stella and I that a friend of us, Beau, had taken at a party a few months before. I knew I could have used my phone to look at more than just one tiny and grainy picture of us if I ever felt lonely, but I had gotten used to having that Polaroid on my nightstand, propped up against the wall, and looking at it helped me feel happy and relaxed before going to sleep. Stella always made things feel better, brighter and kinder.

These were the few items that I deemed necessary, if not essential, for my trip (not including my phone charger, I'd just keep that in my left pocket, along with my wallet), and once I had gathered them all, I looked under my bed and took a small carry-on-sized suitcase.

As I was organizing everything in the suitcase, my phone rang. It was Jude.

"Hey dude, what's up?" he said.

"Not much, I convinced Darlene to let me take the next couple of days off for the trip. What time are we leaving tomorrow?"

Jude meditated for a few seconds, then said. "I think Erin wanted to leave the city by 10 AM so, I think I'll pick you up at around quarter to ten. Does that sound good?"

"Yeah sure." I was fairly sure that Jude would probably pull into my driveway at twenty past ten at the earliest, but I'd still wake up early enough to be ready by the time he suggested, just in case. "Should I eat something here before then? Or are we stopping somewhere for breakfast?"

"We can stop at the coffee shop drive-thru for some breakfast."

I felt a sharp spike of PTSD from my *second* accident of the day, but I tried to dismiss the acid reek from vomit that was being conjured up in my mind. "Uh, sure, as long as you order for me because they may think I'm sick. I'll pay for myself, obviously. They just can't see me."

"Sounds good my dude."

"Okay, perfect. Well, I better go to bed now so I can get a good night's sleep before our trip," I said. "See you in the morning, dude."

"'Kay, 'kay. See you tomorrow."

I was about to hang up, but then I added, "You should go to sleep soon too, it'll be a long drive."

Jude exhaled in an amused sort of way. "Uh, yeah sure, I'll just watch a movie first. It helps me sleep." It didn't, watching movies always kept Jude up and he was well aware of it, but it had been a long day full of excitement, coldness and puking, so I didn't feel like contradicting him or chatting any more.

We said goodbye again and hung up.

I finished packing shortly afterwards, but although I was exhausted, I knew trying to go to bed would be a lost cause.It was going to be my first time visiting Canadian New York, and I was understandably very excited. Homesickness and anxiety were also in my heart that night.

My first thought was to call Stella if she was awake, but she had to go to work early in the morning and if she didn't get her eight hour sleep she'd have a bad day no matter what, so I decided not to bother her this late.

After a few moments I remembered I hadn't talked to my parents in a while, so I picked up my phone again and opened the *FaceTime* app. *They will appreciate a heads up about the Toronto trip*, I thought.

2

The videocall with my parents was brief, but it brought me some much appreciated peace. They told me that my sister, Ely, was preparing her art portfolio to apply to some colleges that she was interested in. She had always been great at drawing, well, except when she was eight years old and started to spend an unnatural amount of hours making colorful stick-figure paintings with titles such as "Me and mom and dad and Marco at the beach". Back then I could definitely recognize her passion for drawing and painting, but talent was still yet to come.

Now, however, Ely was nothing short of an artist. She'd become a proficient illustrator, and while I was never a big fan of her subjects, which nine out of ten times were fictional anime characters, there was no denying that she had a unique visual style and the skills necessary to become a professional. I just hoped that the colleges she applied for didn't have old pretentious teachers giving students a harder time than they should.

After fifteen minutes of chatting with my parents I remembered why I don't tend to call them too often: when I said it was getting late and I was feeling drowsy, our goodbyes stretched out foreclose to ten minutes. Not that there was anything wrong with that, but I thought it was rather unnecessary for my mom to put our dog, Samantha, on the screen and make her "talk" to me, in which mom used her high-pitched baby voice to convey Samantha's *thoughts* to me.

When we at last ended the call I turned off the light and crashed.

3

I think I could have had a decent sleep, but my small bladder forced me to go to the washroom multiple times, so by the time my alarm rang at 8:30 AM my body demanded more rest from me. I refused, and started my day exhausted, experiencing something like an alcohol-less hangover, head pounding and lower extremities aching. It made me feel like an old man.

I opened my mini-fridge, took out a pathetic butter chicken frozen-supper package, opened a small hole in the protective plastic film to let the steam out and threw it in the microwave for five minutes.

While my nutritious breakfast was being defrosted I looked for an extra-strength *Advil* in my drawers and found none. I remembered that Cliff kept all of his over-the-counter medicine in the kitchen cupboards, but since I did not have the energy required to chat with him this early in the morning I chose the lesser of two evils and resigned myself to eating my breakfast with a headache.

As I was having a bite of an underseasoned chunk of chicken, however, I realized that I still hadn't heard Cliff's early morning shenanigans, so I put my fork down and left my room in search of some ibuprofen, hoping that he'd still be dosing.

***

Cliff's snores greeted me in the hallway as I got out of my room. I made my way to the kitchen and looked for the pills I needed for an embarrassingly long time until I found the container of *Advil* with the lid off on the counter next to the sink. *He must have had a hard night,* I thought.

I grabbed a glass from the white (fake) wood cupboard with thin, gold handles and went to the fridge to serve myself some ice-cold water. Just feeling the cool glass of water in my chubby hands gave me some ephemeral relief. I put two pills in my mouth and took a couple of gulps of water to wash the ibuprofen down.

I washed the glass and put it in the drying rack–because Cliff would freak out if I didn't do the dishes the second after I was done using them– and started towards my bedroom when a sleepy middle-aged voice startled me.

"You're up early, my boy. Do you have anything to do this morning?" Cliff asked, squinting and trying to suppress a yawn without much luck. I hadn't even noticed that his snoring had stopped, let alone that he was sneaking up on me. He was wearing the only pajamas I'd ever seen him in, but his signature picture-perfect combed hair was a mess, with some strands of hair rebelling against his head, stretching towards the ceiling, and other locks hanging lazily down his high forehead. It was in situations like this when I suspected he had paid an obscene amount of money to a plastic surgeon to attach a very convincing hairpiece to his head, probably made out of real human hair.

"Oh, actually I do," I muttered. My original plan was to get out of the house, hopefully while Cliff was at the gym, and text him about my trip when I was already out of town to avoid unsolicited travel advice from him, but that was certainly not going to happen now. "I'm going to Toronto for the weekend with some friends."

He stretched his arms, yawned and said, "Oh, that's nice."

I waited for Cliff to try to convince me not to go, to say that it was a stupid idea, or at least to make a follow up comment of some kind, but he didn't. "Yeah, I'm excited about it," I said to break the silence.

"Just don't forget to bring some condoms, you don't want to ruin your future with an unexpected pregnancy." Ah yes, it was never too early for Cliff's birth control advice.

"Oh she's not coming. It'll just be me and Jude."

Cliff threw a suspicious look at me, flexing the corners of his eyes for a second, wrinkling them heavily, and then relaxed. "Oh good, good. Well, please just try to keep it quiet when you head out. I went out to the bard with some buddies last night and I got a bad hangover. Might have had a little too much tequila," he said and tried to wink at me, but failed. He ended up giving me more of a slow double blink and walked back to his bedroom.

4

The cold morning shower and the pill I took did wonders for me, and even my headache faded away. My body still felt tired as fuck though, pardon the language.

I was ready by ten past nine, so sent Jude a message to let him know. By then the hot summer sun was shining potently over the city, the scarce clouds cruising the sky struggling to dim it, even slightly, and I decided to grab my suitcase and sit on the porch to wait for Jude to arrive.

I sank on one of Cliff's old white beach chairs from the porch wearing my sunglasses and a black ball cap with the *Friends* logo. My hair was longer now, way longer than what was socially acceptable back home, giving my ears and neck some protection against the sun. If any of my friends from Mexico saw me now, they wouldn't have recognized me at first. I looked like a picture perfect *gringo* tourist visiting the Mayan Riviera. Even my beer belly added authenticity to the costume.

Willow Street was always quiet, with old (white) retired people living in the houses at either side of it. The few homes that were not occupied by this demographic were young middle-upper class families, where the husband had either lucked out and found a really good job or inherited his dad's business because most residences had a vast, luscious backyard. Cliff's for instance was more of a small hiking trail area than an actual yard. He said that he'd seen bears there a few years before, but the most exotic animal I'd seen myself since I moved here had been a fox.

There was something sweet and nostalgic that came from living in a small city like White Peaks where you could just sit down, enjoy the sun on the porch and maybe, just maybe see an animal that belongs in the forest trotting merrily on the street across from you. I'd like to imagine that fifty years ago, when the city was just a town and most of the land within its limits was raw nature, there was nothing special about sighting a bear or a fox or a skunk, but in 2018 this was sadly becoming a rare occurrence.

I waited for Jude to come for over an hour, sending him texts here and there, never receiving a reply. I didn't mind it though because I got the opportunity to just sit down and enjoy doing nothing. Working at the coffee shop for the summer only added to the satisfaction that this calm morning gave me.

At 10:45 AM my stomach produced some nasty, guttural sounds, so I left the peace and quiet from the porch and went to the washroom. Right before I finished doing my *business* I heard The Mirth's old, wheezing honk screaming at me. I hurried up and went back outside to find a just-got-out-of-bed Jude, hair all frizzled up and eyes bloodshot sitting in the driveway. I took my suitcase and ran to the car.

"Is everything okay, Jude?" I said after I closed the door.

Jude was now pulling out of the driveway and into the road, perhaps on autopilot because it took him a moment to register what I had said. "Huh? Oh yeah, yeah it's all good," he answered. "I just overslept."

"No shit." I joined him with a yawn of my own. I really was tired, but at least the fresh air I got while I was waiting for him had let my body recover a bit. Jude drove east towards the city limit, and I was about to ask him if Erin was still coming when his phone rang. That gave Jude a start.

He took his phone out of his pocket and answered the call. "Hullo?" he said, yawning again.

I could overhear an angry voice shouting from the other side of the line. After a few *Uh-huh*s and *Yeh*s from Jude, he eventually said, "I will be there in 3 minutes," and hung up, making the tires screech from the sharp u-turn he made when he got to the next lights.

I grabbed the safety handle above the passenger's side window. It broke. I looked at Jude, feeling a mix of shame and anxiety. He didn't take his eyes away from the road but nodded. "It's okay," he said and reached under his seat for the bag with his cassette collection. He handed it to me. "Pick something nice for a road trip."

When we drove in The Mirth I usually preferred to listen to new music, but when I saw the *Californication* tape I couldn't say no. After we listened to the first few chords of *Around the World* Jude said with a "The Peppers?"

"Yeah"

He either sighed or yawned once more. Maybe both. "I'm not a big fan but it's all good."

"Then why do you have it?" I said.

"It's my dad's collection, remember?"

"Oh, right. I can pick something else."

"Nah dude, in this case it's appropriate. There's , uh, a song about road trips in it I think, and that's kind of what I wanted anyway."

I was glad to get Jude's approval because *Californication* was one of my favorite albums and I didn't want to pick another one. We arrived at the White Peaks College dorms by the time *Otherside* was starting, and a sunburnt (mostly on her nose and shoulders) Erin was already outside, two suitcases by her side, waiting for and scowling at us. Jude and I shared a nervous look and did not need to exchange a word to understand what we were both thinking: that the Toronto trip was going to be *fun*.

Jude got out of his beloved station wagon and opened the trunk, and when he offered Erin a hand to help her load her suitcases he was rewarded with a cold, nasty frown. He left her alone and jumped back in the driver's seat. "I think you should, uhh, give her the shotgun seat," Jude suggested.

I looked at him, my lips thinning into a flat line. He closed his eyes and nodded, looking like a wise modern-day monk. I exhaled but did not object.

I got out of the car and when I opened the back door Erin said, without looking at me, "You didn't have to give me your seat."

"Just thought I'd be nice."

Erin grunted and took her place at the front of The Mirth. With everyone's butts on their seats and suitcases secured in the trunk, we began our pilgrimage to the big city.

5

We were approaching the lights on the River Road intersection when Jude turned the blinkers on and started moving towards the turning lane that would lead us to a coffee shop.

"We're not stopping anywhere. We're already an hour behind schedule," Erin snapped.

Jude and I looked at each other's eyes through the rearview mirror. He raised his eyebrows and I shrugged. I wasn't starving, but I was hoping I could get a hot chocolate or some other kind of a sugary drink with empty calories, and on the other hand it was easy to tell that Jude had just gotten out of bed without food in his stomach or caffeine in his system.

Jude turned the blinker off and returned to his lane. An angry driver behind us honked and cursed at us. We couldn't actually hear them, but sometimes you could just tell when someone wished you did unspeakable things to your mother.

"I gotta eat though," Jude said despite having already passed the coffee shop.

Erin bent down, looking slightly less annoyed, maybe even a little pleased, and looked inside of her colorful (and enamel-pin-littered) backpack for something. After a few seconds she drew a plastic bag with a peanut butter and jelly sandwich from it. "Here," she said. "I made us some snacks for the trip."

Erin loved to feed her friends, although her cooking skills were questionable at best, and none of us had had the heart to tell her. She handed Jude the bag containing a soggy and leaking sandwich which he–to my surprise–seemed interested in eating. He was not a picky eater, but I was still surprised to see that he didn't seem put off by the humidity trapped within the bag, condensed in tiny droplets of water, moistening his lunch.

When I received my own sandwich I considered telling Erin that I wasn't hungry and that I'd save it for later, hoping that I could secretly toss it in the garbage we dropped her off at Newmarket, but decided it would be smart not to give her any more reasons to be mad at us, so I opened the slimy bag.

The smell of the sandwich was indescribable, but I can swear that the peanut butter had somehow turned spicy based on the whiff I got from it. I've never been a fan of peanut butter–or to be more precise, I always hated it–, just the way cilantro is not for everyone, so I grimaced and took a reluctant bite.

The bread was wet to the point of it falling apart as soon as I put it in my mouth and the jelly was warm and tart. Bite by bite I ate the stinky lunch that Erin had made for me, but I had to keep my fist near my mouth to try to cover my disgust. After what seemed like hours (but was closer to a few miserable minutes) I finished my *slimedwich*.

Jude glanced back at me through the mirror and said, "It was a pretty good sandwich, eh?" Almost tauntingly.

I closed my eyes, trying to stop my urges to throw up, and nodded. "It was," I said. "Thanks Erin."

"You're welcome guys. See? You didn't have to stop at the coffee shop," she replied, smiling to herself.

Well, we did *have to stop there if we wanted to get* decent *food,* I thought.

We drove on the lonely highway mostly in silence for a good two hours and until Erin reverted to her normal (and obnoxious) self. "Do you have an aux cord for me to play some music?" she asked, turning the volume of the stereo down.

Jude chuckled. "Of course not," he said. "This car is older than me. You can pick something from my cassette collection though."

Erin opened the glove box, looking for tapes that were not there.

"Under your seat," Jude corrected her. She looked in the deteriorated white plastic bag that kept Jude's dad's cassettes in one place and picked up a tape with a black and white cover of a black man with sunglasses and an impressive afro holding a saxophone.

What came out of the car's speakers was an angry yet charming voice yelling *What time is it?!* a few times to some invisible audience, and eventually a raw and potent saxophone, presumably the one from the cover of the album, started blasting, followed by intermittent percussion and a funky piano.

The album, I later found out, was called *Nation Time* by Joe McPhee, and it was excellent, but Erin wasn't a big fan of it and turned the volume off. It (unfortunately) wasn't the first time she'd been in Jude's car, so she knew that looking for another tape with the hopes of finding something she'd like was an almost lost cause.

My friends started talking about some role playing game Erin was apparently really into and, as I was not interested in that topic at all, I kind of tuned their conversation out. I was way too tired to force myself to chat with them about LARPing or whatever it was, but at the same time I wasn't tired enough to have a cat nap, so I settled for just resting my head on the seat and looking through the window.

An incredible feeling of awe crept within me when I started to understand just how vast the nature surrounding us on our trip was, most of it still untouched by man. Long stretches of the road were besieged by impressive spruce and cedar trees like a gigantic company of green soldiers, and the fertile land seemed to keep running forever and into eternity, interrupted only by the occasional little rocky lake and shore. The crop fields (of mostly corn) that I was so used to seeing back in Mexico whenever our family hit the highway to go on vacation almost seemed to me like something alien that had come out of a strange fever dream instead of from my own memory.

I was in another country.

I was an outsider.

Eventually, the peace that the northern Ontario nature had given me allowed me to drift into a brief but revitalizing sleep.

6

I was woken up by a sudden and loud snore. I jerked my head up and looked around, my heart beating so fast and loud that if I couldn't actually hear it, I could certainly feel it pounding in my ears. Since nobody else was sleeping–and thank God for that, because if Jude had been snoozing this would be a much different story–I came to the conclusion it had been my own snoring the thing that had brought me back to reality.

I rubbed my face to help me to fully wake up, yawning and feeling grateful for the little extra rest I'd had when a bridge to our left caught everyone's attention. The old and rusty construction itself was not memorable in any regard. It was the simple but final message that was written on it what demanded our attention.

THIS IS INDIAN LAND

The enormous white letters were starting to crack and peel, but I had a feeling that the weather would never succeed in washing it away. The quietness of the moment was broken by Jude. "Now that's a bridge," he said.

"Yeah," was my addition to the conversation.

Jude and Erin then started to talk about First Nations and eventually two words caught my attention. "What's a residential school?" I asked Jude, who always appeared to know more than me. He was about to give me an answer but Erin stepped in before he could.

"What do you mean?" she asked flatly.

"What do *you* mean? I just asked a question."

"You really don't know what a residential school is?"

"No. I'm pretty sure we don't have that in Mexico."

Erin sighed. "Well, they were schools where native children were locked in against their will so the government and Christians could eradicate their culture back in the day." The Christian part made me feel a little uncomfortable, but I said nothing.

"Yeah, it was awful," Jude said."They, uh, closed them all down though. Actually, the university used to be one."

Erin choked on her *slimedwich* mid-bite. *"What?"*

"Yeah."

Erin reached inside her backpack for a blue, scuffed water bottle, and had a few sips. "Are you serious?"

Jude nodded.

"Well now I feel gross for having to study there. Who knows what awful things Christians did in those hallways." After a long and awkward silence, Erin continued the uncomfortable conversation, "Like, they probably killed innocent children there for all we know. They're all just a bunch of murderers with a taste for touching people inappropriately."

"Yeah, maybe," Jude said, his face pale and grim. Both his exhaustion from not sleeping the night before and his usual casual demeanor were gone.

The silence that followed was again broken by a remark from Erin, who no doubt thought it was hilarious. "They should just kill them all."

"Who?" I demanded.

"Christians," Erin said merrily.

"Oh so like you'd like to kill me too?" I knew she was obviously just joking, but I couldn't help myself from getting ticked off. It wasn't the comment itself that I had a problem with, but the underlying intention. Erin always shifted her opinions, political ones for the most part, to impress whomever she was talking to. In this case it was Jude, an outspoken agnostic who, unsurprisingly, had stated his disgust for organized religion many times since we became friends. He did, however, have nothing but respect for people who practiced them.

Erin's eyes widened.

She was about to say something but I didn't let her. "Or do I get a pass because I'm brown?"

Jude snorted but tried to pretend he was coughing, probably because I was the palest Mexican he'd seen.

"Relax dude, you know I didn't mean it," Erin replied.

"Yeah but how would you feel if I was making jokes like that at the expense of minorities?"

"Marco–"

"It's all good dude," Jude interrupted. "You do know she was just being silly."

She was just being stupid, I thought. I took a deep breath and finally said, "I know. I'm sorry. It's just like, not okay though."

Erin shifted on her seat and turned her head over to look me in the eyes. "I'm sorry," she said, and I knew she meant it.

I bit my lip, as if that would help me stop feeling embarrassed for what I'd said. "It's okay. I overreacted."

Jude passed me his tape collection. "I think we should listen to some music again. It'll, uh, make the trip feel faster."

"Sure," I said and started digging through the tapes.

7

When old, decrepit barns and hay-bale-filled plots of land started to appear more and more often to our sides–a sign that we had started to leave northern Ontario behind–,I began to feel sick.

I had spent the last hour trying to ignore the increasingly more violent grumblings coming from my belly, focusing on the music playing on The Mirth's warm speakers, counting the Amish caravans that we were passing on the side of the road and thinking about the places in Toronto that I wanted to visit; none of it helped. *That stinking sandwich. I didn't taste mold in it, but I wouldn't be surprised if it was infested with it,* I complained to myself, silently.

I did not dare to even suggest having a potty-stop because Erin had been quite vocal about how our late start of the trip had messed up her (and her friend's) plans for the night, but as The Mirth's ancient odometer added more miles to its count, my stomach became much less merciful.

Look at good old Marco, spreading out in the back seat to have another nice little nap, my friends probably thought, when in reality I was laying in fetal position to alleviate some of my gastrointestinal aches. Cold sweat was making its way down and around my goosebumped skin while my stomach tap-danced inside of me. I grabbed one of Jude's blankets that were stored in the back of the car and covered myself with it. It only made me feel colder.

I tried not to imagine where the white stains on the blanket had come from to avoid feeling worse. By the time I started to consider jumping off the moving vehicle to visit the nearest washroom—or field, as my body wouldn't allow myself to be picky in this situation—when Jude saw a gas station in the distance, no more than half a mile ahead us and said, "I think we should gas up here and get a little snack or something."

I bolted back up, the stained blanket still covering me and making me look like an old and wise pilgrim and said, "Yes, yes, yes!"

"Somebody's finally awake," Erin noted. "Yeah, sure. I gotta go to the ladies room anyway."

Jude signaled and turned right into the gas station. I got out of the car with as much energy and passion only people with the runs are able to conjure.

***

After my business with the poorly maintained gas station bathroom was done, I sent a message to Stella to let her know how the trip was going. She was still at work and wouldn't be able to see my message until later. That was fine. My stomach was empty and no longer causing me much discomfort, so I was happy.

Walking out of the washroom and into the convenience-store part of the gas station the smell of bread, marinara sauce and cheese let me know that there was a Subway attached to it. At that moment my stomach grumbled, demanding me to fill it with cheap food. I joined Jude in the line up. He still looked tired, but also a lot more relaxed than before, probably because of the hours he had already spent behind the wheel. One of his favorite activities was taking us out on night drives and stopping at various fast food restaurants to try out the newest items in their menus, listening to music and, honestly, just enjoying the moment; so being on a road trip, which was sort of an extension of the night drives, was definitely something that brought him joy.

"Feeling better now?" Jude asked.

"Yeah, much better. I must have gotten car-sick or something."

"You don't have to lie to me," he said. "It was probably the sandwich. It was a little funky, wasn't it?."

I agreed, and before I could say anything else, Erin walked out of the ladies room and stood behind us.

Jude and I got a meatball sub. Erin's pick was a chicken teriyaki salad which lost all of its healthiness with the exorbitant amount of blue cheese dressing that was poured on it. We ate our underwhelming fast food meal quietly. When our plates were empty and our bellies full, we got up, stretched our lazy arms and legs and left.

On our way out Jude stopped at the novelty gifts part of the gas station store. A corn pipe had caught his eye, and after holding it in between his fingers, probably imagining how much better his life would be if he were to acquire the pipe, he proceeded to buy it.

When we were back in The Mirth Jude, with the corn pipe dangling in his mouth, inserted the key in the ignition. He turned it but nothing happened. And to our dismay, none of Jude's subsequent attempts at starting the car worked. He inserted the key again and again, twisting and turning it, pushed (and then kicked) the gas pedal multiple times and even hit the deck but the old car refused to even make a sound. I was worried about being stranded in the middle of the highway, of course, but my main concern at the time was what Erin would do to us if the old station wagon chose this day to die.

She was a small, freckled girl who did not look threatening at all, but looks are deceiving.

"Uhh–" Jude started, but when he looked at Erin, whose complexion was slowly switching from sunburnt-pink to anger-red he decided to get out of the car and check the engine to see if there was anything he could do before flat out admitting that we were shit out of luck. He put his corn pipe away, got out of The Mirth and popped the hood open.

He nodded and after mumbling a few *Uh-huh*'s and some *Hum*'s he snapped the hood shut. When he was back in the car he sat silently for a few seconds, rubbing the top of his forehead–where his hairline began–with the heel of his hands. His long fingers swayed like the tops of palm trees in the wind.

"Well, are we stuck here forever or what?" Erin asked, probably doing her best to try to hide her frustration from us. It didn't work.

Jude remained silent for a second or two, and after a big sigh he said, "No, I think the battery's just dead"

"Oh fuck."

I leaned closer to the front seats and said, "That's not that big of a deal though, right?"

"Yeah, it could have been a lot worse," Jude replied. "I'm, uh, going to need your help to start the car."

Erin and I got out of The Mirth, moved to the back. The evening sun warmed the exterior of the car, like a comfy metal blanket, and it took our hands a little while to get used to pushing it.

"Wait!"Jude cried. "Leave the doors open so you can jump in when we get The Mirth going."

We pushed the car, slowly at first, and when we reached a slight slope we had to use all of our strength and might–which was not much–to get to the top. We were a sweaty, puffing mess by then.

We eventually reached a point in which the car stopped resisting our pushing, and in that moment Jude's foot parted ways with the clutch pedal, and the car came back to life. "Jump back in!" he said, and we did as were told. We hopped back in The Mirth, and were safe back inside, Erin started chuckling, and the joyful chuckles turned into stifling laughter.

"That was kind of fun!" she said after she calmed herself down enough to be somewhat intelligible.

What a strange girl, I thought, but couldn't stop myself from laughing as well. Jude couldn't, either, and soon enough Jude achieved his goal. We were all experiencing a strong feeling of mirth, warm and comforting in our bellies. Even though the trip had not gone according to plan, and I had almost shat myself earlier that day, but I loved my friends and I was glad to be there and then, with them.

8

Jude had told us that we wouldn't be able to turn off the car until we got to Newmarket, but luckily we had a full tank. More than enough to take us to our first destination, if everything went well. "But what if I have to pee?" I asked, half joking, but also kind of not.

Jude said nothing. Insead he reached under his seat and handed me an old root beer bottle. I grimaced and looked at the reflection of his blue eyes in the mirror. "Try not to fill it up, we still have a couple of hours to go," he said.

I sighed but said nothing more. I had a feeling that Jude's bottle solution would not work out if Erin was the one who needed to go to the washroom. She had purchased a tall iced tea can at the gas station store, and she'd put it away after Jude handed me the empty bottle.

"How far away are we anyway Jude?" I said. "Like, exactly?"

"I'm not sure, maybe, uh, two hours more. Maybe two and a half."

Erin did not seem to agree with Jude's estimate, so she took her phone out and after a quick search on her maps app she said, "We're three and a half hours away. We should get to Newmarket a little after dark, then you guys will have to drive for another forty-five ish minutes to get to Toronto."

So a little over four hours left for me and Jude, I thought. That wasn't too bad now that I felt rested and my stomach wasn't mad at me anymore. I didn't really feel like sleeping, but I considered it since it would help me pass the time. I was about to lay down on my back seat nest when Erin interrupted me. "I'm tired. Marco, could we switch spots so I can take a nap?" she said.

I looked down at the comfy blanket on the seat for a moment. "Yeah, sure," I replied.

Regardless of Erin's fun-size, she wasn't agile or graceful. She unbuckled her seatbelt and squeezed her way into the back seat, and I couldn't get out of the way soon enough to avoid her sandaled foot, rapidly approaching my face. I blacked out for a few seconds, and when I regained consciousness I was laying against the window and I felt a throbbing, pulsing pain on my nose, and something warm dripping from it. I wiped it with the back of my hand and saw blood and clear snot mixed together.

"I'm sorry, I'm sorry, I'm sorry," Erin kept saying.

I was about to tell her that it was fine, but I sneezed violently before I got the chance to speak. Erin jerked her head to the side, but some blood made it to her face. She raised her shaking hands up to her cheek, and wiped. "I'm so sorry," she said.

I pinched my nose, tilted my head backwards to stop the bleeding and said, "Don't worry about it, it was an accident."

"I'm sorry," Erin whispered.

I looked at Erin again, in the eyes, and said nothing, but she seemed to understand that I really meant that everything was okay. It had been nothing more than an accident. "Do you have any tissues Jude?"

"Uh, I don't know. Let me see." He opened the glovebox and rummaged inside. "Here," Jude said, extending his hand towards the back seat, offering me a crinkled Wendy's napkin.

I wiped my nose with the raspy and cheap napkin and we continued our way.

***

The sky, somewhat similarly to my nose, had a violent red-orange sunset scene painted on it. The sun elongated and slimmed the shadows of the trees, houses, barns and fences that accompanied us during our long trip down the highway.

My friends and I had reached the inevitable point that comes with every drive of a considerable length in which we no longer cared enough to fill the quiet moments with small talk. We were a tired, squeezed–and now also a little smelly–fellowship on our way to the south. When the tiny blue spot which we could barely see far down the road transformed into a big NEWMARKET– 15KM sign our spirits got a little higher again.

I don't know why I was so excited to be this close to Newmarket, because that still meant we had almost an hour before we reached Toronto, but I still found myself smiling. Erin was, understandably, the most excited of the three of us. She had told Jude and I that even though she was a good two hours late–and had lost her reservation for supper at Ricardo's, an amazing italian cuisine restaurant according to the locals–, she still had time to go somewhere else to grab a quick bite to eat with her friend Megan, with whom she was going to be staying during her visit, and then meet up with their friends from the city to play boardgames as if nothing unfortunate had happened on our trip. This last part of her plans made me feel a little jealous.

I really missed *some* of my friends from Mexico. Not the bullies from my high school who hardly passed as an excuse of a friend due to the lack of actual good people in my classroom, but the ones I had made during the one semester I took at the local university. My friends with whom I used to hang out every Friday night after school, playing party games and being a little slutty while drinking strange alcoholic beverages (made by our self-appointed bartender Carlos) and eating pizza.

I think that the fact that I'd gone to private schools my whole life had substantially increased the amount of assholes present throughout my life, and after my dad had informed me that he was okay with the idea of me taking a gap year before moving to Canada as long as I either found a job or went to the public University, I chose the latter. Up until that moment I had assumed that eighty or so percent of the people in Mexico were arrogant, judgy assholes who thought they were better than you because their parents had more money than yours (and while my estimation was a bit high, it wasn't too far off from reality).

I ended up, however, having a revelation after I finished my orientation week at the university: I wasn't so bad at making new friends after all. Back then I had long hair and a dirty-looking (and modest) beard, so I was quite distinct in appearance from my class-mates who all had short crew cuts and clean shaven faces since they had just gotten out of high school, where having such a plain and "clean" look was always mandatory unless you were enrolled in a private school. This allowed me to be recognized with ease, and people learned my name quickly.

After just a month, not only had I become friends with almost everyone in my class, but I'd also experienced being respected for the first time in very a long time. That semester was one of the hap-piest times of my life, because despite not reaching any milestones or achieving important personal goals during those few months, I was comfortable in my own skin. I was happy. I didn't feel self con-scious all day, worrying about doing something in a funny or stupid way and being caught by someone who would then deem it as *cringe,* and then tell the rest of my classmates about it so that they could tease me for the rest of the year. During that semester I didn't have to pretend that I was stupider than I really was in order to fit in. I didn't have to be as quiet and reserved as I had been my whole life as an act of self-preservation back then. Not in this amazing classroom, and not when I was around my new friends.

When I relocated to White Peaks I was glad to see that people here were more than a little friendly–except not in the cartoonish way that TV and movies depicted Canadians–, and that I wouldn't have to get used to the toxicity that I was so familiar with before I got out of high school, but I'd never forget the huge positive impact that my old university class had on me, my mental health and my self esteem, and now that Erin had mentioned her evening plans I could not shake off the melancholic mood that I'd gotten into.

"We should ask your friends in Toronto if they'd like to play board games with us too, Jude," I suggested.

"Yes for sure, dude. Actually, that reminds me of something." Jude took his phone out of his pocket and dialed a number, making me feel uncomfortable by the amount of time that he spent looking at the screen rather than at the road. "Hey, how is it going? ... Good, hey is it okay if my friend Marco stays with us too?"

"Jude, what the fuck?"

He presented me with his index finger and shushed me. "'Kay, great. We should get there in an hour or so ... Okay, see you ... Bye."

I stared at Jude in disbelief, thinking about the uncomfortable scene that we would have been in had it not been for my last-minute reminder. "Dude–"

"They said it's okay for you to stay over, relax."

I said nothing.

"Yikes," Erin noted.

"Yeah, yikes indeed," I agreed.

Jude's chuckle sounded more like a sarcastic snore. "It's all good, dude. I would have, uh, paid for a hotel or something if worse came to worst." I didn't doubt that he meant it, but the fact that he had lied to me was what bothered me the most, but we were so close to Newmarket, and I couldn't be in a bad mood anymore. Soon enough we'd be in Toronto having the time of our lives, exploring the big city, or so I thought before we stumbled upon another metaphorical bump on the road.

9

Newmarket was larger than White Peaks, but just barely, and they still shared some small-town similarities. By the time we entered the city it looked as though there was a curfew put in place, which was weird because it was seven o'clock. Big chain stores were open, as one might expect, but driving down the street we almost saw no pedestrians at all. Traffic was almost non-existent, rush hour would have taken place an hour or so ago I assumed, so we had avoided it.

Newmarket was in hibernation.

Jude turned right onto Main Street and we passed a shabby church with a big green and white lawn sign that said, *The Church is a Gift From God. Some Assembly May be Required,* we saw a much larger billboard on the other side of the road, picturing a young woman with an ill-fitting gray off the rack business suit that had probably been stylish ten years ago, straight black hair that curved inwards right before it got the chance to reach her shoulders and a fake smile with cold, blue eyes. Her name was Lise McMillan and if the billboard spoke the truth, everything she touched, she sold. The billboard as a whole gave me the impression that she was just another overpaid real estate agent that preyed upon senile house owners who wanted to sell their family home to move to another more quiet place–maybe Mexico–, and were clueless enough to be locked into an unfair contract, one which would give people like Lise a big fat commission.

Someone had ruined Lise's fun though, because anyone who liked to see pictures of themselves as big as the one printed on that huge Main Street billboard would absolutely hate what some graffiti *artist* had done to the billboard. Lise's picture was adorned with a classic fake mustache, round, dorky glasses and a few missing teeth. But not only that, this local *artist* had also made another addition to his canvas, one which, in my humble opinion, was the cherry on the cake: a simple S, on the left to Lise's name, transforming it into *Slise McMillan.*

It was such a stupid little thing, but I tend to find shit like that hilarious for some reason, so I started laughing.

"What's up?" Jude asked, but I didn't need to provide him with an answer, because at that moment he also saw the big *Slise* above us. "Dude," he said, fighting off the urge to chuckle. "That's not even that funny."

"That's what makes it so funny," I managed to say. My explanation was sufficient for Jude to get the absurdity of the mediocre vandalizing of Lise's billboard, because his little chortles matched my roaring laughter shortly after.

"You guys are so dumb," Erin said, making an effort to keep herself from giggling.

My laughter started to slow down and transition into hiccups when, out of the corner of my eye, I saw an elderly black cat slowly crossing Main Street, half-dragging one of his skinny back legs. I panicked, and the only word that came out of my mouth was: "Jude!" I patted him on the arm and pointed at the old cat, words still struggling to crawl out. Jude was still laughing–probably still picturing *Slise's* incomplete smile on his mind–and didn't seem to get that I was being serious. "Jude! Jude! Jude!"

"Jude!" Erin shouted, now also tugging at Jude's arm. By the time our urgent cries finally got to him, it was almost too late. There was no time to stop the car without hitting the cat, so I did the next best thing (or what seemed like it to me at the moment). I grabbed the steering wheel and turned it to the right, hoping we wouldn't hit anything, or anyone.

10

Nobody was killed, mangled or seriously injured, and the only damage to public property we caused when The Mirth drove over the curb was a dent on a mailbox. At some point, before the shock of the event wore off us, we heard a loud pop, followed by a low hiss.

After a few more moments of silence and confusion, it was Jude who finally spoke. "Dude what the fuck?!"

"I, uh, uh," I started, but Erin jumped in before I could put my thoughts into words.

"You almost ran over a cat!" she said.

"What?"

"A cat," Erin explained. "He's still over there."

Jude turned around and found the feline old-timer wandering down the sidewalk, oblivious to what could have been its demise. "Oh, uhh, sorry. I didn't see it." He rubbed his forehead and pink, watery blood stuck to his hand.

"Yeah, I figured," Erin snapped.

Jude closed his eyes and exhaled a long breath before stepping out of the car, with Erin and I following him. He walked to the front of the car and crouched to better inspect the damage done to The Mirth. He bit his lower lip and then made a clicking sound with his mouth. "Looks like a flat tire," he said. "The rim is also a little bent. Marco, can you get the spare tire out of the trunk?" Jude's question sounded more like an exasperated command.

"Yes, of course man," I said and went to open the trunk. While I was digging through layers of blankets, suitcases and miscellaneous items–guitar strings, old DVD's, some books–I overheard Jude and Erin's conversation.

"Don't be mad at him, you almost killed that poor cat." Erin whispered. "He saved it."

Jude sighed. "I know. I'm not mad, just a little, uh, rattled, I guess. It all happened too fast, but I guess I would have done the same as he did."

My friend's conversation ended abruptly upon my return with the spare tire, a hydraulic jack infested with rust and a wrench.

"Have you changed a tire before?" I asked.

"Yeah–" Jude said. "Maybe? I think I might have at some point."

"Oh boy."

"It's all good, man. How hard can it be?"

***

Changing the tire hadn't been hard, but rather impossible. First, we pushed The Mirth off the sidewalk back into the road–because the battery still refused to start–as fast as we could, to avoid the unwanted attention of nosy people's eyes. The last thing we wanted at that time was some sort of ticket or fine. When that was taken care of, Erin stayed inside the car while Jude and I walked a couple of blocks up until we found a pizzeria with an open wi-fi network and signal strong enough for us to connect to it from outside of the restaurant, since none of us had enough cell phone data to look up a video explaining how to change a tire.

It took us a while to find a video in which the jack used to change the tire resembled the one we had, but we eventually found one, and we watched it religiously, pausing and rewinding some sections that we thought were most useful. When we returned to the car we found Erin, standing next to The Mirth and with her back resting on a light pole, typing something on her phone, perhaps letting Megan know of our latest setback. A sour expression on her face. Jude and I looked at each other, and without any spoken words, agreed that it would be for the best to let Erin keep doing her own thing while we changed the tire. She'd had enough inconveniences to last her for the rest of the trip already.

Jude took the jack and slid it under the car. When it was placed in the right spot, he started to pump–with ease at first, slowly finding more resistance. When the flat tire was suspended about an inch above the ground, I went ahead and used the wrench to try to remove the bolts from the rim. I used all my strength, but that wasn't enough, so I got up and stepped on the wrench, putting all my weight on it, but even that wasn't working, so Jude took over.

Jude was a big guy, but even he had to kick the wrench with all his might to loosen the bolts. After an extraneous ten minutes, my sweaty friend was done, a red pulsing vein on the right side of his forehead.

"Fuck me," Jude said, a little out of breath. I stood behind him, feeling ashamed because I hadn't been strong enough to help. Also because it was my fault that the car got even more fucked up than before.

"Let me do the actual tire swap, you go rest for a moment," I suggested.

"Thanks, dude," Jude said and he sat on the pavement, close to me in case I needed *more* help, probably.

I pulled and pulled but the tire seemed to have made its mind: it would not move, regardless of my best attempts. I turned my head just a little towards Jude to see him while I was still trying to take the tire off. He was now laying on the pavement with his arms stretched up above his head, doing something on his phone.

I returned my attention to the tire, but it was a lost cause and I knew it. Here was yet another thing that I couldn't help with. "Need a hand?" Jude asked.

"Maybe."

Jude pocketed his phone, stood up and stretched. "What's up?"

"It's the rim. It's so bent it won't let me take the tire off the car."

"Uh, let me try."

I moved back, still crouching, and let Jude take my spot. He grabbed the tire and pulled. And pulled. And then pulled some more.

His tensed arms were trembling with effort, and his fingers had turned white around the area where they were holding onto the tire. After a few more moments of struggle, Jude let go and color returned to his hands. "Yep, I think we will have to call a mechanic."

Upon hearing this, Erin cringed. "Well, then let's do it now. We're already so–"

"Late," Jude finished.

Whenever I fuck things up I usually try to compensate by showing initiative to try to fix them, so I drew my phone out of my pocket and searched for local car shops. The only shop that was still open was the Newmarket Superstore, so I gave them a call. An automated answering machine greeted me with a robotic, "Hello, and thank you for contacting us. We will be more than glad to help you–" and then started listing various phone extensions. When the pre-recorded message gave me the right number–008–I dialed it. The line beeped seven times until I got disconnected. Jude and Erin gave me a hopeful look, but I shook my head and restarted the process.

After the fifth beep, a raspy yet somehow oily voice picked up my call. "Automotive, Vern speaking."

"Hi, uhm, we hit a curb and got a flat tire and, uh, a bent rim–
"

"Sorry, you'll have to call again tomorrow," Vern interrupted. "We're full for the rest of the day."

"Uhh–"

The man with the oily voice ended the call. I sighed. "They're busy until tomorrow."

"Of course they are!" Erin said. "What else could we expect from this shitty trip?"

I wanted to say something, but again, couldn't, because she was right.

Jude put a hand on Erin's shoulder. "I'll call a cab for you, Erin. Me and Marco will look for a hotel or something and then tomorrow–"

"No, no. Just give me a minute," she said.

It was now Erin's turn to use her phone to try and get some help. She called Megan and after a brief conversation–trying not to let her voice betray her and show how anxious and distressed she was feeling–she smiled and nodded looking at us. "Oh thank you, thank you so much. Okay, we'll see you later then."

11

We locked the doors, put enough quarters in the park meter to last us for an entire day and waited, standing on the sidewalk with our suitcases by our side. After sixteen minutes, we saw a lonely forest green Ford Fiesta from the mid 2000s approaching. *Finally things are starting to get better* I thought, not knowing that our Toronto odyssey was about to start.

Megan stopped her car next to us–behind The Mirth–and rolled down the passenger's side window. She did not look the way I had pictured her. Short, curly purple hair covered half of her pale face–not because she had bangs, but because her hair was so puffy it spread out in all directions at once–, the only traces of color coming from her perpetually blushed cheeks and plump lips. She had a smile on her face but her eyebrows arched upwards, making her look both happy and concerned at the same time. She reminded me of my second grade teacher, Mrs. Trujillo, whose full lips made me and my classmates think of the pink fish from *Shark Tale*.

"Hi guys, I'm sorry you've had a bit of a hard drive down here," she said. Her voice was boyish and kind. "Come on in."

She bent down slightly, pressed a button and the trunk popped open with a squeak. We loaded our belongings in it and got in the car. The air outside was getting a little cooler, but stepping into nice artificial air-conditioning of the Fiesta was a very welcomed treat. Megan was listening to a man with a feminine voice singing in a falsetto about his undying love for some girl he had just met or something like that–it was from a musical, I assumed–but she turned down the volume to chat with us. And after a brief introduction, Megan jumped straight to good stuff and said, "So, how bad was it?"

"It was awful!" Erin bursted. "We just run into problem after problem after problem! We kept getting delayed and then the car being the piece of shit that it is–"

"Hey! Give more respect to The Mirth" Jude said, temporarily losing his cool, but Erin chose to ignore him.

"Then we almost hit a cat because these guys were farting around and not paying attention to the road," Erin continued, throwing us a nasty look from her seat at the front. If she had more complaints (and I'm sure she did), she must have thought she'd said enough after she saw that Jude had his head down and was biting his nails. I was looking out the window, trying to distance myself from the conversation. "And I wasn't the best road trip buddy either, I guess."

"Wow... what a day," Megan said, turning the volume of the music even lower. "But at least it's all over now."

"Not really," I said, still looking out the window. "Jude and I still gotta go to Toronto."

"Yeah, I know. You guys can stay with me and Erin for the night and get your car fixed in the morning."

"Thanks," Jude said, taking his finger out of his mouth. "It's just been a very long day. I think I'm gonna be ready to crash soon, I only got like, uh, three hours of sleep last night."

Megan turned her head back to us and Erin winced, perhaps hoping no cats would walk in front of this car. I don't know if what I saw on Megan's face was either understanding or pity, but I chose to think it was the former. "How about this?" she said. "Let's just grab something quick to eat and then I'll drop you guys at my place to get some rest while me and Erin go hang out with some friends."

I hesitated for a moment, but then made up my mind and said, "Actually, I was thinking about tagging along with you, if you don't mind. It would help me clear my head and what not." Erin looked back at me and I gave her a frail little smile in return.

"Oh I don't mind at all! The more, the merrier," Megan said.

12

We parked outside of a duplex house which had been turned from a typical Canadian working-class family home into student housing not too long ago. The left half of the house–the Megan side–had been subject to less college-party damage than the other half had, but it was nonetheless in need of significant repairs and renovations. The screen door greeted our entry with a rusty creak, like a nice grandma, and the living room, despite being tidy and clean, had more cracks on its walls and ceiling than what I felt comfortable with. The ancient hardwood floor was scratched all over it, and there was a big circular spot of about a foot in diameter at the right corner of the room, which was a darker shade of brown than the rest of the floor.

"Home, sweet home," Megan said. "Come on in. Erin and I will share my room on this floor, and for you guys I hope the basement will be okay. There's a futon down there and I can also let one of you take my inflatable mattress. I already blew it up. You guys can figure out who gets what."

"Thank you so much, Megan." I said, happy to know that even if we were an entire day delayed and The Mirth was at the moment out of commission, we still had a decent place to rest and a (cracked) roof over our heads.

"Yes, thanks a lot," Jude agreed.

"No prob guys. The basement is down that way," Megan said, pointing towards the stairs at the back of the living room, past the dark spot on the floor. "We'll head out in half an hour-ish, so you guys have time to go downstairs and settle in. I'll come down to let you know when we're ready to go to my friend's place."

"Sounds good," I said. Jude and I grabbed our suitcases and we headed down to the basement.

Our temporary home had a strong musty smell that reminded me of the library (and, unfortunately, of Mrs. Townsend). The futon Megan had mentioned had seen better days (maybe fifteen years ago) but Jude claimed it by plopping on it and letting out a big yawn. "This is actually quite nice," he said.

I walked towards the depression-green inflatable mattress and bent down to inspect it. There was sand on top of it, pooling in the indentations of its surface. Not too much, but I took off my shirt and used it to dust the sand off. The city where I'm from was right on the Pacific Ocean, but not even nineteen years of living there made my distaste for sand fade away. It was the feeling of never quite being able to completely get rid of it when you put your shoes back on, after spending a day at the beach, what I hated about it. When I removed as much sand off my bed as I could, I plopped on it as well.

If Megan had been correct when she said *the more, the merrier*, I wouldn't be able to corroborate it, because by the time she and Erin came downstairs I was already fast asleep.

***

My sleep was interrupted at 10:30 PM, when I received a sudden phone call from Stella, who was getting concerned due to the lack of updates about my trip. "Sorry, we're at Erin's friend's house now," I explained when I recovered from my post-sleep confusion. "I was so tired I crashed as soon as I put my head on the pillow."

We chatted for almost half an hour. I tried to be as quiet as possible to avoid waking Jude up at first, but he was the heaviest sleeper I knew, so I eventually decided that my normal voice levels would be just fine for this phone call. No more whispering. I mainly just talked (in great detail) to Stella about all the difficulties we had faced in our trip. When she could hide her drowsiness no more, we agreed that it was time for both of us to go to bed.

"I love you so much and I can't wait for you to come back," she said in a dreamy and whispery tone.

"I love you so much too. I'll be back before you know it," I replied, uncertain about what the next day would have in store for us, and not really wanting to find out.

Part 3: Toronto

1

The basement had no windows, but daytime somehow found a way to wake me up the next morning, and I pretty felt well rested–even though the blow up mattress was wobbly and not firm enough for my taste. I had, however, forgotten all about the events from the day before, and when I realized that I wasn't in my own bedroom back in White Peaks, I felt a bit uneasy. I looked around the unfamiliar room and saw Jude still sleeping, with his left arm outstretched and his hand almost brushing the carpet on the floor. That's when the memories of our road trip came back to me and I calmed down. *I really miss my own bed,* I thought as I sat up on the mattress and rubbed my face. I found my phone laying on the floor next to me and checked the time. It was quarter past nine. I noticed that the battery was almost dead so I got out of "bed" and went to my suitcase to grab my charger and plug my phone in.

It was still early but my stomach was more awake than my mind, and it was begging me for food. "Jude." I said. "Jude!"

The response I got was a dull grunt. I shook my friend and woke him up. "Huh. Hey, what's up?" Jude asked, still with his eyes closed, almost as a reflex.

"I'm hungry."

Jude considered this for a moment, opened his eyes and said, "Yeah, I guess I could eat."

"We should get ready to head out and grab a bite as soon as we can," I said. "Then we can get the car's tire switched and go to Toronto."

Jude was much more awake now, taking less time to process what I was saying. "Yeah, sure. Let me go have a shower first."

I agreed and left so Jude could undress.

***

I went back upstairs to see if Erin and Megan were awake already. I hadn't heard them come back from their friend's house in the middle of the night, but I doubted their game night had been wild enough for them to have to spend the night over there.

The main floor of the house was quiet as a mouse, white light coming into the living room through the big windows. It was an overcast day. All the bedroom doors were shut except for Megan's, and when I walked by I saw a naked freckled back, the rest of the figure covered by a thin pale-blue sheet that had lost its punch little by little with every time it had been washed. The naked back was Erin's, and she was sleeping next to Megan, who had the entire comforter for herself.

No wonder she was upset we were so late, I thought. Erin stirred and I turned around to go back downstairs, making the floor creak.

2

Forty-five minutes later we were all sitting down at the table having breakfast. I had also taken a shower and my body felt refreshed, my hair still very wet because I had the bad habit of never drying it properly–I just grabbed a towel and my head with it until my hair stopped dripping.

Megan had cooked us fried eggs, bacon and toast. Both the bacon and toast were fine–it was hard, but not impossible, to mess them up–, but there was something special about the eggs.

"This is amazing," Jude said, with his mouth half full. "What did you put on the eggs?"

Megan didn't blush, probably because it wasn't the first time people had complimented her cooking–or maybe because her cheeks were already red–, but accepted Jude's praise nevertheless. "Thank you, Jude. I just fried them with some butter and added salt, pepper and a little bit of garlic and rosemary."

"Megan's a great cook," Erin said, smiling and looking at her *very special friend* with dreamy eyes. This did make Megan's cheeks gain even more color, somehow.

"I'm decent," Megan replied. Jude's face both deflated and tightened, and he raised an eyebrow. "Okay, I guess I'm sort of good, but I wouldn't say I'm a great cook."

"She's just modest," Erin said.

I wiped my mouth with the back of my hand to remove some butter off my face. "She sure is," I added.

Megan bit her lip and tried to change the topic of the conversation. "What's your plan for today guys? Did you find someone to fix the car?"

"Not yet, but we will," Jude said after having a big bite of toast.

***

Jude and I grabbed our belongings from the basement and put the thin mattress back inside the couch, making it screech. Little dust clouds erupted and I sneezed violently.

Jude called the Superstore, dialed the correct extension and talked to the mechanic. I could hear Vern's loud gruff coming out of the speaker. Jude, on the other hand, sounded a bit nervous. "Oh, uh, okay. And how much will towing it cost?– *What?*– Okay, uh, thanks."

"So–"

"We gotta call a tow truck first to take the car to the shop and then they'll see if they can, uh, help us out. They said they're very busy today."

Of course they're busy, I thought. "Well, I guess we better do that now so they can swap the tire today and we can get going."

"Yeah," Jude said and paused for a second. "It'll probably be expensive, though."

"How expensive?"

Jude let out some sort of mumbly grunt.

"What?"

"It doesn't matter, it has to be fixed," Jude said.

"I can pitch in for it or–"

"Nah, it's all good, I got it. Don't worry about it."

"But this was my fault, it would be just fair for me to–."

"Nah, dude, don't worry about it. I should have paid attention to the road. Plus it's my car. I wouldn't expect you to pay for my stuff if it got broken."

"But–"

Jude put his left index finger on his lips and shushed me. "I gotta make another call."

3

The tow truck driver arrived at Megan's twenty minutes later. He was a tall, skinny man called Jim, and he had paper-thin skin that allowed the small blood vessels on his nose and around his eyes to be easily seen. He reminded me a bit of the crackhead that had tried to steal my bike at Jude's.

He wasn't much of a talker, and he only spoke to us twice. First upon his arrival to confirm our destination. The second time, a few minutes after we'd hopped on his truck, to ask us if we were from Newmarket.

"No, we're from White Peaks," Jude answered.

"Actually, we live there but I'm originally from Mexico," I said.

Jim nodded, his eyes not meeting ours. I had only been living in Canada for ten months so far, but I was already sick of people saying *No way! What do you think about the winter up here? It must be* so *different from winter in Mexico*, every single time I introduced myself to someone new. In any other instance I would have avoided mentioning where I was from, but that day I was feeling anxious– and therefore, chatty. It was a nice surprise to see that if Jim had anything to say about weather differences between Canada and Mexico, he kept it to himself.

We were dropped off at the Superstore's big garage and Jim gave a yellow receipt to Jude, followed by a debit machine. I was quite a bit shorter than Jude, but I still managed to see the amount due: $135.25 dollars.

"Holy shit," I whispered. Jude ignored my comment, took plastic out of his wallet and paid. "Let me transfer you some money, man," I suggested after Jim had left.

"No, I said it's okay and I meant it dude," Jude said.

We walked into the Superstore's car shop section, and I finally put a face to Vern's name. He was a sturdy-looking man–which is my polite way to say that he was overweight, but probably not obese–, close to sixty years of age with thick, gray hair drenched in gel. His face was clean shaven and covered in acne scars, making his cheeks look like massive oranges. He had a big, bubbly gut, which put a lot of strain on the poor buttons of his shirt that barely managed to keep it shut, and his big hairy arms threatened his sleeves with ripping them open.

"Hello, what can we do for you?" Vern asked, giving us a cool, toothy smile, the way only someone who had been handsome and popular in his youth–but was now starting to live his twilight years, still thinking he was the big shit–could. Something I'd never be able to do or even identify with myself.

"Hi, uh, we called earlier because our car's tire got flat and the rim got bent," Jude said.

"Oh yeah, right. Well we're quite busy today as I said on the phone," Vern said. "We're all booked for the day, but if anyone cancels we'll make sure to squeeze your car in." He smiled yet again and produced a clipboard and pen from under his counter. "Here, write your information down and give us the key. We'll give you a call when we get 'er fixed."

I didn't want to step in because Jude had given me the impression that he wanted to take care of the situation on his own, and I respected that, but when he took the pen from Vern's greasy fingers and started to fill out the form I said, "Uhh, thank you Vern, but we're in a bit of a pickle here. See, we're not from town. We were just driving down to Toronto but got into this accident and–"

"Sorry son," Vern interrupted, not looking sorry. "You should have made an appointment if you were in a hurry."

I was going to speak again, but Jude stepped in. "Well, that's kind of why we called you earlier."

"And yesterday too," I said.

"But you never did make an appointment, now, did you?" Vern replied, his smile still stuck to his face like a bumper sticker that you thought was cool years ago, but has since gone out of style and you keep forgetting to remove it.

Jude said nothing for a moment, and then started writing again on the clipboard. "Yeah, sorry. We've just been under a lot of stress lately," he finally said, giving back the form to Vern along with The Mirth's keys.

"That's all right, buddies. We'll do our best to help you out. You can sit over there at the waiting area, but if I were you I'd go for a walk or something. This might take a while."

Jude thanked Vern and we left the shop. It was now ten past noon and the gray, even clouds were still looming over Newmarket, preventing the sun from casting shadows.

"So what do we do now?" I asked, walking a little behind Jude.

"I don't know, we'll just have to wait I guess."

"Do you think they'll fix The Mirth today?"

Jude made a wondering, clicking sound with his mouth. "Nope. I doubt they will," he said.

"Yeah, you're right. They probably won't."

I kept walking behind Jude.

4

An hour later we were thirsty and stopped at a convenience store to buy some energy drinks for Jude, and a Sprite for myself, since I wasn't in the mood for my usual Diet Coke at the time. I was already at the counter paying when I looked back, and saw Jude returning to the back of the store. After the clerk—a woman in her mid fifties with curly blonde hair tied behind her long neck with a red elastic, who reeked of cigarettes and deodorant—bagged my drink and handed it to me, I walked towards Jude. He was trying on a fake-denim ball cap and examining his reflection on the mirror.

I looked at an identical hat from the pile where he'd taken his from, saw the price on the tag of $35.99 (plus tax), and said, "Jude, you shouldn't waste money on that. I can give you my hat if you want."

"Thanks, Marco," Jude said, still looking at his reflection, "But I have a pretty big head and most hats don't fit me. This one does, though."

"But you haven't tried mine yet."

"Is it extra large?" Jude asked.

"Uh, I don't know, probably not."

Jude took the ball cap off and showed me the tag. On it, XL was printed.

"Regular hats always give me headaches when I wear them," he said, making his way back to the front of the store to buy the ball cap.

We sat on the bench of a bus stop outside of the convenience store, rehydrating ourselves. We still had some time to kill until Vern fixed The Mirth, if he even had time for it, so I took my phone out of my pocket and looked for fun things to do or cool places to visit in Newmarket. It was a fine Saturday afternoon, but Google let me know that there weren't any events in town taking place during this weekend, so we remained planless–unless we wanted to extend our stay and check out the book fair that the local library was organizing the following week.

"Haha, no way dude," Jude said after I jokingly suggested that idea to him.

In the end, we decided to walk another kilometer and a half to visit the Upper Canada Mall to check some stores out–despite Jude's inclination to buy stuff he didn't need and his shrinking budget–and watch a movie.

5

I've never liked walking–not even when I lived back home with my parents and was twenty-five pounds lighter–, so when we finally arrived at the mall and realized there was no movie theater, it was quite a disappointment. Jude and I loved watching (and rewatching) movies, so I was hoping we could catch a showing of the new *Incredibles* movie, but now that wasn't going to happen. We could have taken a cab to the nearest Cineplex, but cabs are expensive and we didn't have money to spare, so we decided to stay at the shitty, movietheatreless mall to kill some time.

We ate yet another snack–a shared bag of cinnamon pretzel bites from the food court–and went to the dollar store after, because, well, we really didn't have anything better to do while we waited for Vern's phone call. We walked down every aisle, browsing. Once in a while Jude would pick up random items–mostly novelty toys–to check them out before putting them back on incorrect shelves. When we were wandering through the clothing aisle I stopped for a moment when a fake-denim hat caught my eye. The price sticker on it said $3.99. Jude glanced at it for a second and moved on, before I could make any comments.

Jude was a few steps ahead of me and when I caught up with him, his phone rang. The store was busy and loud, with packs of obnoxious families bickering left and right, but despite not being able to hear the voice on the phone this time I was sure it was the call we'd been waiting for. Jude didn't say much again, just agreed and said a few *Uh-hu*'s, and then the call was over. His face was neutral, not showing annoyance or excitement, so after a few moments I asked, "What did they say?"

Jude sighed, took his hat off, brushed his hair with three lazy fingers and said, "There's good news and bad news."

"Oof."

"So, uh, they swapped the tire but the car still won't start even though they tried recharging the battery."

"Of course."

"Yeah, they said they'll check out the engine on Monday because they're closed on Sundays and they won't have time to do it today."

My spirits were already low but this sunk them further. "Fuck."

"Yeah."

"So what are we gonna do now?"

Jude scratched the stubble on his chin and said, "All I know is I don't want to go back to Megan's. I didn't feel welcomed there."

"What? I thought they were, well, I thought Megan didn't mind."

"Yeah, it was mostly Erin who made me feel a bit, uh, awkward I guess. She probably feels like we're crashing her party, and I don't like it," Jude said, turning right into another aisle—the food aisle. We stopped at the chocolate section and Jude took some mini Mars bars.

After Jude paid at the cash register he asked the tall asian cashier what the best way to go from Newmarket to Toronto was. "There's buses and a train you could take," he said. "I'd say the train is the best way to get there, it's a little faster and more comfortable."

"Yeah," Jude said. "We'll probably take the train."

We thanked the cashier and left the store.

"Are we just going to leave the car here then?" I asked Jude after he handed me a mini Mars bar.

"Yeah. We can't stay here all weekend. We'll come back on Monday and drive back home."

"Okay."

The next train to Toronto, we found out after visiting the station's website, was scheduled to depart an hour and a half later, so we rushed back to the Superstore to pick our suitcases from The Mirth. We ran for two whole minutes until our burning lungs forced us to slow down to a brisk walk.

***

An hour later we were once more entering the car shop side of the Superstore. Vern was gone–maybe on his lunch break, eating something greasy like his hair–, and in his place was a balding guy of, unfortunately for him, no more than twenty five years of age. "Hello there, what can I do for you?" the guy behind the counter asked, a little startled from seeing our sweaty and panting selves.

Jude took a moment to catch his breath and said, "The Ford station wagon is mine–" and after making another pause to take a deep breath, he continued. "We need to get our stuff from the trunk because–"

"Oh yeah, for sure," the balding guy said, interrupting Jude. We never found out what his name was. "I just need to see your ID and I'll be happy to give you your keys back."

Jude nodded and looked in his pocket for his wallet. After almost a minute of examining and reexamining the contents of all four of his jean's pockets (and of me getting a little more nervous with every passing second) he said, "Oh, yes!" and looked in the breast pocket of his blue chambray shirt. He took his wallet out and handed it to the balding guy.

After verifying that Jude was indeed the owner of The Mirth, he got the keys back and we were led into the garage where they had stored it. We grabbed our belongings and exited the shop.

"How far are we from the station?" Jude asked after finding out that his phone was dead.

"We're almost five kilometers away," I said after consulting my phone. "It would take us close to another hour. We probably won't make it on time if we walk though. Maybe we should get a cab."

Jude frowned slightly, but relaxed when I told him that I'd pay for it. We sat on the floor, looking like boiled shrimp and sweating profusely, with our belongings next to us, and waited for the cab. A few people walked by and gave us weird looks, but we didn't care. We just wanted to get out of Newmarket.

6

For the first time since we started our Toronto trip, things started to work out. The cab arrived on time and we were on our way. When we got to the train station the temperature had dropped down to sixteen degrees celsius, so I had to put on the black bomber jacket I'd packed. Those temperatures were only seen in the winter back in Mexico. Jude was comfortable in this weather–the big sweat stain on his back was now dry–and didn't feel the need to add another layer of clothing.

We bought our tickets with twenty minutes to spare, so we waited inside the station, walking down the long hallways with clear heads and a sense of relief because even though things had not gone the way we planned, we were back on track.

When we reached the west end of the station the sight of the washroom sign made Jude aware that the energy drinks he'd had before had already passed through his kidneys and were ready to come out, so he excused himself.

My bladder wasn't full, so I walked back the way we came. I stopped when I saw the window display of a shop–that among other things, sold cheaply made electronics at ridiculously high prices–in which a portable phone charger rested. I went inside and bought it. Just in case more shit happened.

"What did you get?" Jude asked when I got out of the store.

"Just a phone charger," I said. "One of the portable ones."

"Good. Do you mind if I borrow it for a bit?"

"Your phone dying was kind of the reason why I got it, so yeah."

I opened the box and handed it to Jude. He plugged his phone to the charger but nothing happened.

"Sorry, man," I said. "I guess I gotta charge it first."

"It's all good," he said.

The train to the Aurora station will arrive in five minutes, the voice of an unenthusiastic girl said through the speakers, repeating the same message in French afterwards. We got out of the station and went to the boarding area, where a collection of people–some college students, a McDonald's employee wearing a Wendy's hat and a young couple swallowing each other–were also waiting for their ride.

A few minutes later the sound of the approaching train started to grow louder in the distance, and when it stopped at the station we all boarded it right away, except for the making-out couple, who almost didn't make it in before the sliding doors closed. We chose a row of seats that was empty and sat our tired butts down. The interior was gray and dirty, with lime green accents here and there–around the sides of the seats and windows–, and there was a faint and unpleasant smell of feet or dirty laundry in the air, but I still couldn't help myself from feeling excited.

I've always had a nostalgic fascination for trains and railways, as the sight of one is somehow able to conjure up images in my mind. Images that feel more like memories from lives I never lived. From the lives of people who had lived and died in a much simpler time, when smoking indoors and casual racism were much more common, and accepted by society, even.

I looked out the window and saw Newmarket shrink into a small cluster of yellow lights in the dusk, like a half-eaten corncob, or like the floor of a movie theatre with a spill of popcorn.

7

The same bored voice from the Newmarket station announced our arrival to the big Canadian city, but I still had to shake Jude awake. "We're here. We're finally here my dude!"

He sat upright and looked around, a little confused. "Oh, nice. Let's get out of here," he said.

We grabbed our belongings and exited the train. I was sure the temperature was the same as it had been when we left Newmarket, but Jude must have thought otherwise and put on a brownish-green light jacket. This was another Jude staple, and he wore it from late-summer all the way until the end of November, only switching to wearing his much heavier winter jacket (also green) when the temperature was below eight degrees celsius.

"Where do we go now?" I asked, hoping Jude had a plan or that might resemble one.

"Now we go look for a place to charge my phone and tell Mel to pick us up."

That was better than nothing, but I wish he'd used one of the four outlets next to our seats on the train. "Who's Mel?" I asked.

"She's the friend we're staying over with."

"Oh yeah. Right."

We sat on a bench inside the Aurora station, which was just outside of Toronto, and Jude plugged his phone in. When the screen turned on I had to remind him that he could browse Reddit later, and he agreed. I stood up and went to one of the windows to look at the city, and also to give Jude some privacy for his call. A hooded man was yelling back at his screaming child, a boy of no more than six or seven years–about something that I couldn't quite understand. The boy's screeches reached a pitch almost high enough to break glass and his red, squinty eyes seemed to be ready to pop out of his face. "*I'm done with you!*" the man snapped, and this time I could hear him over the thick windows of the station. "*Come here,*" he said, grabbing his son's thin and fragile-looking arm. What happened next was one hundred percent true. I took no creative liberties. The angry dad lifted his son's shirt up a couple of inches and slid the kid's arms off it. He then proceeded to use the long sleeves to tie the now confused yet still crying boy to the pole of the streetlight to their left. *What the actual fuck,* I said to myself. *The things you see in the big city.*

"She's on her way," Jude said from the bench.

I walked back towards my friend and sat down. The boy's screams were still audible. I glanced back towards him and saw the kid but not his father. *Big oof.*

"So, uh, I gotta be honest with you my dude–"

"She won't take me in too, will she?" I asked. The last day had put me in a *prepare for the worst* kind of mood.

"*What?* No, no. I just wanted to tell you that Mel and I have a bit of a history, but I don't think it'll make things awkward."

"You guys are just friends now?"

"Yeah. I guess you could say that," Jude said, now looking away from me. "We may hook up or something though."

"Oh, okay. Good for you, I guess."

Jude smiled. "Thanks, don't worry though. We will be, uh, discreet if anything happens."

Suddenly, I thought I knew the real reason why we had come all the way to Toronto. "You just came here to sleep with her, didn't you?

Jude didn't reply.

8

Jude's mood soured when Mel arrived and we saw that she was in the passenger's seat while someone else was driving the car. The guy behind the wheel was a tanned guy of around my age, wearing a faux leather jacket and sunglasses even though it was nighttime. He reminded me of one of my grade school classmates, Javier, who once asked me if I liked to smell my fingers after scratching my butt. I did not. He did.

Canadian Javier parked the car on the sidewalk next to us. The window rolled down and Mel gave us a warm smile. She had long, blond hair and big, brown eyes, and she looked like the kind of person that has a smile as their default facial expression, based on the two razor-thin wrinkles around her mouth like two crescent moons. "Hey guys, sorry about all the stuff you went through to get here," she said, still smiling but arching her eyebrows upwards, making her look slightly worried, "But I'm glad you made it. This is my boyfriend, Magd."

The redundant-sunglasses guy nodded. Jude wouldn't have liked him, even if he wasn't sleeping with his former fling. If we had been alone, he would have said something about not trusting people that look as confident as Magd.

"Thanks for picking us up," I said.

"Yeah, thanks," Jude mumbled.

Mel's eyebrows relaxed. "No problem! Are you guys hungry?"

"Yeah, we could eat," Jude replied. "It's been a very long trip."

"Then come on in," Mel said and Magd opened the trunk. Jude and I put our suitcases in it and jumped in the car.

After a few awkward moments of silence, Magd askes, "What happened to your car?"

Jude considered the question, and to my surprise, opened up to him, "We got a flat tire after we ran over a curb in Newmarket, but there's probably something wrong with the engine because we took the car to a shop to get it fixed and now it won't start."

"Could it be the battery?" Magd asked.

"No, they tried to recharge it and it still won't turn on."

"Oh shit," Mel said, turning around to see us.

"Yeah," Jude continued. "The guys from the shop will have another look on Monday when we head back. This is my friend Marco, by the way."

I introduced myself and went over the same spiel that I had memorized about where I was from, why I'd decided to move to Canada (to study film), and all that fun stuff.

"Oh wow, I bet people ask you this all the time," Mel said, and indeed, they always did, "but I gotta know, what do you think of winters up here?"

"I like them up until the day after New Year's." I replied. "I love having a white Christmas, but after that winters are way too long and depressing,"

"Yeah, winters are way too long. Maybe you'd have a better time if you tried skiing or doing something like that to, you know, make the best of it. I used to get bad seasonal depression in the wintertime, before I started snowshoeing."

"Yeah, maybe," I lied. Doing physical activities in nice weather was already too much of a chore.

Our conversation continued sailing smoothly. Mel was very pleasant and easy to talk to, and I could see why Jude wanted to get in her pants again. She was his type. Smart, chatty and blonde.

During the drive Jude kept reaching forwards, towards the passenger seat, where Mel was sitting, causing his seatbelt to attack him and force him to back up when he got too close to her face. Once in a while I caught Magd throwing unfriendly looks to Jude, who didn't seem to care.

When we arrived at Mel's student house, Magd said goodbye to us, kissed his girlfriend and bumped my fist. It was the first time anyone had said goodbye to me like that in ten years or more. Jude hesitated when Magd presented him with his fist, but decided to bump it in the end, probably because he had done us the favor of driving us to Mel's.

We headed directly towards the dining room and Megan took some pasta, a jar of ragú sauce and some butter out of the pantry to prepare us a home made supper, that while not fancy at all, ended up tasting quite good. I suspected the addition of an absurd amount of butter to the already seasoned sauce was what had elevated its flavor. After all, humans love fat. Some, like myself, much more than others.

After Jude and I finished our second helping of Mel's pasta, a round-faced girl–who made me think of a large egg–with thick black hair and lazy stoner eyes entered the house. "Oh, hi Sabrina. These are Jude and Marco," Mel said. "They're staying over for a couple of days."

Sabrina took off her brown sweater, put it on a coat rack on the hallway next to us and waved "Hey, how is it going guys?" I could smell weed now that she'd gotten closer.

"Oh not bad, not anymore at least, thank you," Jude said, speaking for both him and I. "Hey Mel, we should all hang out sometime or something."

"Oh yeah, we could all go to the bar and have some drinks or something in a bit," Mel replied.

Sabrina's face lit up, as much as her marijuana serenity allowed it, and she bared her slightly yellow teeth. "Yeah, definitely. Let me just take a shower and I'm down," she said and excused herself.

I'm not particularly fond of drinking in bars because alcohol there is much more expensive than it should be and loud music in crowded rooms with subdued lighting gives me headaches. "I don't want to sound lame," I said, slightly sinking my shoulders in a quasi-shrug, " but I think I'll pass." I knew that Mel wouldn't feel comfortable having a stranger hanging out alone at her place, so before she could try to convince me to join them, I added, "It'll work out though, because I really wanted to watch a movie on Imax here. We don't have any of those theaters in White Peaks."

"Are you sure you don't want to come to the bar with us?" Mel asked, likely out of courtesy.

"Nah it's all good, " I said, trying to sound casual. "Just go without me."

Jude asked me if I was sure and I reassured him I was.

Mel eyed me for a second, looking like she was trying to see through me to figure out if I was telling the truth, and said, "Okay, let me give you my phone number to tell you where we keep the spare key in case you come back before us." I took out my phone to get her number. I was expecting Mel to dictate it to me but she instead grabbed my phone and typed it herself. When she gave it back I noticed she'd added a sunflower emoji next to her name. When she asked us if we wanted to finish the leftover pasta we declined and she took us to the living room, where two long, comfy-looking black couches waited for us with blankets and pillows.

"Sorry it's not much," Mel said, "but if you need anything else just–"

"What are you talking about?" Jude said, cutting her off. "It's perfect, and free."

Mel smiled at him, maybe the way she used to when they were dating–or when they were fuck buddies–, or maybe not, I wasn't in the country when they were seeing each other, and Jude never told me more about the nature of their relationship.

9

It was the first time I'd been away–in a different city–from Stella since we started seeing each other, and by then we were both a feeling a little sad and needy, so instead of giving her a phone call to let her know that we'd safely arrived to Toronto, I decided to FaceTime with her while Jude was in washroom so that I could have some privacy.

I hadn't understood how homesick I'd been feeling (perhaps due to the overwhelming feeling of anxiety that had taken over me after having so many unexpected inconveniences presenting themselves to us on our way to Toronto, like an STD that never quite wants to go away) until I saw Stella's face on my phone. We didn't have much time to talk, it was getting late and we were going to leave the house soon, so after hearing about her day–which had been uneventful and uninspiring but otherwise fine–I let Stella know of my plans for the night. "Isn't it a bit too late to go to the movies?" she asked.

I hadn't considered this, but said, "Well it's a big city, I'm sure they'll have some late shows."

I heard a door opening and Jude's wet footsteps coming back from the washroom and we said goodbye and goodnight to each other. I turned around, giving Jude my back, and blew a little kiss at Stella before we ended the call.

"You guys are too much, haha," Jude said, chuckling a bit.

I gave him the finger. "That was a private conversation," I said, facing him now. Jude sat next to me on the couch where I'd sleep for the next two nights.

"So, there's a change of plans," he said, leaning closer to me and lowering the tone of his voice. "When I went to the bathroom upstairs I walked past Sabrina's room and the door was open,"–he was getting even closer to me now, almost invading my personal space–"And it wasn't, like, half open my dude. It was completely open and I saw her naked, getting dressed."

"Oh shit."

"Yeah! And she was like, uh, not looking at me but kind of looking at me, you know what I mean?"

"Yeah."

Jude smiled. "I'm going to try to sleep with her instead, because I don't want to make things awkward with Mel while we're here, and also, like, and who would keep her door wide open like that, especially when there's guests?" I was about to open my mouth to answer Jude's question, but he did it himself. "Obviously you'd only do something like that if you wanted someone to look."

At that point it seemed like Jude was expecting me to say something, but the only thing that I thought of was a simple, "Good luck my dude." I feel uncomfortable talking about sex with my friends.

"Thanks, man. I don't think I'll need it though," Jude replied. "With Sabrina leaving the door open for me to take a peek and all that, I really don't need luck. I would have come into her room if I hadn't had to go to the toilet so bad."

At that precise moment, Mel and Sabrina came into the room to let us know that they were ready to head out, saving me from having to continue the conversation. When we got to the front door, I stopped for a second to look at something that had caught my eye when we first got to the house, but hadn't inquired about because I was too eager to go to the kitchen to have some food: a collage of Polaroids, maybe thirty pictures or more, showing a different person in each of them. Some had little scribbles on them, others had signatures . They were hanging from a long, zigzagging strip of copper colored wire with fairy lights.

"Who are all these people?" I asked Mel, still looking at the people on the Polaroids.

"Oh, that," Mel said, sounding proud, " It's a small project of mine. I take pictures of everyone that comes to our place. I'll have to get more film to take a picture of you guys before you go back home!."

"Yeah, that would be cool," Jude said right before his eyes landed on a picture of a guy wearing a pink shirt, standing next to Sabrina. It was the one of the only polaroids that showed two people. The image was rather overexposed–they'd used the flash to take it, maybe by accident–, and their eyes were red and their teeth were a shade of pale yellow, but they looked happy.

"That's Matt, Sabrina's boyfriend," Mel said, but before this could worsen Jude's mood further, Sabrina stepped forward and snatched the picture away.

"He's my *ex* boyfriend," she explained.

Mel gave her a doubtful look, but if she had anything else to say, she kept it to herself. Mel put the Polaroid away in the back pocket of her black skinny jeans. It surprised me that there was enough space in it for her to slide her hand in because of how tight they looked.

Jude and Sabrina shared a silent and mischievous look, and Mel opened the door to let our first official night out in Toronto begin. A very, very long first night out in Toronto.

10

It never ceases to amaze me how obtuse print advertising can be, especially when designed by public sector agencies. As I sat on my subway seat I couldn't stop looking at (and analyzing) an unintentionally offensive poster from the city's mental health association. It depicted what their marketing coordinator must have thought teenagers with depression looked like in real life: a very thin, pale guy with long black hair, who I at first thought was a young Trent Reznor. His long sleeve shirt wasn't actually black but a very dark gray, and he was pictured at the top of a mountain, shouldering his backpack with only one strap (the way *cool kids* do), and his gaze fixed on the horizon, past the camera. Next to him was the message: *Look after your mind, look after your future!* Underneath it, the subtitle read: *Lighten the load.*

It would have been an adequate yet uninspiring mental health sign had it not been for the overly simplistic stereotype of the *sad boy* they chose to depict. But at least it wasn't as bad as an anti-vaping poster I saw a few months ago in a White Peaks bus, in which its illustration of the lungs still had a *Canva* watermark.

The subway's pre-recorded messages noting each upcoming stop sounded just as uninspired as the bored lady's voice from the Newmarket train did. It was as if whoever gave the script to these people to read them out loud included instructions on how to add a long and monotonous drawl at the end of each phrase, so that they could strengthen the feeling of depression that passengers suffered on their commute. I, however, felt none of that. I was way too excited to feel angst that night. For the first time in my life I'd come to a new and interesting place for a (brief) holiday completely on my own, with no younger sister to prevent my family and I from going out late to fun places.

That night I didn't even have Jude and his friends to influence me on how to spend my night out. The last time we'd been out and about in White Pines we ended up going to the dump to see bears, against my will.

When the crackling speakers–which in my opinion needed to be changed sooner rather than later, before they stop working altogether–announced that we'd arrived at my stop I exited the subway with light and eager feet, almost as if gravity had just gotten weaker. I didn't even mind seeing a plump rat dragging a half-eaten Jamaican patty behind one of the subway's convenience stores because of what I saw when I returned to the surface: row after row of enormous buildings with glass windows, shielding them like a glittery tortoise shell, in some cases replacing altogether the concrete walls I was expecting to see. They spread out in every direction down the streets for as far as my little Mexican eyes could see. Waves of people from all different shapes, sizes, smells, colors and nationalities swarmed the sidewalks like ants and moved with unnatural ease, effortlessly avoiding contact with cars, cabs and motorcycles. There was the occasional pedestrian here and there who would almost get run over by a careless driver, but a simple slapping of the hood of the car and colorful curses would be as far as those encounters would go. Nobody had the time or the energy to do more in the big city.

I stood in the middle of the sidewalk taking everything in, rooted to the wet pavement, unable to do anything else for several seconds. For the locals, I became an object rather than a man, and what's worse, an object that was on their way. People who had to walk around me to avoid tackling me, and it was not until a large bald man wearing a navy blue pinstripe suit and smoking a mint-flavored cigarette hit my side with his briefcase and said, "What the fuck are you just standing there for, kid?" when I finally snapped back to reality. I apologized but if the bald businessman–who was now twelve feet ahead of me, crossing the street–heard me, he didn't care and kept walking.

I walked two blocks to the right, following the instructions I'd found online to get to the Regal Cinema. As usual, Stella had been right, because after I entered the cinema and saw the employees cleaning the counters and throwing leftover bags of popcorn into huge, black garbage bags, I looked at the digital marquee above them and learned that the last Imax show had started at 8:15 PM. Almost an hour before I arrived.

Oh well, maybe tomorrow Jude and the others will want to come to the movies with me, I thought without really thinking I could convince them to do so. They all were much more extroverted than me.

I was sure that there would be tons of things to do and tons of places to visit in Toronto at night, but with no friends or knowledge of the city it made finding somewhere fun to go somewhat difficult. I left the Regal Cinema and decided that the best thing to do was to walk around until something caught my eye.

As I made my way down a random street I passed multiple restaurants claiming to sell the best pizza in town, a couple of oddly specific stores–one of them selling baked goods containing weed, the *Wake n Bakeshop*–, and more than a few homeless men in sleeping bags, buried under a variety of blankets, either fast asleep or awake and ignoring everything around them, numb to the multitude of people walking around their rudimentary urban camps.

When I came upon the first one, I looked in my pockets for some change and I placed it in a plastic cup with a cardboard sign behind it that thanked people in advance for donations. Inside it were a few loonies, a five dollar bill and a cigarette butt. However, by the time I'd passed the third one, I had no more change to spare. I thought that once I explored the city some more I'd stop feeling guilty and ashamed of having a place to call home while these people didn't, but that never happened. Most of their faces were covered either by their make-shift beds, but the few ones I did see forced me to wonder *Who are you, and how did you end up here?*

There was another question, however, that I kept trying to ignore and push aside, like an annoying fly buzzing around, and that eventually reached a point in which I could not dismiss it anymore. The question was, *Why do I get to have a good life when they don't?* Is it because of systemic social inequalities that have not yet been mitigated by slow-to-action governments worldwide, or perhaps something more basic and unpredictable like random chance and chaos? If we're all equal then why should they lack the means to live a proper life while we spend an embarrassing amount of free time complaining about how slow our internet connection is?

The moment in which those questions took the forefront of my mind was when I walked past a dirty newsstand ran by a thick man with an even thicker Stalin mustache and wearing a green apron, sitting comfortably behind his counter reading a magazine. All of the various newspapers available had front-page stories that did not interest me–family drama involving the royal family and the new Duchess of Sussex, the American and North Korean presidents having a playdate somewhere exotic, the new socialist Prime Minister of Spain being sworn in–except for one with an ominous picture of a young man of about thirty years old, with long wavy hair, a long and gaunt oval face blackened by dirt and grime, staring absently into the camera with his mouth barely open, showing his two front teeth. Next to his headshot, there was another picture of (presumably) him, sitting on the floor with a dilapidated green tent behind him. The headline read *Toronto Man In the Last Stages of Medically Assisted Death Application*.

I moved closer to the newspaper, skimmed the text and found the name of the man in the picture: Simon Willet. I didn't have coins to pay for the paper, but decided to look Simon's story up on the internet later.

I kept walking for another twenty minutes until I found myself in front of a small italian restaurant-bar was located and I made my way in, partly because every time I went out of town my already lax sense of healthy eating went out the window, but also because it was late, dark and seeing so many people living on the street had put me in a grim mood and, whenever I was in situations like that, I tended to stress-eat. I went in and told the young host that I'd come by myself, and when he offered me a seat at the bar I took it, but not without a touch of hesitation. I'd never sat at a bar before because I didn't like the idea of sitting so close to strangers–bartenders and other customers–, but I figured if there was a good time to do it this was it, since I had also decided that I was going to have a drink or two.

I sat on a bar stool that made me feel more self conscious than usual about my short height when I saw my tiny legs dangling far away from the floor. I was still staring with disappointment at them when the bartender–a tall guy in his mid-thirties with one of those child-like faces that made you question whether he was actually thirteen instead, with short blond hair approaching whiteness and light blue eyes–dropped the food and drink menus in front of me.

"How's it going, bud?" he said with a kind voice. He reminded me of someone I couldn't quite remember.

I looked up at him for a moment, he must have been close to seven feet in height, and said, "Oh, not too bad I guess. It's my first time in town."

"Oh excellent, what do you think of *The Six?*" he asked.

I was about to ask him what he meant by *The Six*, but I'd just told him it was my first time visiting the city so I assumed he was talking about Toronto. "It's great," I lied, trying to get the images of homeless people out of my head. "There's so much to do. I wish I was staying here longer."

"How long are you here for?" The bartender asked while preparing a drink.

"That's a good question. I drove here with a friend but his car got busted in Newmarket. We left it with a mechanic and took a train here. We're supposed to go back there on Monday, hopefully the car will be fixed then. *Hopefully.*"

"Was the mechanic too busy to look at it when you brought it over?"

"Yeah."

The bartender handed me the drink he'd been making. "Here, you strike me as a rum and Coke kind of guy," he said. "My name's Tom, by the way. Are you having something to eat too?"

I'd never had rum and Coke before. I took a careful sip and the earthy and spicy taste it added to my Coke elevated it to new heights, as if it was now complete. "I guess I am a rum and Coke guy now. I'm Marco. What would you recommend me for supper?" I said and took a more generous gulp of my drink.

"Cannelloni. You can't go wrong with that. Unless you're lactose intolerant," Tom said, pointing to the location of the dish on the menu.

"I'll have that," I said after I finished my drink. Tom offered me another one and I accepted it with the condition that he'd use Diet Coke.

A young couple sat next to me (with one seat in between us to get the illusion of privacy) and Tom went to take their order. That was okay, I liked him but I didn't have the energy to keep up with a chatty bartender that night.

11

The bartender's meal suggestion wasn't as spot on as the drink one had been. The cannelloni were fine, but the pooling grease that was left on the plate–which did not mix in with the rich tomato sauce–after I was done eating made my stomach question how much I'd actually enjoyed my second supper. I asked Tom for one final rum and Diet Coke before heading back out into the busy streets of Toronto.

With a drink in one hand and my phone in the other, I took small sips and browsed Facebook. I'd already made the obligatory food post that's expected when you're out having a "good time" in another city, so I started scrolling down endlessly and finding out what my other friends were doing on that Saturday night. Some of my old university friends were having a party at Carlos', Jude had been tagged in a picture dancing a little too close to Sabrina, and my friend Keesha was apparently also out of town. She posted a cliche picture of her point of view from a tub, with a book (The Invisible Library) and a cup of black tea atop a little wooden table designed for bath enthusiasts who like to multitask while they soak in their own bubbly and scented filth. *Best job ever,* her caption read. I replied to her post with a comment saying, *Nice, please let me know if wherever you're working now are still hiring lol.*

I finished my drink and put my hand above my glass to stop Tom from giving me a refill. I asked for the hefty bill ($56.75 plus tax) and paid with my debit card. I was about to leave when my phone started ringing. It was Keesha.

I picked up the phone and said (in an almost unnoticeable tipsy tone), "Hey Keesh, what's up?"

"Hey, not much, I just saw your comment actually."

"My whaaa?"

"I actually meant to call you a little while ago. My boss said he was going to hire some summer students for his business." Keesha replied, and I heard something fall into the tub and splash, maybe her book.

"Isn't it a little too late for him to look for summer students?"

"Yeah he had some issues with his application to get the funds he needed, that's why he just hired me so far."

"What are you doing there anyway?"

"Videography."

"Oh wow," I mumbled. Tom had made my rum and Diet Cokes quite light, but I'd had a few (four or five, perhaps?) and my wobbly voice proved it.

"Yeah, I know," Kesha said. "It's the only film-related job I've found in White Peaks. The guy I'm working for is an author. He made some self help books for divorced men and he also hosts seminars."

"Do you think you could get me an interview with him?"

"Yes, definitely. He hired me to go with him on his trips and record clips for some videos he wants to make. He said he wanted to find an editor too so I'll definitely tell him about you."

"Please do!" I said, minute specks of spit coming out of my mouth. "I've been wanting to quit my job for a while now but it was so hard to get it in the first place, so I haven't."

"No worries dude, I got you. I'll talk to him about it tomorrow when we're on our way back home."

"Thank you so much! What's his name? I want to prepare for the interview," I said. "If he does want to interview me."

"Franco D'amico," she said.

I remember thinking back then that it was a fitting name for a man that based his entire business model in praying on vulnerable men that were desperate to *finally take control of their lives* or whatever he claimed he'd help them achieve.

I thanked Keesha again for hitting me up and ended the call.

"Have a good night bud," Tom said as I was leaving. I waved at him and left, returning to the both depressing and at the same time exciting streets of Toronto.

***

At quarter past midnight my aching legs forced me to sit down on a bench. I knocked down a wet newspaper–and whatever it was wet with would best remain unknown–that was next to me, leaving a trail of something slimy behind it, and I proceeded to look up instructions on my phone to get back to Mel's. The Maps app said that the shortest way to get to my destination was to walk half a kilometer east to the nearest subway entrance, past the next street-lights.

With the exception of attracting the gaze of a skittish man with a long frizzy beard that fell all the way down to his chest, who was wearing an oversized maroon sweater–and who seemed to be using his baggy clothes to hide the fact that he was playing with himself while sitting on the middle of the sidewalk–, everything went well. I was worried I'd fall asleep in the subway and end up at the other end of town, but my fears worked in my favor and helped me stay awake and semi-sober, constantly looking at the map marking the route I was following.

I got in the subway, and after ten or so minutes I got off on Eglinton and walked the rest of the way back to the student house where I was staying.

I thought that even though it was possible that Jude, Mel and Sabrina would already be home, I shouldn't count on it. When I arrived at the empty house and saw the lights off I called Jude. His phone sent me straight to voicemail, maybe because he hadn't charged his battery for long enough and it was dead again. I looked for Mel's phone number (with the pink flower next to her name) and tried calling her. It rang eight times but she didn't pick up, and after calling her a few more times I gave up.

She'd said earlier that they kept a spare key somewhere, so I checked under the rug, and found nothing but grime and dust. There was a little plant in a pot on the right side of the door, and after thoroughly searching it, I still had no key to let myself in.

I could go to the bar they're at and find them, I thought, but I didn't know which one they'd gone to–and even if I did there were no guarantees that they were still there. They could be on their way back, in the subway, in an Uber, in a bus, or perhaps they had simply decided to move their party someplace else. My legs were throbbing because of how used to my semi-sedentary life in White Peaks they were, so I sat down on the ground.

I only got about ten minutes of rest before I noticed that an old lady was staring at me with wrinkly, distrustful eyes from a window in the house across the street. I could see her skinny and frail silhouette, stiffened by age and suddenly felt uneasy. *What if she thinks I'm a burglar or some shit?* I said to myself, and as if in response to my thoughts she reached for her house phone, her eyes never steering away from me.

I got up and went for another nocturnal stroll. If the old lady had been suspicious of me and intended to call the police, I was *not* going to be there for it. A Mexican has to look out for himself whenever he's on foreign land.

I walked for a block or two and went inside a nearby corner store, bought some gum to excuse my presence there and left after a few minutes of loitering, hoping to find the old lady's window empty upon my return.

I was right, and when I got back to Mel's the old lady had vanished, or gone to bed or whatever. As I walked up the front steps towards the door I noticed a tiny bronze spot shining above its frame, reflecting the orange light from the streetlights.

I jumped–because I'm *that* short–, felt a small metal key under some dead leaves and grabbed it. I unlocked the door and headed straight to my couch. I didn't bother undressing or even removing my shoes, I just covered myself with my blanket, sent a text message to Mel explaining how I got into her house and fell into a deep sleep.

I had one of the most pleasant nights of my life.

12

At first I didn't know what it was, but my brain eventually told me that a loud thump had awoken me, followed by a knock on the door. *What the fuck?* I thought and stirred with confusion on the couch. I sat upright and saw a naked body standing up through the big glass panels of the sliding door that led to the small backyard. Jude rubbed his left ankle, and a moment later he looked back at me and covered his penis with his left hand so fast that he accidentally slapped it. He winced and slid the door open with his free hand, then ran towards his couch.

"Dude what's going on?" I asked, tired and still rather disoriented, removing crusts from my eyes..

"*Shhhhh!*" Jude replied and covered himself with his blanket.

Somebody at the door knocked again, and footsteps coming from upstairs announced Sabrina's arrival.

"Shit, shit, shit," she said, making her way to the front door, wearing a fluffy pink bathrobe. Her hair was a messy rat's nest, similar to Jude's, and that's when it hit me: Jude had succeeded in his mission.

Sabrina opened the door and a guy who seemed to be in pain or under massive stress came in. It didn't take me long to realize that it was the same guy from the Polaroid that Sabrina had removed from the wall the night before. The one she'd emphasized was her *ex* boyfriend.

"Hi hon, sorry for coming on such short notice," the *ex* boyfriend said. "Are you ready to go for breakfast or–"

"Almost," Sabrina replied, combing her hair with her fingers. "Why don't you just wait in the car for a couple of minutes? I just gotta brush my teeth and get changed."

"Can I just wait in the living room?"

Sabringa put her arm around her *ex* and gently but firmly pushed him towards the door. "No!" she said, her voice betraying her and breaking.

The stressed guy lifted his eyebrows, making him look even more troubled.

Sabrina smiled and rubbed his shoulder. "Just because Mel has friends over and they're sleeping in there. But it's okay, I just need *five ish minutes.*"

The troubled *ex* looked behind Sabrina, found both Jude and I pretending to still be asleep and reluctantly agreed to wait in his car. Sabrina shut the door with the type of firmness that only comes from getting out of an uncomfortable situation and headed back to her room. She stopped halfway up the stairs and looked at us. We were no longer pretending to be sleeping. "That was close," she whispered. "Are you okay, Jude?"

"Yeah," Jude said and started to massage his ankle under the blanket. "I thought I sprained my ankle from that fall but I think it's fine."

"Good. Last night was fun." Sabrina replied before resuming her way to the bedroom.

I waited until I heard Sabrina shut her door and looked at Jude. "Had a fun night?"

"I suppose I did," Jude said. He stood up, apparently forgetting that he was still naked, and flashed his hairy balls to me. I looked away and Jude immediately sat back down. He grabbed his blanket and covered himself again. "Could you grab my suitcase? I left it over there in the corner."

I picked up the suitcase, which felt lighter than mine, and gave it to Jude. He thanked me and started taking out some clothes: an old blue shirt, jeans that looked too baggy for him and underwear. I looked at my phone for a couple of minutes, to give Jude as much privacy as I could, given our current living situation. I checked some emails and saw that Darlene had already sent out the following week's schedule. I was expected to work Monday, Tuesday, Thursday, Friday and Saturday mornings. *Great.*

I peeked at Jude, and when I saw that he was done getting dressed I put my phone away. "I gotta go back to work tomorrow," I said.

"What time?" he asked and started looking for something else in his suitcase. Maybe socks.

"4 AM"

"Yeah, I don't think we'll get back home until Monday evening. Can you call in?"

I sighed. "Yeah. I guess I'll have to."

He found the pair of socks he was looking for and put them on. "Okay, just tell them you'll be back on Tuesday."

I agreed and started to type a text message for Darlene, but before I hit send I looked back at Jude and added, "I can't miss any more work. Like, for real this time, Jude. Plus this trip has been more expensive than I thought,"–he was preparing to say something, but I didn't let him– "especially for you with the car accident and all that, but also for me. I have to go back to work before I use up all of my savings, and *you* gotta find a new job." I had never felt more like a mom in my entire life.

Jude was silent for a couple of seconds, reflecting on something, and then said, "Yeah. You're right. We'll be back home tomorrow night, I promise."

"Thank you." I sent Darlene the message I wrote and put away my phone to avoid having to see her reply, at least for the time being. "How was your night, anyways?"

Jude chuckled and gave me a summary of the events from his night out. Apparently they'd gone to the bar, met some friends there, drank, danced, smoked some weed. Jude also said that he and Sabrina had gotten very, *very* close that night and decided to go home early to *get to know each other a bit better*, leaving Mel behind. "Where is she anyway?" I asked after I realized I hadn't seen or heard her at all that morning. Not even after Sabrina's *ex* showed up.

"I don't know," Jude said and continued his tale. After partaking in the old *bedroom ham-sandwich* they passed out. Then, early in the morning, Sabrina's *ex* texted her, saying that he loved her and that "It would be stupid to throw away what we have because of a silly misunderstanding" (which I later found out was because he'd cheated on her, and perhaps that's why she'd been so eager to sleep with my friend, or maybe she was just slutty, I never found out).

"I was going to just go back to the couch, but we were still naked and one thing led to another... and by the time we were done that dude was pounding at the door. Sabrina freaked out because he apparently still had a key to the house, so I improvised and got out the window," Jude explained.

"But if he had a key and just decided to come in, he could have seen you naked in the backyard. No?"

Jude's mouth turned into a flat, colorless line. "Oh. Yeah I guess he could have."

I smiled an anxious smile at him. "At least it all worked out in the end and he didn't just come in," I said, hoping that would make Jude feel better. My stomach made another guttural sounding noise, loud enough for Jude to hear it, and we agreed it was a good time to have breakfast. He called Mel but she didn't answer the phone. "Let's just go get some food. She'll come back later," Jude said and I agreed. We finished getting ready and went to the door. As soon as we stepped out we saw the car that had picked us up at the train station pull into the driveway.

Mel and Magd shared a tense moment of silence, not looking at each other at all, before she got out of the car without as much as a goodbye kiss or even an indifferent wave of her hand. She started her *walk of shame* towards the house, stopping when she reached Jude and I.

"Where are you guys going?" she asked in a low, ashamed voice, looking at something on the floor.

"Just going out for breakfast," Jude replied.

"It 's noon," she said. "Lunchtime. Do you guys mind waiting for me to get ready so I can join you?"

I did mind–I was extremely hungry already–, but said nothing. Jude assured her that it was okay and we all went back into the house, a tart whiff reached our noses as Mel walked past us. Vomit was my guess, based also on the brown crusty spot I'd seen under her lips.

13

We waited for Mel sitting in the living room, looking at our phones and not really talking to each other. After close to an hour she came downstairs wearing a pink shirt with tiny fabric balls all over it, the ones that show up after multiple times washed, mostly seen on socks–, pale blue jeans and sunglasses . *Either Magd's style choices are rubbing on her or she's got a pretty bad hangover,* I thought.

We walked for another half an hour, which angered my empty and somewhat spoiled brat of a stomach even more, and ended up stopping at a little Portuguese bakery that sold pastries, soups and sandwiches. There was a sign at the entrance claiming they sold the best donuts in town, and despite my initial hesitation–which had inevitably come after spending countless hours reheating food at the coffee shop–I decided to give them a try.

I was still on *not giving a fuck about what I ate because I'm on holidays* mode, so I ordered a prosciutto and mozzarella panini with a side of tomato soup and a plain sugar donut as a dessert for good measure, purposely pushing away the image of clogged arteries that had flashed in my mind. Jude got the same as I did and Mel just omitted the donut. She didn't take her sunglasses off and chatted very little, often putting her elbows on the table and resting her head on her hands, like a sad kid resigned to endure the torture of doing homework.

I was also not feeling much like talking, so Jude guided the conversation. He was in the middle of explaining to us why the Matrix sequels were vastly misunderstood and not the absolute shitshow that popular culture had labeled them as, when the waitress–a thin and small guy with a rat-like mustache that had more in common with a stain than with facial hair–struggled to get to our table without dropping our food on the floor. His trembling skinny arms holding the tray were shaking and swaying terribly.

Jude got up to try to help our waiter out, but the woman behind the counter stopped him. "No! No!" she yelled, scaring some of the other customers. "He's gotta learn how to do it on his own." Jude sat down and blushed. None of us took our eyes away from the poor waiter.

Our food somehow made it safely to our table. Jude did not resume his Matrix rant. We ate in silence only disturbed by the occasional *mmm* sound and approving nodding of heads that only exceptionally good food deserves. The toasted buns of our sand-wiches were shining with butter or margarine or whatever it was which the cook had used to add the savory, fatty taste that is always welcomed–if not necessary–in breakfast food (or if you're Ameri-can, in all types of food). The soup would have been just okay had it not been because of the addition of real parmesan cheese–not that green bottle crap from the grocery store–and croutons, calmly floating on it. The donut was delightful. It made me forget about how much the coffee shop had made me loathe them.

I finished my meal before any of my friends did, so I returned to the counter to ask for another Diet Coke. After carefully inspect-ing the other varieties of pastries sold at the bakery I got my Diet Coke and a *pastel de nata*, which was one of their best sellers. At that point I felt full and a little lethargic, but my parents were no-where near to stop me from overindulging in gluttony. I sat back with my friends and let them each have a bite. Everything was going well until the guy who had been sitting at the table next to us paid for his bill and left. Next to the now empty table was an old counter with metal, almost mirror-like siding, and what I saw reflected on it made me want to throw up and, to be quite honest, cry. It was the first time that I had ever seen a side view of myself: my white shirt was so stretched out that the bottom of my stomach was ex-posed, as if I were wearing an improvised crop-top. I knew that my shirts were getting tighter and tighter with each passing week, but looking at my stomach flap hanging out like a hairy and beefy tongue hit me hard. It, however, wasn't the thing that upset me the most. That was reserved to my double chin, which I had up until that point, been pretending did not exist. The scuffed metal coun-ter distorted the image of myself that it reproduced, but it was clear enough for me to stop lying to myself and accept that I was proba-bly obese. Not just overweight.

I put my donut down, hands trembling, and I excused myself.

"Is everything okay?" Jude asked.

"N-no," I croaked, walking away from the table.

In the bathroom I slammed open one of the doors of the stalls, got on my knees and wretched. The sour taste of the soup mixed in with the sweetness of the donut made my eyes water. When I was done I sat on the floor, back to the stall, and closed my eyes. It took me a while to realize that Jude was standing next to me. "Hi," I said, panting.

"Are you okay? Did you eat something bad?"

I thought for a moment what to say, opened my mouth but no words came out. Jude sat on the floor and put his arm around me.

"It's okay, you don't have to tell me anything."

"I'm gross," I finally said.

"No you're not,"

"Yes I am. I eat like a pig, and when I saw how I looked today I–"

"Listen," Jude said, "we all like food, and that's okay, but yeah, maybe you have been overeating lately. So what? You're having a small vacation, so it's okay."

I tried to look at Jude but couldn't. I didn't want him to see my quivering lips. I was trying really hard not to start sobbing like an oversized baby.

"I know that you've been trying to lose weight, and I, uh, can't really help you with that," Jude continued. "But I know that whenever you're ready, you will lose all the weight you want. Just don't be so hard on yourself. Give yourself a break."

"I feel like I have been giving myself a break ever since I moved to Canada."

Jude chuckled. "Well maybe, but still. Try not worrying too much about it. A sandwich and a donut won't make you gain ten pounds, and starving yourself or–"

"I didn't force myself to throw up."

"Right, but still, just enjoy the rest of your time here. If you want to try to lose weight, it'll be easier to do back home. You can buy your own groceries and what not there."

I nodded, still not making eye contact with Jude. He got up, offered me his hand and helped me get back on my feet.

***

"Are you okay?" Mel asked. She had taken her sunglasses off and her eyes, though bloodshot, were kind and concerned.

"Yeah he's fine, he just had to take a shit real bad," Jude replied.

Mel laughed and let out a snort. I pretended to laugh too and said, "Yeah, when you gotta go, you gotta go." I felt grateful for not having to tell someone else about the real reason why I had gone to the washroom. It's not that I didn't trust Mel, she struck me as someone who, had she lived in White Peaks, would probably become a very close friend of mine, but I just didn't have the mental strength to talk about how disgusted I was with myself. Soon enough, Jude and Mel were engulfed in their conversation. It had something to do with college.

I had almost forgotten entirely about the whole photocopied ass business with the old and bitter Mrs. Townsend, and of my subsequent PR strategy, so I did another quick internet search on my phone to see how things were going. I looked up the White Peaks Online's website and once I was in, I typed "Library" in their search bar. No results from before 2014–when a fire had been avoided after "devoted librarian and dear member of the community, Evannah Townsend" used her coat to extinguish the flames from a garbage bin that a teenager had set on fire–were found. I tried looking up my name afterwards. I found nothing. I went back to the 2014 article I'd found, which had been written by Rob, so I clicked on his name at the bottom of the page and discovered that his newest article was from ten days ago. Before then he had been steadily pumping out garbage content multiple times a day. *Oh shit.*

I found the website's *About Us* page, and when I scrolled down to the part where they'd added cheesy black and white pictures of their staff smiling against a brick background. Rob wasn't there.. *Of course he's not working for them anymore, what else could I expect with my luck lately?* I sighed and finished eating my Portuguese tart.

When our plates were free from any leftover crumbs and our drinks were gone we went up to the counter to pay. "How's the bill going to be?" The same angry woman who had yelled at the scrawny waiter asked us.

"Just one bill please," Jude replied. "I'm paying."

Mel and I looked at him but before we could argue he took out his credit card and tapped it on the machine.

"You didn't have to pay for us, we got money and it was a lot of food," Mel said on our way out, using her hands to shield her face and allow her eyes (again under sunglasses) to readjust to the brightness of that brilliantly sunny day.

"It's the least I could do for letting us stay at your place for free," he said. "And you also fed us last night."

Mel managed to give him a weak smile which could have been bigger if she hadn't been at the mercy of a hangover that day.

"And I'll get our supper," I said, knowing very well that I'd regret making that offer when I saw the bill, but I was happy nonetheless. Happy to be in the company of such good people.

14

My friends and I continued our walk for close to fifteen minutes before I realized that we were heading in the direction where we'd come from. "Where are we going now?" I asked.

Jude and Mel stopped and looked at each other for a brief moment. "I don't know," he said. "I'm still pretty tired and thought maybe we could go to Mel's for a bit to get some rest."

"Yes, I'm not feeling great either," Mel agreed.

I was hoping we'd walk downtown and explore more of the city. There was a big mall I wanted to check out—I kept pushing away the nagging thought of my shrinking wallet like a persistent and annoying fly—with a couple of stores I was planning to visit to try to find a gift for Stella. Maybe a nice sweater or a stuffed animal (she liked cats and bears).

"Oh okay sure. But could we maybe go to a mall later tonight?" I asked.

My friends promised me we'd stop by the Eaton Centre as soon as they had some time to rest (and nap) and we continued our way to Mel's. My short legs and lack of physical conditioning made it a difficult task to keep up with my friends, who were tall and sort of in shape, so they had to stop a few times for me to catch up. They didn't seem to mind, however, because they were chatting about the good times they'd had back in White Peaks before Mel had moved to Toronto to go to university. They seemed to have a much deeper connection than what you would have expected from two fuck buddies, and seeing them laughing and sort of making each other complete made me feel a little sad and wish that there was a way for them to make things work. But distance is a bitch. There was also the issue of them being still too young (and stupid) to have a healthy, long lasting relationship–Jude was a great friend but not the best at being *faithful,* and even though I didn't know Mel almost at all, I wouldn't be surprised if she was also a bit *lax* when it came to relationships. *Maybe it's a good thing they're not together and can remain friends instead of dating for a year or two and then having a nasty break-up,* I thought and kept walking, listening to Jude's silly comments and Mel's pleasant laugh.

***

Mel invited Jude to *hang out for a bit* when we got the house. They went up to her bedroom and I sat down on my couch. I read my book for a few minutes until my friends upstairs started making Mel's bed creak lightly. It wasn't loud by any means–and they were considerate enough to be *silent* otherwise–but despite my best efforts I could not tune out the sound of the springs from Mel's cheap bed. I stopped trying to get lost in the story of that little bitch Holden Caulfield and put on my earbuds instead. I started playing an eight hour recording of a gentle rainfall that sometimes helped me defeat sleepless nights at home, and I eventually dozed.

15

My eyes opened to a day that was letting out its last dying breath. It was 7 PM and the living room was dark and empty. My body was sore–legs aching, thighs on fire–from oversleeping. It reminded me a little of the couple of times that I'd been hungover myself. Jude wasn't back on his couch, so in my still semi-conscious state I decided to go to Mel's room to see if they were awake.

I made my way up the stairs, almost tripping when I reached the top step–which was ever so slightly smaller than the rest–but managed to regain balance on time to prevent another, most unfortunate accident. The door was half open and I saw my friends cuddling, still fast asleep, covered by a thick pink blanket with white doves printed on it. The adrenaline rush from my almost-trip had helped me wake up and I realized it was quite creepy to stand at the door looking at my friends, post-coitus, sleeping peacefully, so I returned to the living room.

Silence had finally set in the house. I turned on the lights and sat down intending to finish reading my book so that I could move on to the next one when we returned to White Peaks, but the unpleasant scent of day-old sweat and "fun" that emanated from my pits wouldn't let me focus. I closed the novel and I put it aside. I was in need of a hot and relaxing shower.

I made my (slow and again a little drowsy) way up the stairs, trying not to make much noise. I shut myself in the washroom, undressed, placed my clean clothes on the sink, and hopped in the shower–I had made an effort to avoid looking at my grossly plump naked body in the mirror. The stream of water that sprouted from the showerhead was harsh and thin, like Mrs. Townsend, and the space within the cubicle was rather limited. I missed Cliff's extremely large guest washroom, with enough room to host a small orgy within. A shower is a shower, however, and I enjoyed cleaning and refreshing myself.

I turned off the tap and almost, by instinct, took one of the still moist towels hanging on the rack next to me, a damp scent coming off. One was lime green, the other one a pleasant-looking light cream color. I shook my body like a big, wet dog and stepped out of the shower. I looked for fresh towels in the cupboard under the sink, but there were only three rolls of toilet paper inside, some cleaning supplies and two thin hand towels. I closed the cupboard and looked around even though the bathroom was very small, as if spinning around naked and dripping shower water would somehow help me find something that wasn't there, and I (unsurprisingly) found no fresh towels.

The answer was clear: if I didn't want to wait fifteen or twenty minutes to air-dry my body, I'd have to use one of the hand towels I'd found, or both.

I took one of the small towels and dried my hair, face and shoulders. That was everything the first one could handle, so I took the other one and continued drying the rest of my body as best as I could. In the end I was still a little moist, especially around my crotch area, but I wasn't dripping anymore so I started to get dressed.

I was sitting on the toilet seat putting my socks on when I heard Jude and Mel's low voices coming from the other room. I couldn't tell what they were saying but I was glad to know they were awake so that we could head out and have fun on our last night in the city.

I made my way out of the bathroom and down the stairs, making sure to be loud so my friends knew I was up and felt inclined to get out of their little comfy nest. They met me in the living room after the exact amount of time two fuck buddies need to put their clothes on and fix their hair (haphazardly), remove the lipstick stains on their bodies and what not.

16

Jude and Mel did not feel as inclined to go out as I did. "We're gonna have a long day tomorrow, with driving and all that," Jude *kindly* explained to me.

Then, as if they'd rehearsed it, Mel finished their statement in a patient and somehow maternal tone, "Yes, maybe it would be best if you guys stay in to get as much rest as you can before your trip."

I looked at the clock on my phone. It wasn't too late, just ten past eight, and most malls would still be open, but I decided I wouldn't try to convince them to go out anymore. The main reason for this change of heart was because if we stayed in, I could order some pizza instead of paying for everyone's supper at a nice restaurant, which could have been pricey and not a very smart idea given the shrinking state of my chequing account. "Okay, yeah that's okay," I said, trying to sound more reluctant than I was. "I could order a pizza and we could watch a movie or something."

"Yes, that's a good idea!" Mel replied, her face lighting up. "I'll get the pizza, my treat for your last night in town."

"Thank you, Mel," I said and after a short pause added, " For everything."

"It's nothing, anyone who's a friend of Jude is my friend too."

Mel ordered two medium pepperoni and onions pizza–those were the two toppings we all collectively liked–and turned the living room's TV on. After a long browsing session on Netflix we settled on watching *The Disaster Artist*. Jude and I were huge fans of *The Room,* and enjoyed the movie to an almost absurd degree. Mel had never even heard of *Tommy Wiseau* or his bizarre masterpiece, but that didn't stop her from laughing out loud at various times throughout the movie.

The pizza was excellent: thin and greasy. It had stayed in the oven for a little longer than it had to, lightly crisping some spots of cheese in the most delicious way–golden-brown goodness.

When the credits rolled and everything that was left of our supper were two cold slices Mel put them in the fridge and we watched two episodes of *Freaks and Geeks*. At quarter past midnight our last night in Toronto was over, or at least that's what we thought. What it was *supposed* to be. Mel said good night to Jude and I as she walked up the stairs towards her bedroom, as she closed her door we heard the front door open. After a few seconds, Sabrina reappeared. She reeked of cheap weed and didn't seem to notice we were there at all, she just followed Mel's steps and headed straight to her room.

"Well, uh, I guess we better go to bed too," Jude said.

I agreed, turned off the lights and slept. It had been a very ordinary night, but I always look back on it with fondness. Sometimes the best of memories are not the most eventful ones–birthdays, graduations and achievements come and go just the same as any other ordinary event does, after all–, but the ones that can give you a warm feeling of peace when you remember them.

***

I've never been great at goodbyes, but saying goodbye isn't an easy thing to do (unless you're saying *See you later alligator, after a while crocodile!* to a venereal disease after a long antibiotic treatment, that is). So, as you may expect, I couldn't say goodbye to Mel–who I'd just met not even three days before but had proven to be a true friend nevertheless–without shedding a tear or two. "Please don't, or I'll also–" she started saying before she also started crying. When she composed herself again and her eyes weren't quite so red anymore, she gave me a big, tight hug.

"We'll have to come back soon," I managed to say.

"Of course we will," Jude replied with determination. "Maybe for Thanksgiving weekend or something."

My friends had already said goodbye to each other (both in the bedroom, I'm sure, as well as in the driveway, where we all were at the moment), but upon hearing this, Mel lurched towards Jude and embraced him once more. He held her for a few seconds, kissed her on the forehead and ended the hug with a sad smile.

We waited for our cab for a few minutes, enjoying each other's company in silence.

17

Silence was also our companion on our way to the train sta-tion–the radio wasn't working and Jude and I did not feel very chatty–, the sounds of the city dulled by the dirty glass windows of the cab, which sealed us in our own little bubble. I gave Toronto one last look as our destination got closer and closer, and I saw peo-ple walking on the streets and wondered if I'd ever see them again, because even though I was already thinking about convincing Stella to come back with me for a whole week sometime in the near fu-ture, Toronto was a massive city with three million habitants, which would make this a statistical improbability. I sat on my sweat-stained seat, thinking about how strange it must be to live in a place where you are able to blend in the crowd with ease and an-onymity was one of its most valuable perks, something I couldn't do in White Peaks, given that I was one of its only Mexican resi-dents.

The cab driver dropped us off at the Aurora train station the same way he'd driven us there: quiet and unceremoniously. The bored voice from the girl of the pre-recorded messages we'd heard on our way to Toronto welcomed us inside after Jude paid fifty dollars to the driver, who gave us a nasty look when he saw there was no tip coming.

A faint but still crushing feeling of depression was setting over me, and I thought the same was happening to Jude. I was lost in thoughts of dread and anxiety about having to go back to work at the coffee shop for a few days or even a couple of weeks until I got the new job Keesha had talked to me about. If I get that job I'll put in my two-weeks notice at the coffee shop faster than Jude took his pants off for Mel.

The train ride turned out to be the last easy part on our trip. We arrived at Newmarket at 10:05 AM safely and with no delays.

Jude and I had an unspoken understanding of how big of a dent the Toronto trip had made to our personal finances, so even though it would have been comfortable to take another cab to the Superstore where The Mirth was waiting for us, Jude suggested that we took the bus instead and I agreed without hesitation.

We walked half a kilometer towards the bus stop pulling our bulky suitcases behind us, the sun beating us down and making our crevices and flaps sweat. When we were a block away we saw the bus closing its doors after the last guy at the stop had made it inside. Jude turned back to me and said, "We'll catch the next one. I'm too tired to run for it." I nodded and we continued at our slow pace.

Buses in Newmarket ran every fifteen minutes, according to the Newmarket Transit website, so we sat down at the gross bus stop bench—the parts that weren't covered with stickers and obscene messages had chewing gum stuck to it instead—for a short time before we jumped in the next bus. We went to the very back of the bus and sat on the only two seats that weren't taken by pimply college students. The drive was short but awkward, as we kept having to hold our suitcases so they wouldn't roll down the aisle and run over someone's foot.

The Superstore opened at 10:30 AM but when we went into the car shop section at quarter to eleven, Vern was just turning on the lights and starting his computer. "Hi buddies, just give a moment to get this old thing up and running," he said and left us to go into the garage.

He came back into the reception ten minutes later carrying a clipboard in his hands and reviewing whatever was written on the sheets of paper it held. "So you're the guys with the old station wagon?"

"Yes, will you be able to take a look at it today?" Jude asked, his question sounding more like a plea.

"Just did, bud," Vern said and showed us the clipboard. His fingernails had grime underneath. "I don't want to get too technical, but the engine's done. You can look at the report over here."

I felt a knot on my chest tightening. Jude took the clipboard but kept his eyes on the mechanic. "How much will it cost to fix it?"

Vern shrugged. "Too much," he said. "It's an old car and it would be cheaper to just buy a good reliable used car instead, something from this century haha."–His laughter sounded false and re-hearsed–"You can go to Max's World Class Cars and see if he'd buy yours and use it for parts, I think I got his number somewhere–"

"I don't need the number," Jude snapped in a quiet but firm tone. "How much would it cost to fix the engine?"

Vern's confident smile turned into a flat line. "You won't be able to find the part that got busted, buddy. You'd have to buy a whole new engine, and that can cost more than what you can af-ford."

"How much?" Jude insisted.

"Four, maybe five thousand if you're lucky and get a good deal on it."

Jude's eyes widened just a little. "Okay, thank you. We'll think about it," he said and turned towards me. "Let's go, dude."

I stared at Jude as he grabbed his suitcase and left. *We're fucked,* I thought and turned towards Vern behind the counter. His smile was back. "Well, ain't he a *nice* kid? Make sure to tell him to get a tow truck then. We don't store cars for free here."

18

Jude sat on the curb, slouched and staring at the empty parking lot. Upon getting closer, I noticed thick drops of sweat trickling down the side of his flushed face. I didn't know what to say except I wasn't surprised that The Mirth was beyond repair, but I kept it to myself. I exhaled a long, bitter breath and I joined my friend on the pavement. We said nothing for a long time, maybe ten or fifteen minutes. I knew what was happening, however. Sometimes when Jude encountered a particularly big problem–such as the one we were facing that day, when there was no easy way out of our prob-lems–, he shut down.

"What are we going to do?" I said, breaking the depressing si-lence.

Jude sighed something similar to how a deflating balloon sounds and said, "I guess I'll take The Mirth to another mechanic so he can give it another look."

"*What?*"

"Do you have the number of the tow truck we called before? My phone is dead." Jude said, scratching his chin and ignoring my previous question.

I shook my head, trying to wrap my head around what Jude's had said. "Jude, the engine is dead. We gotta find another way home."

"No, they're just trying to like, uh, upsell us or something. The battery's probably just dead."

"*Dude*, they already checked the battery and that's not it," I replied, trying to calm myself, but the frustration within me was getting stronger. Tighter around my chest.

"That's what they said, but we don't know for sure,"Jude replied blankly. "That guy back there works for a huge company, so like, who's to say they didn't train him to lie to people so they can sell them stuff they don't need?"

"*Jude*," I started. My voice was getting louder, but I didn't notice it at the moment. I was fighting the urge to shake my friend (or even slap him) and make him realize how bizarre the things he was saying were. "I'm sure that's against the law–"

"You don't know that," Jude intervened before I could continue.

"*Jude, what the fuck?* The guy didn't want to sell us anything. He even told us to get another car somewhere else."

Jude started to rub his temples, near his hairline, with the heel of his hands, the way he always did whenever he was getting too stressed out. "It's not our car, it's *my car*, and I get to decide what to do with it."

I stood up out of frustration, anger, or maybe both. "I know it's not our car," I said, rubbing my forehead with my left hand. I knew that if someone walked by they'd think this was the beginning of a scene, so I took five deep breaths before I continued what

I had to say. "But dude, you can't just waste another hundred bucks on another tow truck for them to take The Mirth to another mechanic who will just tell us *again* that the car's dead." Jude wasn't even looking at me. He was still staring at the parking lot, and I felt like I was talking to a wall. No, actually, I felt like I was trying to convince a wall that it was, in fact, a door. "*Jude, hello? Did you hear me?*"

And at this, Jude also got up, his pale and sweaty face turning to a light shade of magenta. "*The Mirth is* not *dead!*"

We were just a few decibels short from yelling at each other now. I let out an anxious laugh, not unlike a hyena's, and said, "*Yes it is, and the longer we spend denying it, the harder it'll be for us to find a bus or something. Some way out of this shitty place.*"

Jude considered this for a moment, and eventually crouched to sit back on the hot curb. You could have cooked bacon in no time on the pavement that day. "If all you care about is going back home," Jude replied in a calm and even tone, "then just leave. Nobody's stopping you. I'll find someone who will fix the car and I guess I'll find a way back home."

I suddenly felt a little cold and stunned. I looked down at Jude's face. Serene and relaxed. I also noticed that there were some hairs stuck to the palms of his hands from rubbing his forehead earlier. "Jude, you gotta sell the car," I said, calming myself down a bit. "You can buy another one in White Peaks, but we gotta get out of here soon. We're already running low in money."

Silence.

"Jude, I–"

"Sorry dude, but I'm staying. You can go if you want. I'll see you later." His voice was even quieter than before. He gave me a disappointed look before standing back up. He then grabbed his suitcase and set off somewhere on his own.

"Jude, wait. Don't go yet, let's just talk about this for a minute. "

Again, silence.

"Jude..."

But my best friend kept walking.

19

"Hi there, what can I get for you?" the waiter with the bikini-girl pen asked, preparing to scribble my order on his battered notepad in an almost indecipherable handwriting.

"Huh?

"Or do you need some more time?"

I was still looking at the "menu", if you could call an old piece of laminated paper with its peeling corners and coffee stains a menu. I wasn't very hungry, especially having Jude wandering the streets of Newmarket in a futile quest to save his car in the back of my mind, but it was already 1:00 PM and I hadn't eaten all day, so I scanned the menu quickly and chose the smash burger with fries and gravy.

"Alright." The waiter said, scribbling on his notepad. "Do you want bacon on it?"

"Sure."

"And the works okay?"

"Yeah. Just no tomato." I handed the menu back to the waiter and he left for the kitchen. I took a sip of the Diet Coke he'd brought me earlier and looked around the restaurant. It was clean but old. The stainless steel chairs and tables had red and white accents at the top and around the bottom. The floor had a black and white checkerboard pattern, and another waiter was cleaning a pop spill at the far side of the room, near the bathroom doors.

I think I should add that I was back in Toronto. There were no Al's Diner locations in Newmarket. I'd decided to go back to the big city for one last day when I found out that there were no buses that went from Newmarket to White Peaks. Toronto and Ottawa were my only options within Ontario. And as a matter of fact, the last bus to White Peaks had left at 11:30 AM, so I had to wait until Tuesday to go back home. Having to stay in Toronto for an extra day any other time and under different circumstances would have been an unexpected yet welcomed surprise, but that day, it had made me feel claustrophobic. As if the city had its claws tightening me in their grip and was fighting very hard so I could never leave. I took another sip of my drink.

After about ten the waiter brought my food to the table. I was the only customer at the time. My burger smelled amazing and the edges of the patty were caramelized and crisped to perfection, and next to it was a generous portion of fresh cut fries and dark, thick, rich gravy. I'd be lying if I said that my meal didn't cheer me up a little. Maybe more than a little, actually. I took out my phone, put my earbuds in and picked a YouTube video of a guy explaining what "planned obsolescence" was to distract myself from the loneliness of my situation.

The video was more like background noise while I thought about what to do next. I didn't dare to look for a hotel–even a cheap one–to stay the night for fear of spending another two hundred dollars on this already awfully expensive and long trip.

Another option was Mel. I had her phone number and thought she'd definitely let me crash at her place, but that would mean that I'd have to explain to her what had happened with me and Jude, and I was not in the mood to do so. *Where the fuck are you now?* I wondered.

The least appealing option of the bunch was Stella. Stella had offered to make the seven and a half hour drive to Toronto after work to pick me up. "You can't just stay there all alone," she'd said. "Let me just go and pick you up. It's not that big of a deal!"

I, however, had reassured her that I'd find a place to stay eventually. "Worst case scenario I'll just go to a hotel, so don't worry too much about me, Stella. I'll be okay. I promise."

After discussing my situation some more she (reluctantly) agreed to stay in White Peaks and pick me up the following day from the bus terminal instead.

The YouTube video ended and I finished eating my burger. When the waiter came to my table to take the plate away I asked him to refill my drink, because not only was I addicted to food, but

I was also addicted to Aspartame. I thought that until I figured out a place to stay for the night, hanging out at the restaurant wasn't a bad idea. I was about to look for another video when I received a text message from Stella.

"Have you found a place to stay yet?"

"No, not yet."

"Are there any decent B&B's in the area?"

How the fuck did I not think of looking for a B&B before? I thought and started browsing Toronto listings, sorting them from the cheapest to the most expensive. I scrolled past a few very sketchy shitholes and stopped when I found a basement apartment with its own bathroom and private living room located not far from Al's Diner. It was $65 per night and the reviews were good, so I booked it immediately. I thanked Stella for the suggestion and told her that I'd finally gotten myself somewhere to stay,

I paid my bill, left a five dollar tip and left the restaurant feeling relieved. The check-in time wasn't until 3 PM so I had about an hour and a half to kill. I would have gone to the theater to watch a movie if I hadn't had to bring my suitcase everywhere I went, so I decided to go to the Eaton Centre and look at things that I probably shouldn't spend my money on.

20

I wasn't expecting the mall to be particularly busy on a Monday during work hours, but that was the case. The Eaton Centre was packed like a can of multicultural sardines. Everywhere you looked–on every single one of its floors–was full of groups of people coming and going from one way to another, in and out of stores.

I walked down the hallway and stopped at a small Japanese shop with a bright red sign above it and white words written on it in a language that I couldn't read. They sold various plushies from

Cartoon Network shows, exotic-looking candy and a large selection of novelty gifts, so I went in. I felt terribly out of place in a store with only asian girls so when I found what I was looking for (a reasonably priced stuffed gray cat for Stella) I headed to the counter and paid without wasting any time. The cashier gave me the stuffed cat in a paper bag that was way too big for it, and even threw in some mint chocolates that she had on the counter. I thanked her and left.

I spent the next hour and a half browsing stores that caught my eye, picking up an item once in a while, examining it in my hand and eventually putting it down after looking at the price tag. Sometimes my suitcase attracted unwanted attention from a couple of store managers, but after following me around for a minute or two and deciding I wasn't likely to steal anything they'd lose interest in me.

I had set an alarm on my phone to let me know when I could start walking to my B&B and when it went off I saw a message from my host, saying that the check-in time would have to be a little later than expected. *Feel free to stop by anytime after 4* the text said. The delay didn't bother me though because there was something else I could do in the meantime. I put my phone back in my right pocket and left the mall through a set of revolving doors that smelled like feet.

***

I walked around the busy streets of Toronto and ended up at a little grocery store, "Ahmad & Sons". I bought some pasta (penne), a jar of tomato sauce with a label that said that it contained mushrooms and herbs even though all you could see was an homogenous tomato puree, a package of instant oatmeal and a two-liter bottle of apple juice. The apartment I had booked had a kitchen, so I thought it would be smarter to buy groceries to make my own supper and breakfast instead of ordering take-out, so that I could save some money that way. The grand total came to a little over ten dollars after taxes. I asked Ahmad–or one of his sons, perhaps–to double bag my groceries because the last thing I wanted was to drop them in the middle of a busy street–something that had happened to me once while biking back to Cliff's from Walmart, a few months after I had moved to Canada. Ahmed obliged.

At four on the dot I got to the basement apartment where I was going to spend the rest of my time in Toronto. I took my phone out and looked for the message my host had sent me containing the access code for the door lock, typed it in and after a second or two of suspense, unlocked the door. *Thank goodness,* I said to myself.

Given my luck, I was kind of expecting the apartment to be in a horrible state, with unpleasant moldy smells in the air, dirty sheets on the bed and garbage everywhere, but that couldn't have been farther from the truth. My B&B looked exactly the way it did in the pictures I'd seen. There was a small living room area with a long comfy-looking couch and a big TV across from it. The kitchen was modest but it had a stove, a large fridge and all the dishes, pots and pans I'd need. The bedroom wasn't big either, but the twin-sized bed was soft and welcoming, and the washroom was spotless. It smelled like lemon all-purpose cleaner, a scent that I'd always loved.

I left my suitcase and groceries on the floor next to the door and headed towards the bed. I did not get up for most of that evening.

21

For the first time since my friends and I embarked on our little road trip I lay on a real bed with an actual mattress. I spent most of what remained of the day in the bedroom where I napped, watched two movies on my phone (*Shrek* and *The SpongeBob SquarePants Movie*), and only left to use the bathroom and eat.

Sometimes I do stupid stuff, as you already know, and that night I decided I deserved to do one last stupid thing before going back home. I got out of bed, feeling a strong primal force urging me to reconsider and stay in my comfy nest, and walked to the living room. I took the groceries out of the double bags Ahmed (or one of his sons) had given to me, and put them in the kitchen's pantry for the next person who stayed at the B&B to use. Before I went back to the bedroom to resume my evening of *self-care* I noticed a little basket, presumably left there by my host, with a sticky note on it which read *Complimentary Snacks*. Inside it were three mini bags of chips and two chocolate bars (KitKats). I took one of the bars and returned to bed.

When I was once more all snuggled in bed, I proceeded to order a pizza. I knew it was a stupid idea to order more overpriced food–that was the reason why I'd stopped to buy groceries before going to the B&B, after all–, but the past couple of days had been rough, and I felt if I didn't actually *deserve* to indulge on food one last time before going back home, then at least it would be *understandable*.

I decided to order pizza again. Pizza was my comfort food and, perhaps subconsciously, I wanted to recreate the previous night as best as I could under my current situation: alone, with Mel probably at her own place and Jude God only knew where.

I devoured my supper while still in bed, and when I felt the approaching food coma I set up two alarms on my phone–one for 8:15 AM and the other one for 8:45 AM–to prevent me from oversleeping. I was *not* going to allow things within my control to keep me from returning to Twin Peaks anymore.

***

The threat of a food coma never materialized, so I watched *Shrek 2* before calling it a day at about quarter after ten. I texted Darlene to let her know that I wouldn't be able to make it to work the next morning, given that I'd got stuck in Toronto and all that. She never replied to my message, maybe because I'd ruined her night, but that was okay. I was sure she would figure something out.

I stayed awake until around midnight, when the exhaustion and stress of the day overcame my restless mind and sent me to sleep. I woke up to pee once, but beyond that I had a quiet and uninterrupted night.

22

People make a big deal about the so-called *Mexican time* but I'm usually never late, and the following morning wasn't the exception. I got to the bus terminal–a big concrete building that reeked of depression, piss and gas–an hour early and sat on a bench next to an electric outlet to plug my portable charger in so my phone would last the entire ride home, which would take close to ten hours, thanks to the many stops it had to make on the way to White Peaks.

I started to feel more and more anxious the closer it got to 11:15 AM. *What if the bus gets delayed until tomorrow? Or what if it breaks down in the middle of the highway?* I thought to myself, but my worries disappeared (at least for a moment) when I saw the blue bus with the *White Peaks* sign approaching the terminal.

I gave my suitcase to the driver to load in the luggage compartment and went in the bus almost automatically, as if someone more eager than myself was controlling my body. I sat on a window seat near the back.

I was glad to see that nobody decided to sit next to me, and when the bus driver closed the door and turned the engine on I felt my entire body–in particular my butthole–relax as we started our journey to White Peaks, leaving the city of Toronto behind us once and for all.

The Lying Tongue

Part 4: The Interview

1

The bus ride was slow, long and unpleasantly hot. By the time we passed Newmarket (where Erin would be staying for another couple of weeks with Megan) my armpit sweat stains were getting larger and larger, as if a drunken tailor had sewn a sports jacket's shoulder patches in the wrong spot. But these mild inconveniences did not bother me much, because after more than ten hours on the road–which included not one, but two lunch breaks– I made it back to White Peaks.

Stella was waiting for me with teary eyes on the side of the road. I ran to her and embraced her for a very long time. In her arms, I felt home and, maybe more important, I felt safe. "You're back!" Stella cried after we took a step back to see each other better.

"Yes I am," I replied, and the realization that the Toronto trip was over made me shed a few tears of my own. Stella looked at me and held me tight for another moment. I took a deep breath and said, "Let's get out of here, it's so late already." Stella kissed my cheek and we walked to her car.

"Did you at least have some fun in Toronto?" she asked in a hopeful tone, resting her left arm on her car's window frame. The glass was down and the cool summer air was soothing on my face.

I let out a big sigh. "Yes," I said. "I guess I did, but it was also awful at the same time."

"I'm sorry you had a hard time down there, but at least you're back now."

"Me too. I really missed you."

Stella's brow furrowed in an almost imperceptible way, as it always did when she was trying to make up her mind. "Do you think Cliff will be asleep when you get to your place?" she finally asked.

"Yeah probably," I replied, appreciating the familiar sights of White Peaks we were driving by. Any other day, if I hadn't been so overwhelmed by the Toronto trip PTSD that was setting on me, I would have known what Stella was thinking.

"Well,"she went on. "Do you want to *cuddle*?"

"Wha– what?" I looked at her, startled. "Oh, uh, yes. I'm down. But aren't you going to be, like, super cranky at work tomorrow for being up this late already?"

"Yes, but staying up for another hour or so won't make much of a difference. Besides, I *really* missed you," she said, starting to drive a bit faster.

"I really missed you too, Stella."

***

I walked Stella back to her car sometime after 1 AM, and went straight to my room as soon as her car was out of view.

I sat at the foot of my bed for a moment and looked around, appreciating the four walls that contained all of my earthly possessions (excluding the things that didn't fit in my suitcase when I moved to Canada) and provided me with shelter and a place I could call my own. Before the Toronto trip I almost resented how little I got out of my rent money. The small bedroom with second hand furniture and electronics that were on the verge of becoming obsolete, as well as the lack of freedom to have friends over were not worth $550 a month. That night though, when I lay my tired body on the old mattress, I felt like I was in heaven.

***

Darlene's angry phone call woke me up at sixt thirty in the morning. I felt around the bed with my hand until I found my phone feeling confused, and my still half asleep brain only caught some words here and there.

... so fucking irresponsible... where the fuck are you?... I should just fire you...

When I heard that last bit I yawned, causing my furious boss to curse at me some more, and eventually found myself saying, "It's, I quit."

I put my phone away and tried to resume my snooze, but it started ringing again so I shut it off and threw it to the other side of the bedroom for good measure.

2

In the morning I lay awake in bed, reliving the events of the past five days until I could no longer ignore how badly I had to go to the washroom. I relieved myself and went back to my bedroom, careful not to make much noise to avoid letting Cliff know that I was back. Being questioned about the Toronto trip by him did not sound fun.

I opened the door and found my phone on the floor, sporting a fine crack from top right to bottom left of the screen. *Great.* I turned it on and went back to bed. It was true that I'd only spent less than a week away from home, but the constant delays and unfortunate situations we faced on our way to (and back from) Toronto had taken its toll on me, so I decided I was going to have another *self care day* for my mental health.

When I looked at my phone there were fifteen missed calls from Darlene, ranging from 4 to 6 AM. I was ashamed to have quit my job in such an unprofessional way, especially since I'd judged Jude–even though I've always made a constant effort not to judge people–for just not showing up to work one day, instead of putting in his two weeks' notice. *At least he didn't turn off his phone when Darlene was in need*, I thought. I considered giving him a call to find out how he was, *where* he was, and if he somehow managed to save The Mirth, but decided not to. I was still upset about the way we'd left things at Newmarket.

I understood how hopeless he must have felt when Vern had told him that his car wasn't worth being fixed anymore. He adored that old station wagon more than anything else he owned, and it was only natural to react the way he did—especially after I shouted at him—, but a part of me still thought it was wrong for him to just leave me behind. Maybe we were both wrong.

My belly grumbled angrily at me and I got out of bed to look for something to eat in the mini-fridge. I felt a little disappointed when I saw it was empty, except for two pizza pockets and a frozen butter chicken supper. *I need real food,* I said to myself. *I need something* homey.

Suddenly, an idea came to me. I took a shower, rubbing my body vigorously as if that would wash away the stress I was still feeling and got dressed. I was putting on a clean shirt when I heard Cliff's car pulling into the driveway. *I could get out of here through the window,* I thought, but there was no point in delaying the inevitable, so I finished getting ready and headed out, prepared to answer any and all of his questions.

3

Cliff was in the kitchen looking for bread to make himself a sandwich, when he saw me emerging from the hallway that led to my bedroom.

"Marco, my boy! How was the trip?" he cried, still holding a ziploc bag with bologna in his right hand.

I forced a smile and said, "Oh boy, it was... hard."

"What do you mean, little buddy?"

I rolled my eyes and started retelling my misadventures, omitting the details of how Jude and I had gone on separate ways, and by the end of my story Cliff was staring at me with wide eyes. "You gotta be kidding me," he said after a brief silence.

"I wish I was," I replied, feeling a little lighter. I had expected that going over what happened over the last five days was going to make me feel upset again, but it did the opposite. I was kind of glad to have someone other than Stella to talk to about the Toronto trip. My parents were out of the question, they'd have a nervous breakdown if they knew half the things that happened to me on the trip.

"Well, I won't take more of your time, Cliff. I gotta go to the grocery store to buy some stuff to make soup. I feel like I've had enough junk food to last me until the end of the summer."

"Sounds good, I'll see you later, pal."

"You bet."

4

If I hadn't been so hungry I would have waited until Stella got off work to ask her to give me a ride back to my place from the grocery store, but both my belly and my soul craved some good old chicken noodle soup. I hated riding the bus with my hands full of plastic bags and the unfriendly eyes of strangers on me, but sometimes you gotta do what you gotta do.

That evening the bus was almost empty when I boarded it, the only other passenger was a sketchy dude that seemed to have fallen asleep but would once in a while peer at me from under his ball cap, so I went to the back row and placed my grocery bags on the seat next to me, resting my hand on them to avoid spilling anything when the driver stopped at the red lights. I took my phone out and sent Keesha a message to *kindly* remind her of how excited I was to have an interview with her boss. I waited for a minute, then two, then three, but she didn't reply. *She must be busy,* I thought and put the phone back in my pocket.

As we approached my bus stop, the one outside of Ernie's Mini Mart, I got ready to push the stop button but my phone began to ring. I thought it must be Keesha, but when I saw Jude's name on the screen I froze.

I did not push the stop button. Instead I just stared at my phone numbly.

I let his call go to voicemail and got off at the next stop. I walked back to Cliff's feeling nervous, my hunger gone to a place far, far away. The phone did not ring again, so I pretended nothing had happened and went straight to the kitchen.

I am no fancy chef or anything like that, but the soup I managed to make that day was rather good. But more important than making a decent soup, I succeeded in recreating my ultimate comfort food, and when I took my first sip I felt a warm feeling spreading from my mouth to my stomach, then to my heart. It's incredible what a chicken and rice soup can do to people's nerves. I ate two generous servings and put the rest in my mini-fridge. *That'll be tomorrow's lunch,* I said to myself.

5

I spent most of my evening with Stella, going over everything that had happened in the Toronto trip in great detail. She already knew most of it due to the constant updates I gave her while I was away, but I did it anyway, mostly to hear myself out loud and try to figure out if I was wrong in the way I'd handled things with Jude on the day we parted ways.

Stella listened to my ramblings and backstory-filled tangents with patience and genuine interest. When I was done with my tale, I asked her what her opinion was about the Jude situation. She sat at the end of the bed, biting her lower lip lightly, deep in thought.

"Tell me the truth," I said before she started, "Was it mean to just leave him in Newmarket?"

"Well, no. He's the one who left you in the parking lot, no?" she replied. She moved closer to me. She didn't actually smile, but her face relaxed and made me feel at ease.

"I guess he did."

"But you still feel bad about it."

"Yeah, I do."

"Have you talked to him since then?"

I looked at my lap, where my phone was inside my pocket. "No, he tried to call me earlier but I didn't pick up."

Stella arched her eyebrows. She looked as if she were waiting for me to continue and when she saw I didn't have anything else to say, she asked, "And why didn't you answer?"

"I was scared."

"Scared of what?"

I tried to look away from her, but her eyes were magnetic and wouldn't let me. I sighed. "I don't know. maybe I was scared of him yelling at me or something."

Stella smiled to herself, as if she'd thought of something funny. "Why would he do something like that? Aren't you like best friends now?"

We were. Except, were we? Would you still be friends with someone who decided to go home instead of sticking with you during a time like this, even though you both knew it was no good? I refused to believe that Jude actually thought that he'd be able to fix his car. He was just trying to delay the inevitable because of how much he loved his car. Maybe he's hurt that we went our separate ways, but surely our friendship was strong enough to get over something like this. "Yeah, you're right," I said after a brief silence. "I'm just scared he's, like, disappointed in me."

"I don't think he'd be trying to get in touch with you if he was."

"Yeah, I guess I'll give him a call back later. I guess I've just been bad at picking up the phone."

Stella's questioning look returned to her face. "Who else did you ignore?"

"Uhh, my boss," I muttered.

"Were you supposed to work today?" Stella said. Her eyes wide, both terrifying and beautiful.

"Yeah, but uh, I kind of quit."

"*What?*"

I told Stella about my conversation with Keesha and the whole job interview thing, trying very hard to convince her–and myself–that it was more of a formality than anything. "He's hiring a bunch of summer students, who knows, maybe I'll get a job for Jude too."

"Why would he need another?" she asked, her frustration at us only growing stronger the more I talked. "Did he also quit?"

"Uhm... Yes, a week ago or so,"

"Jeez Louise, you guys better get this new summer job before you run out of money. You both *love* eating out and spending money in stu– silly things."

"Yeah, yeah. You're right." Stella was always right.

6

I was back in my bedroom, sitting at my desk and eating another bowl of soup when my phone rang yet again. I was starting to hate that ringtone and made a mental note to change it. I let it ring for a few seconds before I gathered enough courage to take it out of my pocket and see if it was Jude calling.

It was.

I took a deep breath and answered. "Hello?"

There was a pause on the other side of the line. I thought maybe he'd butt-dialed me, but then I heard Jude's deep voice. "Hey."

"Hey." I didn't know what else to say. "What's up?"

"Did you make it back home?"

"Yeah. You?"

"Yeah, uh, actually I'm on my way now," he replied. There was something in the background making noise, perhaps the wind.

"Did you fix The Mirth?"

There was another pause, longer than the first one and somehow more tense. "No, she's dead," he finally said.

Of course it was dead. "I'm sorry my dude."

"It's fine, the other mechanic said he was surprised the car lasted as long as it did. Apparently that model was not very reliable or something."

I was glad things seemed good between us after all. Our conversation was sad but fluent. "So what did you end up doing to get here?"

"You probably already know," he said in a more stiff tone. "I sold it to some guy and used the money I got to buy another car.

Well, that wasn't enough to pay for it all, so I maxed out my credit card to pay the difference. Hopefully it'll, uh, last me a while."

In any other situation I would have enjoyed saying *I told you so* to him, but didn't. Jude really did love The Mirth and now it was gone. Probably not in one piece. "I'm sorry I left you alone down there," was what I said instead.

"It's all good, dude. I'm the one that pushed you away."

"I still feel bad, I should have stayed with you."

We went back and forth, trying to make the other feel better until I changed the subject and said, "I quit my job at the coffee shop."

"Oh shit, why?"

"You know how awful it was, it messed with my mental health way too much. The pay wasn't enough to make up for it," I said.

"Yeah, it really does suck working there."

"Yeah, but I might be getting another job soon."

"Oh. Right on, I gotta find a job too so I can start paying off my debt." You didn't have to know Jude to tell that there was something in his voice that said that he wanted in on it too.

I thought about telling him that I (or actually, Keesha) could probably get him a job interview with Franco but I didn't want to get his hopes up, so I didn't. I'd still try to get him one, but it was best not to mention it until it was a reality. "When will you be back in town?"

"In an hour and a half or two, why?"

"Do you wanna have breakfast tomorrow with me and then drop off some resumes at the mall?"

"Yes, definitely." Breakfast food always cheered him up.

"Okay, I'm gonna get ready to go to bed now, but text me in the morning whenever you're ready to hang out."

"Sounds good my dude. See you later."

"See you."

It was good to know that I still had my best friend.

7

The next morning I slept in again, not as late as I had the day before though. I knew I'd be lucky if Jude stopped by sometime after noon–he would need a big sleep to recover from the traumatic Toronto trip, as well as the long drive home–so I didn't bother setting an alarm for myself.

At 1:45 PM I had already been waiting for almost half an hour sitting on the hot porch. I was glad I'd thought about having a snack–a bowl of cereal with no milk–after I woke up in case Jude was later than usual. About ten minutes later I recognized Jude in the distance, driving a nondescript dark blue sedan with the windows rolled down, allowing me to hear some George Harrison song I didn't know blasting through the speakers. He stopped the car when he reached Cliff's driveway and I went in, unable to feel the familiarity and cozyness I'd come to expect from his old station wagon. "It's not bad," I said on our way to McDonald's. "It's just a bit–"

"Different, yeah," Jude added. "It's just not the same. It doesn't have the same *personality*."

I shuffled on my seat and looked around the new old car. I noticed that Jude's phone was plugged to the stereo. "At least now you can play newer music."

Jude kept his eyes on the road but his face turned grim. "Yeah, I guess," he said. "It'll have to do since I lost my dad's tapes."

"*What?*"

"I left them in The Mirth. "

The feeling of guilt that I had started to overcome returned, stronger. If I'd stayed the extra day in Newmarket with Jude I would have remembered to take his dad's tapes with us. "I'm sorry, man."

Jude gave me a dismissive wave of his hand. "It's fine, most were getting pretty messed up, anyway."

We drove around town for half an hour listening to music and relaxing, something impossible to do in a big city like Toronto, and it helped me feel better. Not much, though. I was still waiting to hear back from Keesha and her boss, and I really wanted to send her another message about my interview but didn't do it so I wouldn't seem too desperate. I still had enough savings to last a month or so– if I resorted to a frozen chicken and rice exclusive diet–, including rent money, but I hoped I'd start the new job before I had to use them up.

We found ourselves in the McDonald's drive-thru, holding up the line of angry people with no patience for a couple of dudes with their minds set on getting their McMuffins and hashbrowns well after two o'clock in the afternoon.

When the horns of the people behind us started to disturb the still summer air Jude turned up the volume of the stereo, upsetting the guy at the end of the line enough to pull out and give us the finger as he drove away, probably to get his burger and fries from Wendy's. "People these days are so disrespectful," Jude said. "They'd live longer if they chilled a little."

I'd be quite mad myself if I were one of the people waiting for us to get our McMuffins, so I said nothing.

Jude, however, must have felt at least somewhat bad because as soon as the girl with braces from the pick-up window gave us our food he wasted no time in hitting the gas pedal and leaving McDonalds.

***

We finished eating at the library's parking lot–because Jude had lost all of the copies of his resume, the ones he'd printed the day I got banned, and needed to get some more copies made before we could actually start looking for a job–listening to music in the car. It did feel odd to be able to listen to post 90s songs at first, but I got used to it rather quickly.

"Nothing can beat McDonald's breakfast," Jude said after he had the last bite of his McMuffin.

"What about homemade breakfast?"

Jake seemed to consider my question thoroughly before answering, "It depends on who made it I guess." He turned off the car and got out. He had already taken some fifteen steps towards the entrance before he realized I'd stayed behind. He shook his head and walked back to the car. "What are you doing in there?" he asked, unlocking the passenger door.

I raised my eyebrows and waited for him to make the connection, but he didn't. "I'm banned, remember?"

"So?"

"What do you mean *so*? So I can't go in."

"Nah, man. Those things don't mean anything."

I raised my eyebrows even lower, creasing my forehead. He didn't care to elaborate. "Yes they do."

"What are they gonna do? Kick you out?"

"Knowing that old bitch from the library, yes, they'd probably kick me out."

Jude sighed. "Come on dude, let's go. That old fart probably won't even be there. Maybe it's, uh, her nap time or something."

"No."

"Ugh, are you serious?"

"Yes. Unless you want to tell Mrs. Townsend the truth about whose ass it really was."

Jude stood looking at me for a moment blankly, as if he was trying to weigh the pros and cons of my suggestion, and closed the door. "Whatever."

Jude went to the library and after a moment or two I opened the door a few inches to let in some fresh air. I took my phone out of my pocket and checked my notifications to see if Keesha had finally texted me back. She hadn't.

I shuffled on my seat anxiously and typed, *Hey, have you had the chance to talk to your boss yet?* I looked at the text for a few minutes, rewriting the same message over and over again with just the slightest variations when a raspy cough startled me.

Mrs. Townsend was outside. She was wearing a purple dress with black lace adorning the bottom of the sleeves and she had her wrinkly arms crossed around her chest. Jude stood by her side. I glanced at him. He looked away.

The old librarian cleared her throat again and said, "Would you get out of the car for a moment?"

I did.

Mrs. Townsend exhaled a frustration-filled breath. "You were very rude to me," she started in a way that made me think she'd rehearsed what she was saying. "But I must admit, I was also being a bit unfair to you."

"Uh–"

"Let me finish," she snapped. "I could not, in good conscience, refuse the opportunity to check the security footage when Brad from I.T. came to the library a few days ago to update the computers.

I tried not to smile, but didn't do a very good job.

"The tapes from that day, however, had already been deleted by then," Mrs. Townsend continued. "And as I'd rather not ask you to show me your, um, birthmark to unequivocally prove whether or not you were the one who vandalized the copier..."

The horny old bitch was blushing, I thought. My smile was now gone.

"... I decided I'd find the middle ground and lift your ban under the condition that you provide me with a written apology letter promising not to cause further damage to the library's equipment."

I shook off my head the disturbing image of Mrs. Townsend checking out my naked butt when she cleared her throat again, expecting an answer from me. "Well?"

"How did you know I was here?" was what came out of my mouth.

"Your friend came to talk to me about something, and given that I'd seen you both hanging out at the library in the past I asked him if he'd help me contact you. He said you were at the parking lot and here we are." She then turned towards Jude and asked, "What did you need, anyhow?"

"What? Uh, nothing. I uh, forgot," Jude said.

Mrs. Townsend didn't seem convinced, but let it slide and turned back to face me. "Well? Do you accept the conditions for the lifting of your ban?"

"Yeah, sure." I was more interested in Jude's anxious behavior. He was shaking and fidgeting with his hair, curling strands of it in his index finger and letting them spring back into place.

"Perfect, please come in. I'll get started with the paperwork while you write your apology."

8

To whom it may concern,

I, Marco Daniel Lopez, am writing this letter to promise that I will take care of the equipment from the White Peaks Public Library whenever I use it.

I would also like to apologize for my previous "bad" and "childish" behavior towards the librarian, Mrs. Townsend, and for being rude to Mrs. Townsend. This was never my intention.

All the best,

Marco Lopez-Lopez

***

Mrs. Townsend scowled the entire time she spent reading my short apology letter. When she was done, she held it in her boney hands with sagging skin which reminded me of a pug's chubby face for a few moments and exhaled sharply. She gave me a disapproving look but my letter must have been good enough, because she filed it in a cabinet behind her. Her office smelled like old woman's perfume—which oddly enough always smelled the same regardless of the brand and who was wearing it—and was filled with mountains of books and folders stacked on chairs and little elementary school tables. The lights were all off except for two thin lamps at each side of her desk, irradiating warm light. They were so old and thin (like Mrs. Townsend herself) that it looked like even the lightest breeze would be able to topple them down.

She rose from her ancient burgundy chair and took something out of her pocket. "Here," she said, handing me a new and shiny library card. "The letter leaves a lot to be desired, but in this case it will suffice. It's not like I'm grading you." It took me a while to realize that she had just made a joke, but not only that, she was even laughing. She sounded like a rusty accordion.

I smiled and pretended to chuckle. "Tee-hee-hee."

"See? I do have a sense of humor," she said before putting her resting bitch face back on. "But some might say that mine is more *refined.*

"Yes, some might," I replied. *Someone from the eighteenth century, maybe.* "So uhm, can I go now?"

"Yes. Yes you may. I have lots to do today and so little time."

"Thank you." I walked towards the door but stopped for a moment.

"Is there anything else you need?" Mrs. Townsend asked, her gaze fixed on her laptop.

"Yes. If you *were* grading me, what would it be?"

Mrs. Townsend looked up, removed her glasses and rubbed her temples gently. "Hmm, to be honest, I wouldn't give you a number. I'd just write *Exceeds expectations.*" Her accordion laugh returned.

9

With a new library card in my pocket I headed towards the computer area, intending to meet with Jude, but he was nowhere to be seen. I considered updating my resume and printing more copies including the date I resigned my job at the coffee shop, but didn't.

Maybe my resume will look better if it shows that I'm still working at the coffee shop, I thought and exited the library. Jude was in his car, typing something on his phone, maybe a message to Mel. He didn't seem to hear me until I opened the door and scared him enough to make him drop his phone. "Sheesh dude, why would you do that?"

"Why would I come back to the car?" I asked with a tinge of sarcasm.

"No, did you sneak up on me?"

"Sorry," I said and closed the door.

"It's okay," Jude said and reached under his seat, trying to find his phone. He sat there with his body bent like a lame contortionist from a cheap circus for a few moments before giving up and getting out of the car. He pushed a handle on the left side of his seat, making it jerk violently backwards. "Ah! There it is."

Jude got his phone, fixed his seat and jumped back in. He continued tapping his phone, tilting it towards him just enough so that I couldn't peek at it. I wouldn't have cared to look if he hadn't done that, but his secretive actions made me curious. "What are you hiding from me, Jude?"

"Hmm... What?" he said when he finished writing his confidential message. "Oh, I was sexting Mel."

"Oh shit, sorry for interrupting, then."

"No worries." Jude said and turned on the ignition. The engine made a concerning clicking sound for a second or two and the car started.

I hope this car doesn't turn out to be a piece of shit, I thought. "Oh, uh, Jude?"

"'Sup?"

"I almost forgot to ask you, were you planning to actually tell the librarian that you photocopied your ass instead of me?"

Jude looked at me for a brief moment and replied with a short and flat "Yeh."

"Thank you."

"You don't have to thank me for anything. I didn't actually have to do anything, remember?"

"Yes but still, thanks. I really appreciate the intention."

Jude nodded and turned onto Lake Avenue. Our next stop was the White Peaks Mall.

10

The White Peaks mall was long past its prime, that was for sure, and it had a depressing amount of empty units–some still with merchandise from the last business owner that had occupied the space and fled the country in the middle of the night. You couldn't walk past three or four stores without seeing at least one vacancy. I was growing anxious because Keesha hadn't even acknowledged any of my previous text messages yet, so I tried to make a good impression when Jude and I talked to store managers and gave them copies of our resumes in case my interview with Franco never happened.

I'd only brought about twenty copies myself, and regardless of how deserted the mall was, I was convinced they wouldn't be enough if I wanted to apply at every half-decent store. The proliferation of big national retailers replacing–or buying out, in some cases–small locally owned businesses had proven me wrong, however. "Sorry, you gotta apply online now," was the most common response we got that day.

By the time we were done job hunting I still had eight copies of my resume even though we'd stopped by other places outside the White Peaks mall, such as the call center on Green Street. Out of every place we visited, that call center would have been my last pick. Nobody liked getting yelled at by angry Americans in need of roadside assistance, and their turnover rate reflected it.

Finally, we agreed that we were done for the day and hopped back in Jude's car. "What's this one's name, anyway?" I asked.

"I don't know. Big Piece of Shit, maybe," Jude replied. "I wouldn't be surprised if it breaks down in a month or two, to be honest."

"It's not that bad," I lied.

"It does the job, I guess. Are you hungry?"

"Always," I said, this time being completely honest, my belly was a bottomless pit after all, and at that moment my phone began to ring.

"Oh shit, you're getting job offers already?"

I ignored Jude's comment and took my phone out. It was Keesha. "I wish," I said and answered the call.

"Hey, sorry I'm just seeing your texts now," Keesha's voice said. She sounded distant and breathy. She was probably hungover.

"It's okay. What's up?"

"I'm with my boss right now and he wants to know if you can meet him on Friday for a quick interview."

I tried really hard not to sound as excited as I felt. "Yes," I said. "Definitely."

"Okay good."

"Ask him if he's free at 3:30" I heard a second, raspy voice say to Keesha. It made me think of a brick for some reason.

"Can you come at 3:30?" Keesha asked.

"Yes for sure," I said. I glanced at Jude, who was giving me a strange look and added, "Oh uhm, is he still looking for more than one summer student?"

Keesha whispered something I couldn't quite understand to the raspy voice. "Yes, do you know anyone looking for a job?"

"Yes, Jude."

There was a pause. "Okay, tell him to come in on Friday too at, let's say, four."

I smiled at Jude and gave him thumbs up. "Okay perfect, thank you so much!"

"No problem. I'll text you the address, and *don't* be late. Franco hates it when people are late."

I promised I'd be there on time, thanked her once more and hung up. Jude gave me another look of cautious optimism and I said, "We got our first job interview this Friday, my dude."

"Awesome! What's the job?"

I paused for a moment, trying to find an answer that was not there. "That I do not know."

"Oh?"

"Keesha got hired for the summer to film a guy that wrote self-help books or something like that. I think I'll be his editor and I know that he was looking for more students to work for him over the summer, but I have no idea of what you'd be doing."

Jude shrugged with his hands still on the steering wheel and stopped at the lights. "Beats not having a job."

"True." My phone buzzed with Keesha's message. *122 Longview Road.* "Do you know where Longview Road is?"

"Yeah I think it's like forty minutes out of town. Why? Is the interview there?"

"Yeah. Could you give me a ride? It's only like half an hour before yours, so–"

"Yeah, for sure. It's the least I could do for hooking me up with that writer dude."

We rode the Big Piece of Shit around town, full of cheer and giving each other advice for our upcoming interviews until Jude announced that he had to *go home to lay a brick.* "You can come over and hang out with me after I finish my business," he said.

"Nah it's okay, I better go home now. I also must cut a cigar."

11

I'm no stranger to falling deep into rabbit holes of useless information. I've spent countless hours watching people talking about random topics such as steroids, analog photography, origami, book collecting (mainly about how to spot first editions, even though I still don't own any myself), and many more thanks to YouTube's recommended videos algorithm. Needless to say that for the days leading up to my interview I spent most of the free time that unemployment gave me researching ways to impress potential employers and *ace* my interview.

I also read an ungodly amount of articles with topics that ranged from *Ten Things to Consider to Make a Good First Impression* to *Five Signs That You Will Definitely Not Get A Job Offer,* and by the end of the week my brain was so saturated with random facts and tips that I was surprised my brain didn't turn into a gray mess of mashed potatoes.

***

I spent Thursday night at Jude's to make sure we wouldn't be late for our interviews. I woke up at 8:30 AM after a long night of unrestful and interrupted sleep and spent the next three hours rehearsing my answers to the various imaginary questions I'd prepared over the past couple of days.

When Jude finally woke up he made us scrambled eggs, bacon and toast with raspberry jam for breakfast. On any other day I would have demolished my plate and asked for seconds, but that morning my stomach wasn't cooperating. *Oh great, I just hope I don't get diarrhea as soon as we get to the office,* I thought to myself as I drank a glass of apple juice.

I tried to practice mock interviews with Jude later that morning, hoping it would help me feel more relaxed, but he declined saying that, "I do better when I don't, uh, think too much, it makes me sound more genuine."

"Oh."

"Yeah, employers don't like it when it's obvious that you memorized your answers."

"Fuck."

Jude told me not to worry and turned the TV on to help me *forget* about the answers I'd spent days carefully crafting to impress Franco. We watched a few episodes of *Malcolm in the Middle*, followed by half of *The Big Lebowski* until my alarm went off at two o'clock and we started getting ready.

Jude took a shower while I changed into my interview clothes: black dress shoes, a pair of brown slacks and the only dress shirt I owned–white and wrinkly. Everything was fine until I reached the two buttons right above my belt, which I managed to do up when I exhaled and deflated my stomach. When I breathed in, however, the buttons tightened up and my shirt looked like it was about to burst, just the way Vern's looked, back at the Superstore in Newmarket.

"Tell me the truth, does it look bad?" I asked Jude as he came out of the shower with a towel wrapped around his bottom half.

"Yeah, but it's fine," he said, walking towards his bedroom. "Just a sec."

I waited for him, regretting every burger and slice of pizza I'd eaten in the last year. *That shirt fit me perfectly when I first moved here*, I thought. *Now I look like a fat tamal.*

Jude returned a moment later holding a thick, orange tie with blue circles. It looked like something my uncle Jose would have worn at his wedding back in 1978. "There you go. It'll cover up the buttons and make you look more professional."

Yeah, right, *professional.* I took Jude's tie trying not to grimace and thanked him. He helped me tie it around my neck.

"Snazzy," Jude said.

"Thanks my dude."

"Anytime."

The tie, ugly as it was, did its job hiding the strained buttons of my shirt quite well.

***

We left the apartment an hour early to Jude's annoyance. "We're gonna end up waiting in the car for half an hour," he had said.

"No we won't. We'll get there ten or fifteen minutes early at most."

"For *your* interview we might, but not for mine."

He was right about that. "Oh. Sorry."

"It's okay, I'm sorry for being a turd, it's just that I'm a bit nervous myself and the more I think about the interview the more I get stressed out."

"We'll both do fine. It's just a summer job after all."

"Yeh."

Jude turned up the volume of the stereo, maybe to help us get distracted and stop worrying about the interview, but it didn't work for me, unfortunately. Random bits and pieces of the answers I'd spent the last few days memorizing for my interview kept flashing through my mind until, after a very long and rather quiet drive, we pulled into the long driveway of 122 Longview Road.

The property was kilometers past the last cluster of country houses we'd seen, and we would have missed it if there hadn't been a small but elegant black rectangular, with white letters printed on it which read *D'Amico Residence - 122.*

The stone driveway divided neat rows of tall and fragrant firs, and beyond them, to our right, was a rough path which led to a small pond. *How can someone own a place like this?* I thought. The answer came back to me almost immediately. *Money.* Tons of it.

We parked next to a black Range Rover, ruined by a bumper sticker that said *Alpha Mentality,* in front of an enormous three-storey house with impressive window panels that invited strangers, almost teasing them, to take a look inside the lonely residence.

You could see a grand piano on the second floor in a sort of study, its walls covered with bookshelves and an indented *chaise longue* that reminded me of the time my mom took me to a psychiatrist who helped me stop wetting the bed when I was nine. That study looked more expensive than my entire house.

The living room was enormous, but the most impressive thing about it wasn't its square footage but its height–it must have been at least eight meters tall. It had tainted glass, which made it harder but not impossible for visitors to see. There was a gigantic TV of at least seventy or eighty inches at the far end, hanging over a slick fireplace. There were three three long black leather couches and a white coffee table in the middle. The stairs did not have a handrail: they instead were long slices of wood stuck to the wall, none connected to each other.

There were a lot more rooms, including a white kitchen which was probably bigger than the room I rented from Cliff, but Jude suddenly interrupted my admiration of the D'Amico residence. "That's sick. How can someone own so much fancy shit?" Jude asked, mirroring what I had just thought a few moments before.

"Writing a couple of best-sellers I guess."

We were not the only ones visiting 122 Longview that day. Three men from a moving company were unloading a hot tub from a U-Haul truck, supervised by Keesha and a skinny guy in his forties with long curly hair pushed back from his face with a white headband. It gave him the appearance of a retired pro tennis player who had started to let himself go. He had no chin and plenty of belly. "Careful! Careful!" he squealed. "We don't want to break anything, do we?" He was holding a clipboard under his right arm and would occasionally write notes on it.

"I guess we should wait here for a few minutes," Jude suggested, but at the same time the headband guy shot a nasty look at us. Keesha followed his gaze and said something to him, making his expression soften.

"Maybe not," I said and got out of the car. I made my way to Keesha and her companion and introduced myself.

The headband guy scanned me up and down and offered me–almost reluctantly–his hand. "Ron Gray. I'm Franco's personal assistant," he said. His hand was wet for some reason. "Hey you! Don't drag that on the ground!" he snapped and went over to the truck guys to torment them.

"What a nice fellow," I said to Keesha when Ron was out of earshot.

"He's alright as long as you're on his good side. Are you ready for the interview?" Keesha said, grinning. She was a short First Nations girl of about my height with long black hair, big eyes and almost no lips. She had a tongue piercing that sometimes made her sound like she'd just eaten ice cream and her mouth was numb. That day she was wearing jeans and a light blue sleeveless shirt.

"As ready as I'll ever be," I replied

"You'll get the job, Franco already told me."

"*Are you serious*?" I said, not believing how nonchalant Keesha sounded.

"Yeah, he's already interviewed another guy and a girl and they he offered both of them jobs right away. I think he just wants to get started on whatever he's doing this summer."

"Well shit, I hope you're right because I've been stressing over this interview all week. Plus, I'm still technically unemployed, even if you say Franco already made up his mind and is hiring me."

She touched my shoulder for a second and said, "I'm always right. Come on now, let's go meet Franco. He's a bit, um, eccentric, but I think you'll like him."

Keesha led the way and we walked around the beautiful house–almost a little mansion, in fact– towards the back of the property, which faced Lake Superior. The backyard extended for at least fifty meters into a small private beach with white sand, as fine as the one you'd find in the south of the equator. In Cancun, maybe, and he must have certainly brought it from somewhere exotic because you could see a clear line where the soft sand ended and where the rocky dirt that you'd expect to see in a northern Ontario shore started.

Down by the water there was a stone fire pit with six white lounging chairs around it. There was a man sitting on the middle one. Franco, I assumed. He was holding a glass of red wine in his left hand and a cigarette in the right one. His pink shorts were tight on his skinny legs and gave him a sweaty–and very tanned–muffin top. He had no shoes or sandals on.

"What is it?" he asked with his sandpaper voice, turning his head towards us but not enough to actually see us. He was wearing round sunglasses.

"It's me," Keesha said. "I got Marco here for his interview."

He said one single word that made my stomach contort. "*Who?*"

That's it, I thought. *I'm not getting this job.*

"Marco. My friend from film school," Keesha replied and then looked at me, mouthing: "You'll be fine."

"Oh yes, yes. Sorry," Franco said, getting up from his chair. He turned around, dropped his cigarette on the floor and stepped on it with his bare foot. "Franco D'Amico. Nice to meet you, old timer. Keesha has said nothing but good things about you." He offered me his hand. I shook it. "Good grip."

"Nice to meet you too, Mr. D'Amico," I said, thinking it was fitting for him to be one of those people that make a big deal out of how strong you squeeze their hands. Exactly what you'd expect from someone who has written several self-help books.

"Oh, please. Call me Franco," he said in a dry and emotionless tone that made me feel like he actually preferred it when people called him Mr. or sir. "Let's go to my office."

I walked behind him, following his trail of cigarette smoke, alcohol and tan lotion.

12

Franco, or rather, a massive twenty-two by thirty-six inch portrait of Franco delivering a passionate speech, stared down at me. It hung on the wall behind a beautiful cocobolo desk, where a brand new laptop rested, with a white Beethoven bust to its right and a silver Newton's cradle to its left. The fact that there weren't any framed photos of family or friends anywhere in the office didn't strike me as odd back then, but now, in hindsight, was one of the first red flags that presented themselves to me. Franco loved no one but himself, it seemed.

I gave my back to a reproduction of a famous Japanese painting of an octopus kissing and *stimulating* a woman while I waited for Franco to come back.

"Okay old timer," he said from behind me after a few minutes passed. He walked to his desk now wearing a black polo shirt tightly wrapping him. He still had his pink shorts on and no shoes. "Tell me a little about yourself. Keesha says you're a good editor."

"Uhm. Yes, I–"

"*No.*"

"Sorry?" I asked, trying not to let my voice shake.

"Don't start your answers with an 'um'. That shows weakness. *Are* you weak?"

"No...?"

Franco bared his teeth. His canines were unnaturally long and sharp. Another one of his physical attributes that reminded me of a shark or some other carnivore. "Then be firm. Be *confident*. Let's start again. Hi Marco, please tell me a little about yourself."

I cringed at his *advice* but went along with it. "I'm a freelance filmmaker."

"Go on."

"I'm currently enrolled in the Digital Film program at the college and I hope to–"

"*Hope?*"

"And I will be a film director after I graduate. I'm planning to move to Toronto then," I said, the words coming out of me with less resistance than before. "I've been editing videos for years over the past three years or so, when I was still in high school."

Franco nodded in approval.

"I know I don't have much work experience,"–Franco raised an eyebrow at that–"but I'm a hard working individual and I'm also a fast learner. If you'd like I can email you my resume and a copy of my demo reel–"

"That won't be necessary. I just have one question for you."

I could feel the palms of my hands sweating. I bit my tongue and asked, "Yes?"

"What would you say is your biggest weakness?"

Anxiety, self doubt, poor organization skills. "That I care too much about work," I lied, hoping that my answer, which I'd memorized the day before, would please Franco. "I find it difficult to separate my work and personal life, and sometimes I end up working after I get back home."

Franco smiled again, allowing his smoke-scented breath to reach me on the other side of his desk. He offered me his hand and

I shook it for the second time that day. "Can you start on Monday?"

"Yes, sir." *Of fucking course I can,* I thought to myself.

I got another whiff of wine and cigarettes as Franco's smile stretched out to impossible lengths for anyone who doesn't have the help that botox injections provide.

"Now let me tell you something about myself, it's only fair, don't you think? You had your turn, now it's mine."

"Yes, Franco."

"Do you know what I do for a living?"

I was going to say I knew he was a successful author, but the question was rhetorical. "I'm in the life-changing business," he continued before I could answer. "When I was your age, not too long ago," –now it was his turn to lie– "I wasn't very different from yourself. Smart, but not ambitious. My self esteem was very low and my classmates loved to tease and ridicule me at any chance they got. I even thought about committing self-harm a couple of times, if you want me to be completely honest, until one day I realized something." And at this, he made a pause.

I took this as my cue to participate in the talk again. "What did you realize?"

Franco's smile disappeared for a moment. His expression grave. "I realized it was all my fault. I was the one who let myself down by not believing in myself, and that's when I decided I would never do it again. But it was not easy, I'll tell you that! I had to 'fake it 'til I made it', as some people say, but it was worth it in the end. I got a new haircut, bought new clothes with the money I'd saved up from my job as a grocery clerk and the rest is history. From that moment on I decided I'd never let anyone walk all over me no more." Hot anger replaced the coldness in his eyes. He opened one of the drawers of his desk and took out a picture, much smaller than the one on the wall behind him, and gave it to me. It showed a fifteen year old version of Franco with braces and acne all over his face. He was wearing a yellow dress shirt and a bolo tie with a red, shiny clasp around his neck. "This is me, the year I changed my life. I keep this picture always near me, to remind myself of how far I've come."

He stared at his past self for what seemed like a long time, so I said the first thing that came to my mind. "I'd be honored to work for you." Utter bullshit, I know, but I guess my subconscious decided it was fitting.

Franco's smile returned but the anger in his eyes did not vanish. "And you will, old timer," he said. "So, anyway, I eventually went to university and after graduating I worked as a counselor for a couple of years because I wanted to help others to achieve their full potential. It made me happy, for a while, but I knew I could, no, *should* help many more people than what my job allowed me to, and that's when I came up with the idea of writing books."

I nodded.

Franco opened his computer, looked something up and showed it to me. A video of male Calvin Klein models walking on a runway. They were tall, blonde, and had about twelve percent body fat. I wasn't sure what the point of the video was, so I just watched it and kept nodding periodically. "I want you and Keesha to help me make videos like *that*. I want to look elegant, *powerful* like them. Can you guys do that for me?"

I had access to the college's cameras, lenses and steadicams, so yes. I was certain we could produce videos of that quality, if not better. "Absolutely."

"Perfect. I want you guys to film snippets of my seminars. Do you drive?"

"I don't have my license yet."

"Too bad," he said and paused the video. "But it's okay. I'll drive or we'll take a plane next time I have a seminar. But before then, I'd like you to help me record a trailer or something like that for my YouTube channel."

My participation in the conversation was optional, as Franco seemed more than happy to keep talking all by himself for hours, but I thought I should say something. "Yes, we should definitely do that sooner rather than later, so we make as much content as we can over the summer."

"Precisely. I may hire you part time after your contract is over, depending on how well we work together, but for the summer I'll need you full-time, Monday to Friday."

Where had I heard that before? The vague promise of job security, I thought. *Oh yes, at my last work placement, two months before they hired someone else instead.*

"I want you to get some shots of me at the lake, wearing a cool outfit, maybe some other ones inside the house. It's a beautiful house indeed, I'll have to give you a tour later. I also just got a new hot tub, maybe you could record me talking in it, drinking wine and looking like a *winner.*"

I cringed again, harder than before. "Yeah, we can do that."

"Good. I will get my assistant to send you a contract. Bring it signed Monday morning at, let's say nine thirty."

13

I wandered around Franco's house listening to more stories of his youth. They were all the same: he was nothing, a loser if anything, then through hard work and perseverance, he got to the top. "Here's your office." he said as we walked downstairs to the basement. "Actually, it's the office space I set aside for you and the rest of my summer students, but you know what I mean. Ha ha."

The possessive way in which he referred to us as *his* made the hairs of the back of my neck stand in discomfort, but I didn't care. I was way too excited about having a new job that did not require me to wake up at three in the morning.

Our *office* was a large room with not much in it. Four long tables standing one next to the other in the center, all of them covered with enough tools and toolboxes to make it hard to tell what was underneath. Franco saw my eyes linger on the tables and said, "We'll get that cleared off on Monday so you guys can have space to work."

The walls had green painter's tape around electrical outlets, as well as on the edges of the floor and ceiling. *Another one of our Monday tasks,* I thought, half joking. Little did I know how right I was. Our *office* space also housed an array of different house appliances and miscellaneous items, like the brown bamboo blinds laying on a corner beyond Franco's eclectic tool collection.

The house tour ended when Franco showed me his three spare bedrooms and noted that if I ever wanted to stay over with some friends 'or girlfriends' for a weekend he was happy to allow it. "And that's about it. What do you think? Are you excited to start working for me? Wait, no. *How* excited are you?"

"Very much so," I replied.

"Excellent. Just one more question," Franco said, looking in the direction of Jude's car. "What's your friend's name again?"

"Oh, Jude."

Franco rubbed his five-o'clock-shadowed chin. "Is he also as hard-working as you?"

"Yes, definitely," I lied. Jude was a lover of relaxation.

"Okay good, and do you know if he's got any graphic design or marketing skills?" he asked, his eyes still fixed on Jude's Big Piece of Shit.

"Uhh, he made some posters for a club at the college last semester."

"Okay good. Maybe he'll be our marketing coordinator for the summer. Anyway, have a good weekend and I'll see you next week."

I offered my hand to Franco and he squeezed it hard. He seemed excited himself. "Sounds good Franco, thank you for the opportunity."

"Don't thank me, prove to me, no, to yourself, that you deserve it."

14

Jude's interview took way longer than mine, and at quarter past five I saw Franco opening the dark oak doors of his house to let my friend out, but they stayed chatting at the doorstep for another ten minutes.

"How did it go?" I asked when Jude finally got in the car.

"Pretty good actually," he said. "He offered me a marketing position or something like that right away, and we spent most of the interview talking about, uh, random stuff."

"Good for you my dude. I guess we will be coworkers again."

Jude turned the car on and we left the D'Amico property. "He's a bit of a character, isn't he?" he asked after a few minutes of quiet driving.

"Just a bit?"

"Okay, he's really something else, I guess," Jude said, chuckling. "But you know what dude? I'm just glad I'm having an income again so I can pay my rent and stuff."

"Yeah, me too. I'm just glad I won't have to reheat any more donuts."

***

Jude dropped me off at my place after having a couple of scoops of celebratory ice cream. I could see through the living room window that Cliff was watching something on TV but I was in such a good mood that even his nosy questions could not ruin my mood.

"How is it going buddy?" he said as I locked the door behind me.

"Not bad. Not bad at all. I just got a new job, much better than the one I had at the coffee shop."

"That's awesome! Where are you going to be working now?"

"I'll be editing videos for a local author," I replied.

"Who?"

"His name is Franco D'Amico. He's also–"

Cliff turned the TV off, his expression growing serious. He turned around to face me and took a deep breath. "You can't work for him."

"Sorry?"

"I think it's better if you have a seat."

I joined Cliff on his leather couch, making a squeaky noise as I sat. Cliff sighed.

"You gotta go back to the coffee shop. Ask your manager to take you back. I'm sure they haven't had the time to hire anyone to fill your position yet."

I had never seen Cliff look so serious, his dad-joke humor and lightheartedness were nowhere to be seen. "But why?" I asked.

Cliff shuffled on his seat, as if by rubbing his butt on it would help him come up with the right words. "D'Amico is, uhm, troubled, to say the least. Have you met him in person?"

"Yes."

"Then you already know he's... really out there."

I did. But being full of yourself wasn't a crime last I checked, so I said nothing. Hell, Cliff himself was like that sometimes too.

"You see," Cliff continued, "my son Mike and one of his buddies worked for him a few years ago and they both quit within a couple of weeks."

"Why?"

"Because Franco D'Amico is a bully, and he basically tortured them. He woos you into thinking that he's your friend and that he'll help you develop personal skills or whatever bullshit he's selling nowadays, but he's nothing more than a big old bully." Cliff's wrinkles suddenly looked deeper, his skin paler. "And what's more, there's some other allegations against him."

"About what?" I found myself saying.

Cliff sighed again, more deeply this time. "I shouldn't say, he never did anything to my son or his friend, but they heard some stories. Stories from other people who worked for him, and they said that sometimes when Franco got, uhm, intoxicated he could get quite *physical..*"

Oh fuck.

Cliff must have read my mind, because his serious expression morphed into one of worried concern, and he put his hairy arm around my shoulders. "I shouldn't have said that because I don't know it for sure, but based on what I did see with my own eyes and what David told me I can tell you this: you better put as much distance between someone like D'Amico and yourself."

"But I don't know if I can get my old job back."

"Then find something else, you just have to stay away from him."

"Crap. Okay, I guess I'll try to find something else," I lied (again). "But I won't go back to the coffee shop. It really fu— messed me up."

"I understand. I'll keep my eyes open in case something comes up," Cliff said, his body relaxing again. "But I'm sure you'll find a job in no time."

I had a feeling that there was something that Cliff wasn't telling me. I wanted to ask him so many things, but I didn't. I had way too much stuff to think about as it was.

"I guess I'll go to my bedroom now and start looking for a job online," I said. "Most stores at the mall won't take physical resumes anymore."

"What?" Cliff mumbled, apparently deep in his own thoughts. "Oh yes, you go do that."

15

"I just can't go back to the coffee shop. I hate it so much," I said to Stella, trying not to let my eyes water. We had just finished *cuddling* and were now sitting on her bed. A guy with long, messy blond hair from a poster of an early 2000s boy band—I forgot the name, it was a Chrsistian band—had his eyes on us. I turned away. "It's so fucking awful to have to wake up every day at three in the morning, and don't get me wrong, the rest of the job sucks too, but the worst part by far is how fucked up my sleeping schedule got while I was working there. I just can't go back. I just *can't*."

Stella put her hands on mine and smiled. "You don't have to go back."

"But what about everything Cliff said?"

"People change." Stella always liked to see the best in people, which over the years caused her to get hurt time and time again, yet she never changed. "Maybe he's exaggerating too. We just can't know for sure until you see for yourself. How was he, anyway?"

"He was very full of himself, and I don't know, he could be an asshole like Cliff said, for all I know." I closed my eyes and tried to calm down. It didn't work. "I just can't go back to the coffee shop. I never got how much I actually hated the job until now that I don't have to work there anymore, but Cliff won't let that happen. He's too much of a control freak, thinking he knows better than anyone else just because he's old and has money."

Stella's grip on my hands became more firm yet it still was gentle. "You won't have to go back," she said. "Listen to me, you have two friends that are going to be working for– what's his name again?"

"Franco."

"Right. You won't have to be on your own there, and if things get, uhm, *messy* you can always quit. Even better, start looking for other jobs now so you can have a back-up as soon as possible." her grip loosened just a smidge.

"Yeah, I guess I could do that."

"And you don't have to work for him for too long, anyway. Don't you have to go back home for a couple of weeks before the end of the summer?"

For a moment, shame swept over me. I hadn't given any thought to my visit to Mexico–or to my family, really–for a while. "You're right," I said.

"There you go. Just go to work on Monday and don't tell anything about it to Cliff."

"That'll be hard, but I guess I'll try."

"Why will it be that hard?"

"He's extremely nosy."

"How bad can he be?"

"You have no idea."

16

I did not sleep much that night. I spent hours laying on my bed, reliving the conversation I'd had with Cliff. The words *he could get quite physical* refused to leave my mind until dawn. *Surely I can handle this, I'm an adult,* I thought. I switched positions with the hopes of managing to fall asleep, even for just an hour or two. *I've got two friends on my side, don't I?* Plus, in this day and age it would be nearly impossible to get away with abusing your employees without attracting the attention (and wrath) of the media. *White Peaks is a small town and gossip is its currency.*

When the first rays of sun entered my room, warming it up by a few degrees in the process, I gave up and decided to search the internet for concrete proof of Cliff's allegations against Franco. I had to dig under a few dozen articles from the White Peaks Online kissing Franco's ass–headlines like "*Local author receives national award*" and "*Franco D'Amico pledges to use his social media platform to bring attention to social inequalities*" flooded the website–until I found an entry from May 15ht, 2006. Its heading said, "*Beloved resident of White Peaks gets convicted*".

Cliff was right, I wish I would have listened to him.

The Lying Tongue

Part 5: Franco

1

I decided against my better judgment to accept my new job working for Franco. It took me the better part of the weekend to let the revelation from the article really sink in. Franco had a drinking problem, alright, which had led him to get into a physical altercation with his former assistant Payton Kevill, who had to be put in a medically induced coma for a week after being hit on the head with a brick. A fucking *brick*.

The White Peaks Online reported that after a long legal battle, Franco's infamous lawyer accomplished the impossible and convinced the defense to drop all charges out of the blue. There were rumors floating around about how Franco's legal team had *somehow* stumbled upon Payton's personal emails that could have tarnished his reputation. Some people only even said that D'Amico had offered his old assistant an absurd amount of money outside of court, but no one knew the truth. Just Franco, Payton and their lawyers.

The fact of the matter was that Franco was indeed a dangerous man.

I know I lie more often than what most people would consider acceptable, but I always make a big effort to be truthful and open with people close to me—especially Stella—but I intended to keep my knowledge of Franco's legal and drinking problems to myself. There was no point in her stressing over me. After all, if worse came to worst, it would be three against one. I knew Jude and Keesha had my back, and I had theirs.

Or so I thought.

2

Jude picked me up from Cliff's porch the following Monday. It was an overcast day but the weather report promised clear skies in the afternoon. I was wearing my bomber jacket over a Red Hot

171

Chili Peppers shirt that, as most of my clothes did back then, fit me well enough from the neck to the bottom of my chest, but was rather tight around my stomach area. This made the Pepper's log, a red asterisk, look more like a dash.

"Did you have breakfast already?" Jude asked and lowered the volume of the stereo. He was playing some grim instrumental from a band I didn't know.

"No, you?"

"No. Wanna get a McMuffin or something?"

I looked at the Big Piece of Shit's digital clock. It was quarter to nine. "Do you think we have enough time?"

"Sure."

I didn't actually believe him, but I was too nervous and I didn't care. Being a few minutes late didn't wouldn't be the end of the world. Jude joined the McDonald's drive thru line behind five other cars.

It took us fifteen minutes to get to the pick-up window and by then we only had about twenty minutes to make it to work on time, so the moment the sleepy-eyed McDonalds employee gave us our food Jude floored the gas pedal.

Jude drove thirty kilometers above the speed limit, but somehow no police officer stopped him. He eventually slowed down and made an unexpected stop when we turned into Kenorah Road, just before leaving the city limits. I was so busy thinking about what to do if Franco ever got funky that it took my brain a while to process that we had taken a slight detour and entered a residential area instead of continuing our way on the highway.

"What are you doing?" I asked Jude as he pulled into a random driveway.

"We're picking up Keesha."

"Oh crap, we'll be very late dude."

Jude grabbed his phone and played another song, one with actual lyrics now, and said, "Nah, we'll make it just on time."

I looked at him and arched my eyebrows. "Really? Is she ready?"

"Yeah, she should be," he said and honked the horn to let Keesha know that we were waiting for her.

It took three long minutes that felt more like half an hour for Keesha to come out of her townhouse. Her hair was a frizzy mess and she was still in the process of putting her make-up on. She was wearing black denim jeans and a mauve long sleeve shirt. Her purse and backpack—one of those trendy ones with the red fox logo that were too small to actually be functional—were dangling from her left arm. She opened the door and jumped in the back seat of the car. "Sorry I'm late."

Jude started the Big Piece of Shit again. He had turned the engine off and rolled down the windows while we were waiting for Keesha to save gas. "It's all good," he said.

Keesha smacked her lips and looked at her tiny mirror to make sure her lipstick was applied properly. "How are you guys doing today? Excited?"

"I feel sick," I said truthfully.

"Why?"

"Don't listen to him," Jude intervened. "He's just nervous because he thinks we'll be late."

"We *will* be late Jude."

Keesha looked at the car's digital clock. 9:15 AM. "Oh shoot, it looks like we will be a bit late."

"No, I'm pretty sure we'll make it," Jude said, raising the speed of the Big Piece of Shit.

Keesha looked at me through the rearview mirror. She didn't seem convinced of what Jude had said. "Didn't you have another car?" she said, now looking at Jude. "An old station wagon?"

Silence.

"We don't talk about that," I said.

"Oh?"

Jude rubbed the right side of his head, near his hairline, with the heel of his right hand, the other hand still gripping the steering wheel, thankfully. "It died," he said.

"What happened?"

"We went on a road trip and got into a small accident," I replied. "The engine died."

"Now it's probably in some junk yard in Newmarket. I sold it to a guy that wanted it for parts," Jude added.

I grabbed my phone and sent a text to Keesha.

The car was pretty old but the accident was kind of my fault,
so please let's change the subject

Okay, sorry

"You guys are going to love working for Franco," Keesha said after a long, awkward silence, in an attempt to lighten the mood. "He's so chill."

I really doubted that, but for the sake of changing the subject I nodded.

"Yeah, that'll be nice. I need a chill job after my last one," Jude said and I cringed, remembering what I'd read about Franco and the brick. The fucking brick. The eczema patch on my left hand began itching like hell and I scratched it.

"Where did you work before this?" Keesha asked, her hair tamed and no longer looking like she'd been electrocuted.

"At the coffee shop. Marco worked there too but we both quit. It was *extremely* hectic and there was a lot of yelling and, uh, screaming," Jude replied. "I'm looking forward to having a change of pace."

"Yeah, me too," I said in a small voice.

"Then you're definitely gonna love working for Franco. I've been working for him for a couple of weeks already and most days I just sit down in his living room and listen to podcasts with my earbuds until he tells me to help him make a post on his Facebook page or shit like that," Keesha said from the back seat. She had completed her morning routine and was now looking at her phone.

"I could do that, yeah," Jude said. His mood seemed to have changed. His words were softer.

I felt too nervous to talk–not only because I kept imagining how out of his mind Franco must have been to hit his assistant (and maybe even friend) with a fucking brick, but also because of Jude's speeding– so my friends continued their chat without me. *If things start getting out of control I'll tell them everything. Every single thing I found out about Franco,* I said to myself. *Even if I just see him start drinking a little too often.*

3

Jude had to drive at 120 kilometers per hour once we left town, but we somehow made it on time. We got out of the car and Keesha rang the doorbell after I attempted to use the door knocker, which ended up not being functional at all, its purpose solely being for decoration. We waited for a few moments but no sound came from inside the house and nobody came out to let us in.

"He's probably getting ready," Keesha said. "Let me give him a call."

Franco didn't pick up, but a few seconds after the call went to voicemail we heard a dull thumping sound coming from the other side of the door. Keesha put her phone back in her purse and Franco emerged from his house.

"Early risers," he said. His hair was wet and slicked back. He was wearing nothing but a blue velvet bathrobe and fluffy maroon slippers. "Come on into the living room while I finish getting ready. And let the others in when they get here, if you don't mind."

***

I had a feeling that Franco must have gone back to bed for a quick nap because he didn't come back to meet us for almost another hour. In that time, two more college students joined the Franco ranks: Dakota, a tall, young man of about eighteen or nineteen years of age with short, black hair straight as an arrow (and frosted tips); and Bailey, a short, chubby girl of about the same age

175

who I was surprised to find out was not irish despite her red hair and heavily freckled face.

By then Jude had already inspected every inch of the living room, or rather, everything that had interested him, and he sat down on the couch in between Keesha and I. In front of us, on the opposite couch, our new coworkers pretended to be on their phones, probably to avoid small, awkward talk. We had exchanged names when they arrived, but that was it. I was about to get up to try to find a bathroom when Franco's chainsmoker voice startled me and I sank back down on the couch.

"Hi team, is everyone here already?" he said. He was now wearing tight jeans with rips at the knees, a blue dress shirt with the top four buttons undone—letting his brittle chest hairs peek at us–, a dark gray blazer and a black fedora hat. He looked like a middle-aged youth counselor from a Christian summer camp. And of those ones that gave you predatory vibes.

Nobody answered our boss, but whether no one did out of shyness or cringe, I do not know.

"Looks like you're a quiet lot, we'll have to work on that. Confidence is everything," Franco said. He'd brought a stool and placed it to our left, in between both couches, and he looked at each one of us, smiling a mirthless smile.

"Uh... We're ready?" Jude finally said.

Franco eyed him, got up from his stool and walked towards him. "Am I detecting team-lead energy?" The comment had attracted everyone's attention, which in turn caused Jude's cheeks to blush.

"Y– yes?"

"Excellent!" Franco said with enthusiasm. "You and Keesha will both be our team leads. Let's start the day with introductions." He reached his right hand into his back pocket and produced a small silver ball. "Let's start with you, Jude," he said, passing him the ball. "Just tell us a little bit about yourself."

Jude gave Keesha and I a quick, panicked look and cleared his throat. "Hi everyone, uh, my name is Jude and–"

"Hi Jude!" Franco exclaimed, interrupting him. "Come on everybody."

"Hi Jude," the voices of Keesha, Bailey, Dakota and myself sang in a monotonous unison.

"Hey, hi," Jude continued. His face was beet red now. "I'm studying General Arts and Science at the college. I, uh, I like cooking, music and video games. Oh, and I also play the guitar and piano."

"Ouuu! We got a virtuoso here," Franco said, putting a hand on Jude's shoulder. "Good job Jude, now pass the ball to someone else."

I received the ball next. "Hi, my name is Marco and I'm from Mexico."

The sad chorus greeted me back, "Hi Marco."

"I moved to Canada to study film. I like watching movies and reading." I glanced at Franco, saw that my answer had apparently pleased him–he was still smiling and he was now looking at the guys from the other couch–and decided to finish my introduction. "Thank you."

"Very well," Franco said, his hand still on Jude's shoulder. "I'll be sure to make use of your videography skills."

I passed the ball to Keesha, who mentioned that she was also studying film and was interested in shopping and hiking. She gave the silver ball to Bailey. "Hi everyone, my name is Bailey and I'm studying Social Work at the university. I'm originally from Timmins but I moved here for school as well. I like to knit, swim and paint in my free time, and I'm working on writing a poetry collection."

"See? I'm good at choosing promising summer students to work for me," Franco said, still grinning, like a nasty dog.

Dakota, the last one of the D'Amico cult, had the shortest introduction. He stood up slowly, as though his back had some enormous weight on it, stared at the floor and said, "Hi, I'm Dakota and I like contemporary dance." He handed the ball back to Franco and sat down. It's worth noting that I hadn't noticed that he also had a bit of a beer belly, making Jude the only one of us that could be considered skinny.

"Very well," Franco said, sitting back on the stool. "I think I got a very *diverse* group of students this year and I'm sure we'll do great things together. Now even though you all know me already it's only fair for me to say a little something about myself." Every time he talked about himself, his smile grew bigger, but it never managed to reach his dark eyes. "My name is Franco and I'm an author. A bestselling one. I've written three extremely successful books and I'm currently working on writing the next one. I hired you folks because I see talent and skills in you, as well as weaknesses that I will help you overcome this summer."

My hand started hurting. I looked down for a second and realized I'd started scratching it without noticing, and it had started to bleed. I wiped it on the back of my pants and shifted my attention to Franco.

"Now, let's all go down to the office. That's where you'll be working most of the time, but I'll have to ask some flexibility from all of you. Some days we'll have to go to the city for some events I have scheduled, and some other days I'll take a couple of you with me out of town to help me with my seminars. Don't be jealous though, you *all* will get the chance to come on a trip with me."

Jude nodded, then everyone else mirrored him.

"Okay, now follow me."

4

Franco—or more likely, his new assistant—had moved half of the large collection of tools from the tables to the floor, and added five chairs along the cleared area. In front of each one of them was a two-page contract and a pen. We all took a seat—Keesha, Jude and I still not mixing with Dakota and Bailey, who had sat opposite us.

"Review the contract and sign when you're done. It's all pretty standard," Franco said, standing behind us.

I made sure to read through the entire contract to make sure no funny business was present, and on the contrary, I was pleasantly surprised when I discovered that we'd be making almost three dollars above minimum wage. After a couple of minutes I scribbled my signature at the bottom of the second page. When we had all signed our souls away to Franco and were officially hired, our new boss took our contracts away from us and replaced them with a scrap of paper. "I'll be paying you bi-weekly via e-transfer," he said, "I just need you to write down your emails and that should be it."

It was only my second job ever in Canada, but that way of payment seemed a bit on the sketchy side of things to me. If anyone else found it odd, though, they kept it to themselves.

"Amazing, welcome aboard. This will be a fun-filled summer you won't forget." That, at least partially, was one of the few truths that came out of Franco's cigarette-stinking mouth.

***

Franco's new assistant, Ron, stopped by at around noon. "Hi Franco, how are you new recruits? Everything that you wished for?" he asked as he walked down the stairs to the basement, I mean, "office".

"Yes, I think we got a solid group this year," Franco replied. He had made us go through another one of his *personal-growth* activities in which we, one at a time, had to stand on top of a table and fall backwards, arms crossed and eyes closed, only to be caught after a brief moment of panic and fear in the arms of the rest of us. The only problem with this activity was the time when we barely managed to grab Dakota, mere inches before he could hit his large head–which reminded me of a watermelon for some reason–on the hard floor.

"Good, good," Ron said. "Do you mind going upstairs to your office for a moment, though? I need you to help me straighten out some bookkeeping stuff."

"Yes, yes, of course," Franco said. "Keesha, you're in charge now. You and Marco are the techy ones, so you can grab a laptop and continue with the project we started last Friday." I looked at Keesha, confused. She gave me a sly smile and agreed. "Okay good," Franco continued. "The rest of you can keep sorting and filling the toolboxes. I know it may feel like a tedious chore, but it'll help you develop patience, which is a *core* skill if you want to be successful, and who knows, if you make good progress today I may have a little surprise for you at the end of the day." He winked at us and left the room with Ron tailing him.

"What are we supposed to do now?" I said to Keesha, who had started walking to another room.

"You'll see."

I went after her, and before we left the "office" I looked back. Jude and Bailey had started a cheerful conversation, their attention drifting away from their job while Dakota kept sorting the various tools around him with an almost robotic precision that went well with his expressionless face.

Keesha brought me to a much bigger room. A rec room I assumed, with a pool and air hockey tables at the back, a modern chandelier-like lamp made out of long, rectangular pieces of glass shining above. Behind the tables was another huge TV, not as big as the one from the living room though. I sat on a black *La-Z-Boy*, imagining I was ten years older, living in a house not unlike Franco's and enjoying a day off work. Keesha dropped a laptop on my legs, interrupting my upper-middle class fantasy. "The password is *damico68*, all lower case."

"Okay," I said and turned on the computer. The space bar had an oval shiny spot of wear, but besides that little flaw it looked unused. "What are we supposed to do?"

"There's a folder in the desktop with a bunch of pictures of junk Franco wants to sell on eBay."

"Oh?"

"There's not much left to upload to his account, so we can just take it easy and stretch it out as long as we can so that we don't have to sort more tools," Keesha said and sat on the *La-Z-Boy* next to mine.

"Do you think Franco will be able to tell that we're just farting around in here?"

"Are you kidding? I don't see him half the time I'm here. You just won the lottery with this job. Just do whatever he tells you to do, be quiet and drag things on as long as you can."

I could do this all summer, I thought, the prospect of easy money making me forget for a bit about Franco's violent past. "Okay, but when do you think we'll actually do some film stuff?"

"Ha! I don't know. I only ever shot one of his talks so far, and I've worked for him for almost a month now," Keesha replied. I peeked at her laptop and found the *Just Jared* homepage on her internet browser. "Maybe by the end of the week, but I wouldn't count on it."

"Oh well, we'll have tons of stuff to film when school starts anyway."

5

If Keesha ever did some actual work that day, I never found out. She spent the next two hours reading God knows what on the computer and putting her earbuds in once in a while to watch some videos or listen to a podcast or something. I really don't know.

Less than an hour had passed when I finished creating item listings of Franco's junk, which he never ended up selling because who in their right mind would be interested in buying things like a *North Face* rain jacket–*Worn only once!* as stated in Franco's notes I'd found in the same folder that contained the pictures–from ten years ago for eighty bucks when you could buy a brand new one– *sans* cheap cigarette smell, mind you–for a few dollars more at any mall?

I spent the rest of our time in Franco's den updating a Google Doc file with ideas and a rough outline for my next big film project: a feature length movie script. I had been aching to write one since I was a fifteen year old *film bro* who though he'd discovered a world of arthouse cinema after having watched *Pulp Fiction* and *American Psycho* for the first time, but thanks to my short attention span and to the lackluster short film scripts I'd written in the past I had put my screenwriting plans on hold until I got into film school. *Surely by then I'll have the skills I need to write,* I'd thought.

I still sucked however. My best idea (and the one I was developing at the time) followed the story of a divorced high school teacher whose rebellious son had died of a heroin overdose, a tragic situation that had for some reason fucked her up enough to make her start trying to get pregnant again, now nearing her fifties, by any means necessary—which included inappropriate interactions with one of her students—to fill the void in her heart, or something like that. It was still a rough idea.

I must have rewritten the first page of that document at least eight times alone that day until Ron walked into the room with a cup of tea, a lemon slice adorning the rim. "Are you done?" he asked, dragging the first syllable of "done" in an insufferable tone as if he were a *valley girl*.

Keesha looked at my computer screen and I immediately minimized the window with my bad script ideas. "Yes, just finished actually," I said and closed the laptop.

"Okay great," Ron said, squeezed lemon juice into the mug and sipped his tea. "Franco wants you all to meet him in the living room." He provided no more information, he left the room, swaying his hips from side to side slightly.

"Is he always that obnoxious?" I asked.

"Yeah, you better get used to it."

"Great."

We went to the living room and sat on the couch in front of Jude and Bailey, who were apparently getting to know each other very well. "Well that's the thing, people thought Moondog was just another bum living in the streets of New York when in reality he was a stupidly good musician and composer. He even created some *unique*, uh, musical instruments and—" Jude said while Bailey just sat there, staring at him with adoration in her eyes. I felt irritated and betrayed on Mel's behalf–Jude was clearly enjoying the female attention. Dakota was somewhere else in the house.

"Okay guys, how was your first day of your new job?" Franco asked. Ron was standing behind him, smiling at his phone like a teenage girl texting her boyfriend.

"It was great," Jude, our "team lead" said, cutting his Moon-dog lecture short.

"Yes it was good!" Bailey added with too much excitement in her voice, which annoyed me even more.

"Awesome, that's great to hear. We will continue to mix good *honest* work with social development activities to make this a great summer for everyone. Now, I–" Franco trailed off. "Where is Dakota?"

Jude scratched his chin. "Uh, I think he's in the bathroom."

"For fuck's sakes," Franco said and walked out of the living room. "Where did he go now?"

"This will be good," Ron said, still smiling at his phone.

We heard Franco's footsteps in the distance. *Knock, knock, knock.* No response. Franco turned around and reappeared for a moment before he walked downstairs. *Knock, knock, knock.* Louder this time. "Tree nuts," I thought I heard a voice say, followed by more knocking. "*I said just a minute!*" It was Dakota.

We all sat in silence until Franco came back to the living room. He took a deep, raspy breath. "Well, it appears like Dakota's priorities are mixed up," he said. "We're going to help him with that. But anyway, as I was saying, when people work for me I also work with them, helping them get closer to who they *can* be. Today has been an extraordinary day, and I know it's not five yet, but you're free to go now."

"Oh thanks boss," Jude said, getting up from the couch.

"There is just one condition, though," Franco said, looking for something in his pocket. "Here, take this." It was a gift card.

"Oh, uh, thanks?"

"Don't thank me, it's for work. You have a car, don't you?"

"Yeah."

"Well, this will be your first *team lead task*. I want you to take the team out to grab something to eat so you can get to know each other better. The base of a good team, one in which you know you can rely on, is trust, but before you can trust each other you gotta get to know them really well." Franco gave Jude a light slap on his back. "Okay now off you go. See you all tomorrow at nine."

As we made our way out of the lake house I thought I heard Dakota saying something and Franco cursing again, but I was scared to look back and see what the fuss was. Franco had sounded quite upset when he'd knocked on the bathroom door. If anyone else heard them, they also ignored the exchange.

6

I walked at a fast pace—or at least what I considered a fast pace, given that I have short legs—so that I could have the front seat instead of Bailey, leaving the rest of the team behind.

"What's the rush?" Keesha said when she made it to the car.

"I'll tell you later," I said, a little out of breath. "Where's the gift card from, Jude?"

"What?" He was again lost in his conversation with Bailey. "Oh, Gino's Pizza."

"That's a very nice place," Bailey said. "They got the best pizza in town."

"I mean, it's alright," I replied and jumped in the Big Piece of Shit. "But Arturo's is better." Normally I would have said *I think* Arturo's is better, but as a fat man, and a pizza connoisseur, I knew I was right. Gino's Pizza was too doughy and they used canned mushrooms

"That place is so overrated," Bailey said, continuing our conversation inside the car.

"I just think it was a very nice thing that Franco—" Jude said before Dakota's "yelling" stopped him.

"Wait. Wait." His voice was slow and unconcerned.

We looked around and found Dakota jogging towards us, his beer belly bouncing up and down and his frosted tips undulating in the wind. "Thank you," he said when he reached us. He sat in the back seat between Bailey and Keesha, squeezing them both towards the doors with his broad shoulders and wide torso.

"You're welcome," Jude said. He turned the engine on and drove off.

***

There was something odd about Dakota, something that for some reason made us all less eager to chat, and which in turn caused the drive to Gino's feel longer than it actually was.

Another unpleasant thing about Dakota was his smell: a tangy scent of sweat and chili that refused to dissipate, even after Jude rolled the windows down. By the time we got to the parking lot I almost lept from my seat to put as much distance between me and Dakota.

"Looks like someone's hungry," Bailey said, walking next to Jude.

I chuckled. "Ha. I guess you could say that." She wasn't wrong. All I'd had to eat that day had been a little McMuffin.

Gino's Pizza was the typical family restaurant people go to for mildly special occasions, such as when your grandparents come to visit for a few days and your parents don't want to cook but also don't want to go to a place that will charge them $250 for five entrées, not including the drinks.

Our waiter, who was also an Elvis impersonator on the side, led us to a booth and told us all about the day's special–honey garlic ribs with a side of mashed potatoes and seasonal veggies, which more likely than not were just buttered green beans–before he left to give us some time to look at the menu.

"What do you guys feel like having tonight?" I asked, trying to decide if I was in the mood for pasta or pizza.

"You just *have* to get pizza when you come to Gino's," Bailey said. "Would anyone want to share one with me?"

Not me, I thought. *She's probably one of those people that think pineapple belongs in pizza. Yuck.*

"I'd be down," Jude said. "Which one did you want to get?"

"I was thinking about getting the *Greek Extravaganza*."

"I'll have to pass. I hate olives and half the things on it. Sorry."

"I'll share it with you," I replied, almost to my own surprise.

Bailey frowned for a moment, seemed to consider my offer and relaxed. "Sure," she said. "Why not?"

"I think I'm just gonna get a salad," Keesha said, putting her menu down. "And maybe a caesar."

"Salad? That's not even real food." It was Dakota this time. It was the first time he'd said something since we left Franco's.

"Yes it is, but I think I'm actually getting one of these bad boys instead," Keesha replied and pointed her index finger to the margaritas on the drinks menu. When fake Elvis came back to take our order, we all followed Keesha's example and got a different kind of margarita.

***

I must admit that for the first time so far, one of Franco's team building activities worked. The food (and the margaritas) had loosened everyone's tongues, allowing me to give Bailey a second chance–she wasn't that bad once you got past her snotty exterior, and I also found out that we both loved Brandon Sanderson–, Jude to make everyone laugh with his silly jokes, and Keesha to smile once in a while. Even Dakota told us a bit more about his love for dance. He'd apparently performed in national dance competitions when he was in high school and was hoping to move to a bigger city after college and become a ballet instructor. We had all laughed when he said this, but after seeing that he was serious Jude changed the subject.

"How do you want me to split the bill?" the waiter asked half an hour later, passing his fingers through his voluminous dark hair. He had also brought a container for the leftover pizza.

"Just one bill is fine," Jude said and took Franco's gift card out of his pocket.

"Certainly," fake Elvis said and grabbed the gift card. "I'll take this with me and I'll be right back with the receipt."

"Thanks."

"We should *definitely* do this again," Bailey said. She was tipsy, almost drunk now. "Maybe we could all go out for supper on Fridays after work, and have a few drinks too."

We all agreed and started discussing other restaurant options when the waiter came back, with what looked like a receipt and a debit machine. "I'm sorry, but the gift card only had a twenty-five dollar balance. Here's the bill with the outstanding amount. Do you want me to split it in fifths?"

"No, it's okay. I got it," Jude said.

"Very well."

A long and deep *Oof* came out of Jude's mouth when he saw what he had agreed to pay.

"How much is it? I can pitch in," I suggested after I peered over his shoulder to see what we owed.

Jude declined my offer and proceeded to pay with his credit card, adding fifty more dollars to his debt. This, however, didn't seem to bother him too much.

We went back to his car, all of us feeling a bit more comfortable now that we'd had time to interact with each other outside of work, so that could drop us off. My place was the last stop of the night. I was expecting Jude to invite me to go over to his apartment or something like that but he surprised me with a different request when he stopped in my driveway. "Hey, um, on second thought could you actually send me some money for the pizza and all that?"

I couldn't blame him. Not after the Toronto trip. I just wish he'd said something at the restaurant, when there were another three people that could have pitched in for the bill. "Oh, yeah for sure," I said. "How much?" *Hopefully not half,* I thought.

"Maybe ten or fifteen bucks? To cover your part?"

"Sounds good, I'll send you the money in a bit," I said on my way out of the car.

"Thanks my dude."

"No problem. See you tomorrow."

"See you."

7

The first thought that came into my mind when the strong scents of eastern european food that I had come to love hit me was *I wonder what Anna's cooking today*–most of her dishes smelled rather similar, yet their taste varied wildly–, followed by *Where the heck is everyone?* after I found myself all alone in the kitchen. There was a pot of a simmering, deep-red stew on the brink of spilling over and burning, one trickle at a time, so I turned the burner off.

I left the kitchen with the intention of retreating into my room when I saw Anna in the distance, through the glass sliding doors that connected the dining room to the backyard. She was standing with her back to me, smoking a cigarette and looking into the vast nature that, at least legally and on paper, belonged to Cliff. I slid the door open and walked towards her on the damp grass.

"Hey."

"Oh fuck, you scared me," Anna said and took another hit, blowing smoke through her nostrils. "You're so quiet." She rolled her R when she said "you're".

"Sorry. I just wanted to tell you that I turned the stove off. The stew was–"

"You should have let it burn," Anna said, cutting me off. Her voice was bitter and tired. "Get Cliff to spend the next three hours scrubbing his precious kitchen with a toothbrush."

Do I really want to know what happened? I thought. *Yes, I un-fortunately do.* Few people understood how exhausting living under the same roof as Cliff could be, so I didn't want to miss this opportunity to discuss it. "Where is he, anyway?"

"I don't care. Probably in the living room watching something on TV, or in the bedroom, doing the same. That's all he ever does."

She was kind of right. A gust of wind blew Anna's cigarette smoke straight into my eyes, making them water. "Is everything okay?" I asked, rubbing my eyes.

"Sorry, do you want me to stop?"

"No, it's fine."

"Do you want one?".

"Sure," I said, squinting my irritated eyes. "I'll save it for later." I accepted the cigarette and put it in my back pocket. Soon it would join my collection. I must have had enough of them in my bottom drawers to fill three packs by then. I still don't really know why I never told Anna that I didn't smoke.

"I don't know," she said, inhaling again. "Sometimes it's so hard to be with him."

"I can imagine."

"I knew dating Cliff was not going to be easy, but lately it's becoming almost unbearable. Do you wanna know what happened today?"

Yeah, that's kind of what I asked you a minute ago, I thought, but the word that came out of my mouth was: "Sure."

"You know how obsessed he's with losing weight lately?"

"Yes, of course. He still wants me to weigh in every other week to see how much fatter I got." I sat down on the grass, next to Anna. It had been a long day, a good one, but I was tired nonetheless.

"He's trying to do that with me too! That's why I haven't been staying over as much lately. Every single fucking morning, as soon as I go to the potty" –Anna's occasional silly phrases always made me laugh, but I tried to remain looking serious– "he takes out the stupid scale and makes me step on it." At this moment she sat on the ground and I did the same shortly after. "Well, I've been going to the gym at night for the past two weeks, killing myself in the elliptical to get this weight loss thing over with so I can have my morning poop in peace without worrying about Cliff shoving the scale on my face when I get back to the bedroom, and it's been working! I've lost six pounds so far," she had started pulling stray clovers off the lawn.

"That's awesome, Anna. I wish I could do the same," I said and started to help her pluck clovers.

"Thank you, I was so proud of myself so today I decided to come to his place and surprise him with our favorite dish. So I got here early and started cooking to have everything ready before he came back from his mother's house." She tossed her cigarette butt behind us and continued her story. "After two hours of cooking and stirring that stupid stew he comes home, and guess what's the first thing he says when he looks at the pot."

"What?"

"'We're not eating that, are we?' so I said to him, 'Yes we are.' And he started going on and on about how he's on a keto diet now and he can only eat twenty percent carbs and how my food has God knows how many of those."

"*Wow.*"

She made a pause and took a long breath. "And then he said, 'You can eat whatever you want, but that's the reason why you've been gaining weight while I'm shedding it off *so* easily.'" Tears started to drip from her blue eyes, silently. I didn't know what to say, so I decided to pay her back. I've always had a knack for finding new ways to make things awkward.

"He can be a bit insensitive sometimes," I said. "But he doesn't do it on purpose. He probably thought he was doing you a favor or something."

"I know, but I never even got the chance to tell him I'd lost weight. I don't know. Maybe I am being stupid."

"No, I don't think you are," I said and removed my hand from her back. "But I'm sure if you go talk to him about it he'll apologize."

"Yeah, maybe, but I think I'll wait for him to come to me first. I think I at least deserve that. And it's nice out here."

"That's fair," I said, getting up.

"Thank you for listening, Marco."

"Anytime." I started to walk back into the house but stopped before making it to the sliding door. "Do you want me to tell you something that may cheer you up?"

"Yeah, sure."

"I'll have Cliff all over my ass when he finds out I didn't listen to him and started working for someone he hates. At least by then he'll for sure stop bothering you with the scale."

"What do you mean? Who are you working for?"

"He's a writer, his name is Franco D'Amico."

"Never heard of him, but I'm glad you didn't let him control you."

"Yeah, I guess I am too."

8

Cliff must have a way with words, because by the time that Stella came to pick me up to hang out later that night, a rhythmic clapping noise accompanied by panting and the squeaky sounds of a rocking bed was coming out of his room. *I guess he did end up apologizing,* I thought, hurrying to get the fuck out.

I wanted to do some *cuddling* of my own with Stella, but she'd had quite an eventful day at work herself, so we spent most of the night just talking. She'd had to change twelve diapers that day and, fifteen minutes before her lunch break, had somehow managed to get out of the way before one of her kids threw up on her. "I felt so bad for him. I kept pushing him away after he threw up because he was trying to hug me but his hands were soaked in puke," she said.

191

"You did what you had to do. You could have gotten sick your-self if you'd let him touch you."

"I don't know, he was fine after that, which was good because his parents never came to pick him up after we called them anyway. It must have been something he ate."

"Do parents ever pick up their kids early when they're sick?"

"*Pffft,* no. They'd send them to us even if they were dying." She shook her head. "On weekends and holidays too, if we were open."

After she finished talking about her day I told her the short ver-sion of what had happened at Franco's: how we hadn't worked much and instead spent a lot of time talking about ourselves and doing some housekeeping work–because that's exactly what it had been–, and all about how Jude had offered to pay for the rest of the bill when fake Elvis let us know that Franco's *generous* gift had only been good enough to pay for a third of our food. It was at that mo-ment when Stella closed her eyes and started replying with uninter-ested *Mhmm*'s to what I was saying until she eventually fell asleep.

I lay on her comfortable bed, watching her chest peacefully rise and fall with every breath she took, wondering what I had done to deserve to be with her–based on past experience, I was half expect-ing to end up marrying an abusive girlfriend that I'd been too scared to break up with. I fell asleep (with a little smile on my face) not too long after Stella did.

9

A song I'd never heard before woke me up. The room was still dark and when I reached to grab my phone on my nightstand to turn off the alarm, I found a wall instead. *The fuck?* I rubbed my eyes and tried to adjust them to the lack of light, and that's when I heard a yawn. Stella stretched her long arms and smacked me on the face. *Oh crap.* "Morning," I whispered.

I covered Stella's mouth before she could let out a scream of surprise. "*Shh, it's okay.* I just fell asleep here. Sorry."

It took her a minute to understand what had happened, but she eventually got it, and her eyes grew wide and concerned. She took a deep breath and removed my hand from her mouth. "Crap. Does my mom know you're here?"

"I don't think so, I didn't have to pee in the night or anything so I guess I never left the room."

Stella sat up on her bed. "Let me have a quick look, maybe she's not up yet and you can just sneak out." She got her answer before she had time to get out of bed, however, when a knock on the door just about made her screech.

"*Stella, there's barely any hot water left in the tank, so try to shower as fast as you can.*" Mrs. Levinson said, almost yelling, unaware that she was speaking to two people on the other side of the door instead of just one.

"Okay, mom." Stella's calm and even voice did not match her jittery body.

"*Do you want me to make you some tea?*"

"No, that's okay, thanks."

"*Okay, and again, just be quick when you shower. I'm next!*"

Stella and I shared a look. "So, um, should I leave now or...?" I asked.

"I don't know what to do."

"What do you mean?"

"I... it's just that—" Stella said, wide awake and looking around as if the words she was looking for were scattered somewhere in her bedroom.

"What?"

"I don't know. She can't find out you spent the night here and I don't know what to do. She doesn't work so who knows when she will leave the house."

"I mean, she'll get over it if she finds out, no?"

Stella got out of bed, undressed for a second and put her pink bathrobe on. "She won't. She'll freak out on me and think I'm a slut." Her voice started ringing with panic.

"Stella, you're twenty four. I'm sure she knows we're sleeping together, she may not like it but I'm *sure* she knows. We're not in high school anymore." I yawned, which was not the right thing to do because at this, Stella gave me a look of incredulity, as if I did not consider our current situation as serious as she did. Which was kind of true, but I hadn't meant to express that. I was just sleepy.

"I... may have told her I hadn't slept with anyone after I broke up with my last boyfriend."

I laughed. "No, really, why would she freak out?" Stella made no reply. "Are you serious?"

"Yes," she said, rolling up the curtains and letting warm morning light flood the bedroom. "You know how *Christian* she is."

"I thought you were Christian too," I said, again squinting my eyes to adjust to the light.

"I am, but she's old school and–" Her words trailed off, she fixed her eyes on the window. "I know what we can do."

"What?"

She nodded her head towards the window.

"No."

"You made me get out through the window at *your* place!"

"What about my shoes?"

"What about them?" she asked with a smile on her face and started to take her outfit for the day out of the dresser.

"I left them at the front door."

"Well, just wait here until I leave for work and I can pick up your shoes and leave them in the backyard for you."

That was it, Stella had made the decision for both of us and there was no way to talk her out of it. *I guess I deserve it,* I thought. Too bad if I didn't like it, that was just the way things were going to be. "Okay, fine. But now we're even."

10

Stella spent close to an hour showering, and when she came back to the bedroom I could almost see steam coming off her body.

194

What's up with how girls use boiling hot water every time they have to clean themselves? That was one of the reasons why we didn't hop in the shower together as often as I'd like to–the other one was due to both of our living situations and the lack of privacy that our *roommates,* if you could call her parents and my Cliff roommates, inflicted on us. I'm a man who can't handle extremes, no hot baths or cold swims for me.

One painstakingly slow breakfast's length of time later, my girlfriend came back into the bedroom where I'd been waiting for her to go over the plan once more before I made my dramatic exit. "I feel like I'm forgetting something," she said after we triple checked everything. Stella was a thorough girl.

"I doubt it. Let's get this over with," I replied and walked over to the window.

There was one crucial difference between my bedroom window and Stella's, however. Mine is about four feet above ground level while Stella's was at least three times higher. We removed her hairbrush, stuffies and other personal items from her old beat-up and sticker-covered dresser–which was placed directly underneath the window–so that I could step on it and not stab my feet.

"Good luck," Stella said when I had already had an entire leg out the window.

I bent down and gave her a kiss. "Thanks."

I looked down at the floor, closed my eyes and jumped.

***

I slipped on the cool dew-covered grass, my flabby ass taking some of the impact. I winced in silence for a moment, and when I looked up I saw Stella covering her mouth with her hands. "I'm okay," I whispered, rubbing my butt. I'm sure she couldn't hear me, but she got the message and she retreated from the window.

My socks got soaked after I took a couple of steps on the path between Stella's house and the fence with peeling flakes of white paint that served to mark where her neighbor's property started.

195

There were a few missing planks of wood as well, and it was through one of these gaps where I saw a deep blue eye with eyeliner circling it staring maliciously at me. *Oh great.* I looked away from the eye, hoping that if I acted like nothing fishy was happening the eyeliner guy would just go back to his gardening, and quickened my pace.

"Hey, *hey!*" A voice called after me when I reached the sidewalk. "*Come over here! What were you doing back there?*"

Fuck, please just go home, I thought, still walking and not turning around.

The flipping and flapping of the eyeliner guy's sandals intensified with every step forward I took. "*I'm going to call the police if you don't stop!*"

At this, I could no longer ignore him. I turned around and discovered the rest of the man's facial features. He had a bowl haircut (straightened) with a red streak at the front, partially covering the eye I hadn't seen yet. He had a silver ring piercing the left side of his lower lip and a septum piercing that was barely visible. "What were you doing back there? I saw you coming out the window," eyeliner guy said, resting his fists against his hip and looking like a cowboy with a male crop top and denim shorts.

I froze. *Surely Stella will come out of her house at any second now, with my shoes and an explanation for this guy,* I thought.

"Say something or I will call *the police!*"

I tried to say that I was Stella's boyfriend, but what came out of my mouth was an incomprehensible whisper.

"*What?*"

I stepped closer to him so he wouldn't raise his voice more and attract the attention of nosy neighbors. "I said that I'm friends with Stella."

The man stared at me, probably judging whether or not a burglar could have said to him the name of the girl next door. "*Friend,*" I said again, making air quotes. "I spent the night at her place but her mom doesn't know me and..."

"Ohhh!" eyeliner guy said, understanding finally dawning on him. He patted me firmly on the shoulder and laughed. "I'm sorry about all that. There's been a lot of robberies on this street lately, so... Wait, where are your shoes?"

"I left them at the side of the door last night. Stella was supposed to bring them to me after I fell out the window," I said. "I don't know what's taking her so long."

"Oh well you can't just stand there in the middle of the road with no shoes. Come on in, you can wait in my house until Stella *finally* decides to come out."

"Thank you, that would be very nice."

The eyeliner guy–Devon was his name–took me into his living room and gave me some fresh socks and shoes that were four sizes too big for my tiny, wet feet. I sent Stella a text explaining my situation and asking her to bring me my shoes to Devon's.

"So, are you my neighbor's *special friend*?" Devon asked after I put my phone back in my pocket.

"I'm her *very special friend,*" I corrected him.

"Good. You seem like a decent guy. And you don't smell like ketchup like the last guy she saw did."

"Thanks. That's good to hear," I replied, scratching the growing eczema patch on my left hand. "Sorry it's taking her so long to come here. It shouldn't take too much longer."

"Don't worry about it. I have nothing to do all day today anyway. I work seasonally on movie sets. I'm a set dresser."

But the doorbell rang and I had no time to let Devon know that I was taking film in college. "That must be her," he said and got up from the couch and went to let Stella in. He came back a few moments later, Stella–and my shoes–following him.

"I'm *so* sorry about this, Devon," Stella said. Her face was beet-red and she was slightly trembling.

"Don't be sorry. I'm the one that should apologize. I thought I caught your *special friend* stealing. I was about to call the police. Hee-hee."

Stella did not reply, she simply crossed the living room and gave me my shoes back.

I removed the oversized pair Devon had lent me and I started to roll down the dry socks that he'd lent me.

"Oh, you can keep those," he said.

"Are you sure?" I asked, one sock on, the other one off.

"Yeah, it's fine. They're just socks."

After I put my own shoes back on Stella started towards the door. She had gone from having a massive blush spread all over her face to looking rather pale. "We'll get out of your hair now, Devon. Thanks again for not calling the police."

Devon chuckled. "You're very welcome guys," he said, and as we walked through the doorframe he added, "You gotta tell your mom to stop by sometime, we'll have coffee with Tayte." I thought that was a girl's name, but based on the chubby man in his early fifties that always stood next to Devon in the pictures from the living room, I assumed it was one of those unisex names. It was 2018 after all.

"What? Oh yes, sure," Stella said.

"Oh and don't worry. I won't tell her anything about today or your *very special friend*. Hee-hee."

Stella started to walk faster.

"Yeah, let's just uh, keep walking," I mumbled after I caught up with her.

11

No one answered when Jude knocked on the door. Not the first instance—nor the second or third—in which this had happened. "Do you think he's still sleeping?" he asked.

"Maybe," Keesha said. "Let me call him."

While she waited for our boss to pick up the phone a car started to drive down the gravel path. It was an old yellow Beetle, a bright splotch of red peering behind the steering wheel. Bailey. She parked next to Jude's car and turned the engine off.

Keesha put her phone back in her purse and shook her head.

"What's going on?" Bailey said and slammed her car's door shut. It made a rusty screech that made me cringe.

Jude frowned, almost as if he were looking at something very bright. "We, uh, don't know where Franco is."

"Oh."

"Yeah, maybe we should–"

"Wait," I said. "Do you hear that?" My friends (and Bailey) perked up, trying to listen for the sound I was talking about. It was a low rumbling and splashing, which slowly started to get louder and louder, coming from the lake. Jude walked down the front door steps and followed the mechanical sound. Keesha, Bailey and I followed him. *I guess he kind of is our* team lead, I thought.

A muffin-topped figure, wearing orange swimming shorts and a violently yellow life jacket tightly wrapping a jiggly and hairy torso was riding a jet ski in our direction, making ripples in the calm water, trailing behind him like faithful acolytes of a self-help cult leader, or in other words, Franco, our boss.

"Hey guys, what do you think of my new toy?" he asked once he reached the shore, leaving the jet ski floating a few meters away from the fine, imported sand of his little beach.

"Not too shabby," Keesha observed.

"Just got it yesterday. You guys are more than welcome to hop on it if you want to stay for a bit after work."

"No way, that's awesome," Jude said. "I think I'm down."

Franco unbuckled his life jacket and shook his hair despite it not being wet at all. "Excellent. You see, I like to treat *my people*."

Yikes.

"Come on in, let's all go inside the house and get the day started."

12

Franco invited us to dig into his fridge and "take whatever you want".

"Make some sandwiches or something while I shower," he'd said. "I want you guys to feel like you're home when you come in to work. *Mi casa es su casa.*" I tried not to show my revulsion at how horrible his pronunciation was, but after he left Jude grinned at me and I burst out laughing. "Mee ka-zuh as too ca-zuh," he said with half his head in the fridge.

"Hahaha. Shut up, due."

"Do you think he'll mind if I fry some hot dogs?" But Jude did not wait for an answer and took out a package of wieners.

At first I hesitated, given the fact that I'd already eaten a BLT–minus the lettuce and tomato–at home, but when I smelled Jude's hot dogs frying on the pan I decided to have a look inside Franco's fridge myself.

By the time Franco met with us we had all relocated to the living room and I'd devoured a prosciutto sandwich. "Very well, team. Today will be a fun day," he said, scratching some red spots on his neck, below his beard. "We will split up again for the first couple of hours. Marco and Keesha, you guys can help me down in the basement while Jude, Bailey and Dakota organize the shed."

Bailey's face betrayed her for a second, showing a *Did he just say we'll* clean *his shed?* look. Jude seemed oblivious to the oddity of the task.

"Where is Dakota?" I asked, feeling a little ashamed because I hadn't realized his absence earlier.

"Excuse me?" Franco said. We all looked at each other, as if it was possible that Dakota was simply hiding behind us. "*He's not here yet?*"

There was silence and Franco breathed in, closed his eyes, breathed out and reached inside his pocket until he found the familiar shape of his pack of cigarettes. He took one out, held it with care between his lips and lit it with his golden lighter. "Let's go, team. He'll join us whenever he gets here I guess." He let a little puffy cloud of smoke escape through his mouth. "He must have had a *personal emergency* or something like that."

***

"Here," Franco said, giving me a pile of newspapers as tall as a cat standing up. "And here," he said to Keesha, who grabbed the two buckets of paint that Franco gave her. "This week is all about team-building activities, with a healthy dose of office *beautifying*. Today you guys will give the office walls a fresh coat of paint. Just make sure to cover the table and the edges of the floor and all that so the paint doesn't stain them."

Keesha's lips arched down.

I placed the stack of newspapers on one of the tables that were still littered with unsorted tools and our boss turned around to head back upstairs, probably to provide instructions and life lessons to Jude and Bailey while they cleaned the shed.

"So, is this normal?" I asked Keesha, who had discarded the cans of paint on the floor and was now scrolling down her Instagram page.

"Yeah, you could say that."

"So no videography today either?"

"I suppose not," she said, her eyes glued to the screen.

I sighed. "I guess I better get started then."

"Sure. Good for you."

I spread sheets of cheap newspaper over every surface in risk of getting stained: the tables, the collection of toolboxes half empty, the electric outlets. I was just about done preparing the "office" for our paint session when Keesha looked up and put her phone away. "Oh fuck. Looks like we got a whole week of bitch work to do, doesn't it?" she said and grabbed one of the paint cans.

"Yeah. Do you know how to open those?"

"No."

"Great." I went to the toolboxes and selected one of those flat screwdrivers. The steel was stained with something black and it smelled like oil. "Me neither, but I've seen my dad doing it a couple of times. Can't be that hard." I inserted the tip of the screwdriver in between the rim of the paint can and the actual lid, and it made a little *tap* sound. "See?"

Keesha clapped unenthusiastically twice. "Wow, you're a real man now."

"Yes I am. Now I just gotta get one of those wife-beater shirts."

"Wow."

"Too much?"

Keesha nodded.

I pushed the handle of the screwdriver down, with more strength this time, expecting the lid would break free, but it didn't. "Hmm."

Keesha lifted her right eyebrow and studied me.

"It's okay, I got it." I said and started yanking the screwdriver. When nothing happened, I tried to force the screwdriver deeper into the can, which made it slip and fall violently on the floor. It scraped its way to the corner of the room, leaving a thin white scratch on the fake hardwood floor. *Oh crap,* I thought and bent down, licked the tip of my index finger and rubbed it on a small part of the scratch, which then faded. *Oh good. I'll just mop that later.*

I picked up the screwdriver and stabbed, smacked and shook the stubborn can of paint until my forehead started sweating and my hands were red, but the can remained closed. "Fuck it. I'll go ask Jude for help," I said to Keesha.

"Mhmm." She had her eyes glued to the screen of her phone again.

***

The air in the shed was so full of dust that a thick, grayish cloud was almost visible. Franco was standing at the door, yelling instructions to Jude and Bailey and letting them know what was usable and what was junk. To me, it all looked like junk. "Hey Franco," I said, my nose starting to tingle.

He turned around and looked at me, almost as if he was seeing something wet and gross. Like his own face. "Oh, it's you," he said. "What's up? You're not done yet, are you? Or are you just waiting for the first layer of paint to dry?"

First layer? I thought. *Great, more bitch work.* "No, we're having di–" I started to say before I had to cover my nose to shield Franco from my aggressive sneeze. "Sorry."

"Bless you."

"Thanks, we just wanted to... *AT-CHOO!*" I rubbed my nose and started breathing through my mouth. "Sorry."

"Are you sick?" Franco asked and took a step back. "Do you want to go home? I don't want you getting everyone sick."

"No, it's just my allergies."

"Oh. Good. I got some allergy pills behind the bathroom mirror if you want some. The one on the main floor."

I rubbed my nose again. "Okay, thanks. I was also wondering if someone could help us open the cans of paint." Franco raised his eyebrows, probably marveling at how useless I appeared to him. "We got everything ready to go other than that. Everything is covered and protected. The lid of the can is just stuck."

"Oh. There's a paint can opener in one of the tool boxes," he said.

"Okay thanks." I had only walked a few meters back in the direction of the house when Franco stopped me.

"Do you know how they look?"

"Yeah, of course." I did not, but I thought I'd figure it out. I didn't want him to think I was more useless than he already did.

13

Either he's a very sick man, I thought when I opened the bathroom mirror and looked inside, *or he's one of those doomsday freaks that want to be prepared for a nuclear apocalypse. Or maybe he's both.* There were enough sleeping pills, cough syrup bottles, skin (and hemorrhoid) creams, band aid boxes and prescription drugs to open a successful clandestine pharmacy if Franco decided to pursue a different career path. *Advil, Tylenol, Aleve, Aspirin, Pepto, Tums, Alka-Seltzer, Benadryl, Claritin, NyQuil, Buckley's, HemRid, Preparation H, RectiCare, Polysporin, Vagisil, Canesten, Xanax, Ambien,* trazodone, *Valium,* even fucking *Infermiterol* and *Quaaludes*–you name it. If it existed, Franco had it in stock.

The most concerning thing I saw, other than the (vaginal) yeast infection medication conveniently placed next to the hemorrhoid cream was the sheer amount of discontinued anti-depressant pills Franco had. *Maybe that's why he's not violent anymore,* I thought after remembering the things Cliff and the White Peaks Online had relayed to me. I grabbed the *Benadryl* and went to the kitchen to have a glass of water to wash the pills down.

Once properly drugged and rehydrated I returned to the basement, where the head-numbing chemical smell of paint informed me that I didn't have to figure out what a paint can opener looked like after all. "How did you open it?" I said to Keesha and sucked snot back into my sinuses.

Keesha, who was applying paint on her rolling paint brush, said "You gotta stick the screwdriver in and all around the lid and then pull down."

"That's the first thing I tried though."

"No,"–she was now rolling the brush against the wall with barely any strength but not much paint adhered–"you did it once and when it didn't work you started smashing it open. And then–Wait, are you crying?"

"No I'm not crying," I said between sniffles. "It's just my allergies." I took another brush and started painting the office.

An hour later we had made very little progress. Keesha had painted about a quarter of one of the longer walls from top to bottom while I–as the impatient man in my early 20s that I am–created an irregular oval splotch on half of my wall, opposite hers, never getting closer than a foot away from the floor or ceiling.

I had just put my earbuds on to listen to *Station to Station* by David Bowie when I thought I heard Keesha saying something. "Sorry?" I said, removing my left earbud.

"*Shhh!* I think Franco's yelling at Dakota."

"He's back?"

"*Shhhhhh!*"

I could barely make out what Franco was saying, so I left the "office" and got closer to the stairs. Keesha followed me.

"*–that's not even an excuse, Dakota!*" Franco said, sounding beyond exasperated. "*You have to start taking your job more seriously. Do you know how many other students* wished *they had your job?*" If Dakota made an answer, it was so quiet we could not even hear it. "*Listen, I get it, you're young and sometimes you don't get to appreciate the opportunities you get in life, so I will just leave this as a warning, but don't ever be this late for work again, okay?*" There was a pause. "*Okay good, now go downstairs and help Keesha and* Marlow *paint the office.*"

"Did he just call you *Marlow*?" Keesha asked. I wanted to ask her if that was an actual name, but we heard Dakota's lazy footsteps approaching so we walked back to the "office" as fast as we could before he got the chance to figure out that we had been eavesdropping.

Dakota dragged his feet as he entered the room and muttered to himself, "This is bullshit, yesterday he was hours late and now he's–"

"Hi, could you give me a hand?" Keesha interrupted, ignoring Dakota's angry ramblings.

"What do you want?" he asked her back. I stopped pretending to be working and looked at him, a little concerned about his bluntness.

Keesha took a step closer to Dakota and smiled. "Can you hold the ladder for a sec?"

I started stroking the wall with my brush again once I saw Dakota unclench his fists, but I made a point to stay close to them as we made our slow progress painting the "office".

14

"Very well, great job today team." Franco said to us in the living room. He was sitting on–or rather, squatting over–a black leather ottoman he'd brought from another room. "Thank you, well, thank *most of you* for another day of good work." Dakota shifted on the couch, but seemed fine otherwise. "I know it's not five yet, but you are dismissed. I'll pay you for your full day, so don't worry about that."

"Oh wow, thank you," Jude said.

"*No problemo.* I have an amazing opportunity for whomever would like to take it though." Franco gave us a smile and examined each one of us with eyes devoid of emotion, the way people who are not really happy look when they force out a smile. That was the first time I noticed the slight pale-yellow tint in the whites of his eyes. When nobody asked him about this mysterious new opportunity, he started to explain it. "I have a dream. A dream of offering something more than just life-changing books and seminars. I want to partner with local masseuses,"–everyone's eyes widened with curiosity at this–"and, maybe next year, add one-on-one life coaching stays here for a select few of my fans who are willing to pay the price of such a unique chance of personal growth. I think it would be extremely beneficial to incorporate some acupuncture or stress-relief chinese massages as well to make this a holistic experience. Being able to sleep under the same roof as me is also a bonus."

I didn't have to look around to know that my coworkers were all trying to keep a straight and undisturbed face. I had a hard time at it, so I bit my lip.

"That sounds like a great idea," Jude lied.

Bailey agreed. "Yes, I'd like to come here for one of those retreats myself!"

This pleased Franco, whose smile looked almost genuine now. "Well, I'd like to say that I will offer you a lot of personal-growth knowledge over the next couple of weeks, free of charge, of course, but if you'd like to purchase a package, I'll make sure to give you a discount." He winked directly at Jude. "But before I can do this, I'd like some help building a deck down by the lake, so that people can get their *Feng Shui massages* in a more peaceful place than inside the house. So, here's the deal: if you want to stay and work some extra hours at the end of the day and help me and Ron build the deck, I will feed you supper and you can bank these hours so that you can have some days off whenever you need them. So now, who's ready for some overtime today?"

I had no intention to stay and do more bitch work for him, and I expected everyone else to refuse, but Jude agreed to my surprise. "I'm in," he said.

"Excellent! I can already see how much your leadership skills are developing, Jude. Who else wants to join us today?"

Bailey was the next one to accept, followed by Dakota.

"I can't stay today, I got a baby shower," Keesha said. "But maybe I'll stay some other time.

"I'm also busy today as well." I said, starting to scratch the back of my left hand, then reluctantly added only after I saw Franco's beginning to darken. "I got some evening classes, but I guess I could stay some other time."

"That's okay, we got the *core team* staying today anyway, that should be enough," he said. "But please do stay whenever you want. We'll have lots of fun, maybe we can all hop into the hot tub and have some wine at the end of the day."

I gulped despite my mouth feeling quite dry that day. I couldn't believe that our boss had actually asked his summer students not only to stay late to work but also to build him a fucking deck, drink alcohol and soak next to him in his tub. *What did I get myself into?* I thought. *Maybe I should have listened to Cliff after all.*

15

With Jude staying at Francos until God knows what time, Keesha and I had no way back home, unless we wanted to spend a few hours walking. We sat on the steps below the front door, our clothes stained here and there with little splatters of beige paint. "How much do you think a cab would cost?" I asked.

"I don't know. Probably sixty dollars," she replied.

"*What?*"

"That's what it cost me to go from the city to the airport last year. I think that's roughly the same distance here, I think."

I sighed. "Well, do you want to go half and half?" I suggested.

"No. It's too much even then. I could ask my sister to pick us up, but she works late so we might as well stay here and build Franco his deck. Getting some days off later doesn't sound too bad."

"I can call my girlfriend. She can give us a ride, but we should offer her some money or something."

"Sure."

I waited half an hour until Stella was off work to give her a call. "We'll give you gas money," I said, trying to sweeten the deal. "I can also offer you some *cuddles.*"

She laughed. "If you think I'll wanna sleep with you today then you're not as smart as I thought you were," she said. "You're lucky you have a cute butt."

***

Stella had a lot of daycare (paper) work to catch up on at home, so we didn't end up cuddling after she picked me (and Keesha) up. Instead, she dropped me off unceremoniously at my place. The TV was so loud I could hear it before I reached the front door, but Cliff still managed to hear me coming in. "Marco, my boy! How are you doing buddy?" he asked and lowered the volume of his show to much more pleasing levels. It made the people with dwarfism dating tall blondes from California look a bit more surreal that way.

"Not bad, how about you?" I closed the door behind me and reluctantly went to the living room.

"I'm doing *great*. Lost another three pounds this week."

"That's good to hear," I said, preparing to excuse myself to my room. "I–"

"How's your diet going? Do you want me to weigh you? I got the scale right here, Anna lost–"

"Oh maybe some other time," I cut in. "I'm just a bit tired from work and I wanted to lay down for a bit."

Cliff turned off the TV and leaned on the couch towards me. "Oh good, you got your job back," he said stiffly.

Crap. What am I going to say to him now? "No, I, uh... I got another job."

"Well don't just stand there. Come sit over here and tell me more about your *new job*. It's not working for that son of a bitch, is it? *Ha!* No, you know better than that..." Every time Cliff used real swear words instead of the usual *shoot, heck, dang* and *son of a gun* it disturbed me.

I was not prepared for this, and I was as surprised as him when I sat on his noisy leather couch and the next words came out of my mouth. "No, of course not! I got a job at the call center."

Cliff shifted his nose, as if he could smell the sourness of my lies. "Oh, *really?* That was fast, you getting hired and all."

"Yeah, they're always desperate for new people," I found myself saying with too much ease. "The job can be tough but it pays well."

"Oh good, how much?"

"Eighteen dollars an hour." *Where's all of this coming from?*

"Oh, good for you, my boy," Cliff said, either believing me now or not wanting to bother to ask me what was really going on.

"Thank you. I'm just doing my two week orientation now, so it's been a bit boring but not too bad," I said, relaxing a little. "At least they're paying me for it!"

"You're *dang right!*" Cliff said in approval. "They *have* to. I bet it's a hard job with all those angry people calling you for road-side assistance."

"Yeah, they're really good at giving me strategies to manage those tricky situations," I said, marveling at the amount of bullshit I was spilling. "But yea, I'm tired so–"

"Yes, of course, don't let me keep you. Go have some rest."

"Thanks."

I went to the bedroom, closed the door and let out a big sigh of relief. *For real, where the fuck did all that call center shit came from?* I thought, and the answer came to me after I sank on my bed. I had pretty much regurgitated word by word what my classmate Colter had told me and Keesha about his last summer job over lunch at the college a few months back. He, not unlike myself, also lasted less than two months working at that awful place. *I'll have to give him a call one of these days to ask him more about the job, if I want to keep fooling Cliff.*

16

Jude's face looked older, more tired, as if gravity had become stronger for him since I last saw him. Which made no sense, because that had been less than twenty four hours ago. He was quietly drinking a can of *Red Bull,* and his clothes smelled of booze. "'Sup," he rasped out.

"What's up with *you,* my dude? It looks like you had a rough night," I said, fastening my seatbelt.

Jude started the car again. "Nah, it wasn't the night that was rough, just the evening building that stupid deck for Franco."

"Ah."

"Yeah, you really should stay over with us today, hopefully we'll get this over with in a day or two more that way."

"I don't know, dude. I like my free time, and I'm also bad at physical work." *My laziness just won't let me do much more than the bare minimum these days,* I thought.

"It's all good, we just need an extra pair of hands. I'll ask Keesha to help out too, because to be honest, hanging out at Franco's after we finished was quite nice."

"Really?"

Jude ignored the question, turned on the stereo and the funky latin textures of *Day of the Baphomets* blasted out of the speakers and started to fill the warm summer air. When the song reached the craziness of the eight minute mark, Keesha got in the car and promptly told us to shut it off. "Play something more *normal*."

Jude handed me his phone and I looked in his music app for something we'd all enjoy. I settled for *Two Kinds of Happiness* by *The Strokes*.

"Ah, much better," Keesha said from the back seat.

"Hey, um, I was talking to Marco and he said he'd stay to work on the deck with us after work."

"I did?"

Jude gave me a dismissive wave of his hand. "Yeah, so like, would you like to, uh, stay with us too?"

"I don't know," Keesha replied. "I don't really want to."

I turned around to face her and said, "Me neither."

"Don't listen to him," Jude continued. "He's just horsing around."

I shook my head.

"Come on, it was fun. I'm sure we'll have a great time if we stay late together. I also would appreciate it if, um–" Jude cleared his throat. "If you guys can help me put some distance between me and Bailey."

"And why is that?" Keesha said, sounding interested in the conversation all of the sudden.

Jude squeezed and rubbed the steering wheel, making it squeak. "I let her suck me off last night. She wanted to fuck but she was on her period, but anyway, I thought we both wanted to be very casual about it but–" The steering wheel squeaked again. "I don't know, after I came we cuddled for a bit and she got all excited and started coming up with a bunch of plans. Cutesy couple stuff."

"*Oof.*"

"Oh Jude, it looks like you got yourself a nice little girlfriend," Keesha said, grinning.

"No, it's nothing like that yet. Or, uh, I don't know. I don't want anything serious like that *at all*. But if I don't give her the right signals she'll believe we're like, uh, a thing. So I don't know. Could you guys help me spend less time with her? Maybe you can even flirt with me?"

I smiled and covered my mouth with the palm of my hand. "Oh Jude, you make me blush, but you know I'm taken."

"Shut up, dude. I was talking to Keesha."

I pouted and Keesha chuckled. "Sure, why not," she replied. "She's so annoying anyways, always following you around like a sad pup."

Jude frowned. "You don't have to be mean about it, but you uh–"

"Got a point?"

Jude sighed.

"We're not really being *mean*," Keesha continued. "We're just talking shit behind her back, but when she's around we're polite."

"Indeed," I said.

"That's even worse!" Jude said and the steering wheel screeched.

"No, it's not," I said. "Listen, we just don't like her. So what if we talk shit about her to each other? We didn't try to make each other dislike her because we already did, and we won't try to convince anyone else that she's lame."

"That's right," Keesha said.

"But on the other hand, if these hypothetical people *also* disliked her–"

"Whatever," Jude said. "Will you guys please stay to work on the deck with me at least? I don't want Franco to leave me alone with Bailey again."

I looked back at Keesha and she shrugged. "Fine," I said. "Just today though."

17

"Today I have some very special news for you, team." Franco's hair was wet again, making the thinning on his crown more noticeable. He had the *wet rat look,* as my dad used to say. Franco had moved the living room's coffee table somewhere else in the house, and in its place a single bar stool stood where he sat and preached his treacherous gospel to us. "The key speaker for the Take Your Life Back convention in North Bay just canceled, and guess who's going to replace him?" He didn't pause to let us answer. "*Spoiler alert*, it's me!"

Bailey started to clap unenthusiastically, and soon we all did the same.

Franco bowed low to the floor, floppy strands of black, greasy hair almost brushing the hardwood. "Thank you, thank you. Anyway, that means that I will select a few lucky members of the *D'Amico team* to go to the convention with me for additional support. I have a few ideas of whom I'd like to bring but I'd rather ask you if you'd like to come first." His eyes went straight to Jude, who was looking at the thick firs through the window. "What about you, *team lead*?"

Keesha nudged him on the side of his belly. "Uh? Yes? What?"

"Perfect! I knew you'd step up to the task, Jude."

"What task?"

"*Hahaha!* You're both effective *and* funny, Jude." Franco's eyes moved over to Dakota and a nasty smile appeared on Franco's face. "And you, Dakota? Do you want to come too?"

"Is it free?"

"Is it– Are you f–," Franco said, his smile quivering for a second. "Yes, of course it is, old timer!. Haven't I already told you how I like to take care of *my people*?"

"Will you feed us too? Or are you going to make us–"

"Yes I will pay for the whole trip, Dakota."

"Okay then I guess I'll go," Dakota said, and then muttered something to himself that was barely audible. Franco ignored it but I caught the words "... won't be any landscaping to do in North Bay."

"Okay then," Franco continued. "There is one more spot. Keesha? I would really appreciate it if you bring your videography skills with us on this trip. What do you say?"

"Yeah, sure."

Franco smacked his hands together. "Alright! The *dream team* is coming to North Bay. But for those who couldn't make it for this trip, don't worry. You'll have priority for the next one."

Jude looked at Keesha and mouthed *Thank you,* and she replied by placing her hand on his thigh and smiling, much to Bailey's irritation.

"When will that be?" Bailey asked, her flushed face resembling her hair.

"Thursday, Friday and Saturday from next week," Franco said.

"And what are *we* going to do while you're gone?"

"I'll leave you some tasks that you can do from home, so you don't have to come all the way over here. Unless you'd like to stay over and house sit for me, I need someone to water my plants and make sure the place doesn't burn down," he said, letting out a raspy chuckle.

Suddenly, an idea formed inside my head. "I can do that," I said, already imagining all the things I could do with Stella at the lake house.

Franco nodded. "Okay, that will work out wonderfully. You can stay here and I'll get Keesha to send you the videos she takes every night, so you can start putting something together for the YouTube channel, because by now you all must know I don't like slackers." That was the only thing Franco said that day which actually sounded serious. "We'll talk more about that in the coming days, but now it's time for another team-building activity. Come on. Let's go down to the rec room."

18

I set up some lights on flimsy stands, a videocamera on an old and bulky tripod–which if I had to guess, I'd say was last used in the 90s, maybe for some awfully dated head shots for Franco–in one of the corners of the rec room, behind the pool table while Franco explained to the rest of the team what we'd be doing that day.

"All ready to go?" he asked, dragging a high chair over to our little improvised filming set.

I finished wiping out the memory card from the camera and saw that we had about fifty two minutes of footage available. "Yep, all good."

"Excellent," he said and waved at Jude to go to the white wall, illuminated by the two LED lights Franco had bought a few weeks before.

"Isn't it a bit too bright?" Jude said, squinting. "I feel like I'm, um, staring at the sun."

"Oh Jude, don't be so stinking dramatic. We want to be able to show your pretty Greek face to everyone online!" Franco replied.

Jude signed. "Okay, fine."

"Okay, are we rolling?" Franco asked.

I pressed the little red button on the camera and gave him a thumbs up.

"Do they all have to be here?" Jude said, still squinting but not as hard as before. Bailey was somewhere upstairs, rearranging one of the many guest rooms in the house, but Keesha and Dakota were sitting on the *La-Z-Boys* on the other side of the room. None of them were paying attention to us.

"Come on, Jude. We're rolling," Franco said behind the camera, to my left. "Let's not waste any more time."

"Okay."

Franco cleared his throat and brushed his hair back with his fingers. "Now, tell me how much of a positive impact on your life our little personal development sessions have had so far."

"Uh, it's made a huge impact on me, Franco."

"No, no, no. Start by rephrasing the question, and pretend I'm not in the room, like someone else was interviewing you. No, even better, like no one is here other than yourself and you just *really* want to say to the world how great it has been to be hanging out with me."

"Okay."

"And don't be afraid to make some... *artistic decisions.* Remember that these testimonials can potentially convince people to come to me. People who really need me. *You* can help me change their lives, Jude."

I can't believe the levels of bullshit that Franco is capable of spewing, I thought to myself. I couldn't avoid shaking my head lightly, but Franco was too focused on Jude and he didn't seem to notice.

Jude took a deep breath. But if it was out of frustration, defeat or something else, I didn't know. "I started working for Franco a few weeks ago and–"

"Say my last name too."

"Uh, okay. I started working for Franco a few weeks ago and he's made a huge positive, uh, impact on my personal and professional life."

Yes, yes, go on! Franco mouthed. His cigarette breath reached my nose and I started breathing through my mouth.

"He's helped me develop, uh, leadership skills at work that I can also use at home..." Jude said and looked at me, seemingly at a loss. I shrugged, and after a few moments of awkward silence he said, "And I can't recommend his books enough."

"*Bravo!*" Franco said and clapped his hands. "That was perfect. Did you get it?" he asked me, as if we had just witnessed Bigfoot doing a cartwheel or some shit like that.

"Yep. We got it all on film," I said.

"Amazing, Keesha, you're next!"

***

To say that Keesha was a natural was an understatement. The moment she stepped in front of the camera, she made the cheap spotlight hers. She said all the *right* words: how Franco's life-changing teachings were the reason why she "got clean and found an honest job"–which was a lie, she wasn't clean and our job was not honest in any way, shape or form–and why anyone with common sense should immediately buy all of his books to find the secret to happiness.

"That was brilliant," Franco said when Keesha's little performance was over. "You almost brought tears to my eyes."

And a boner, I thought cringing.

Keesha went back to her *La-Z-Boy* and Franco called Dakota to come. "Are you ready for your close-up Mr. DeMille?" Franco said and half laughed, half snorted .

"I guess so," Dakota replied lethargically.

Franco signaled me with his finger to start recording. I didn't know if he'd done it on purpose, but the finger he used was the middle one instead of the index. I ignored it and gave Franco a little nod.

"Okay, Dakota. Tell me a little bit about yourself and how working with me has impacted your life. And, you know, try to get a good answer like Keesha's or Jude's."

"I guess it's good work experience."

Wrong answer, I thought.

"Ahem," Franco said, biting his lip. "Try to give me good, *full* answers. Repeat the question and then say your actual answer. It's gotta sound natural, okay? Let's try again."

"Okay," Dakota said. "Hi, my name is Dakota and working with Franco has given me good work experience." His answer sounded as robotic and lethargic as you might expect from someone who did not care about his job and didn't feel comfortable being in front of a camera.

"No, no, look at the camera, not at me." Franco said, starting to let her exasperation permeate his tone. "And say my full name. Got it?"

Dakota sighed and looked at the camera. "Hi, my name is Dakota and working for... Wait, what was the question again?"

Franco bared his teeth. "Tell me how working with me has impacted your life." He took his cigarette pack from his pocket and lit up a smoke. "In a *positive way*, mind you. How much more time can we shoot, Marco?"

"About twenty minutes."

"Okay, Dakota. Let's not waste any more time."

He opened his mouth, ready to give us a great speech, perhaps, but closed it back after a moment. "What was your last name again?"

"*Are you fucking kidding me?*" Franco yelled. His cigarette flew out of his mouth and fell on the floor, minute sparks flashing as it landed. I stepped on it because I'm scared of fires and tried to brace myself for what was coming next.

"No, it's just that it's a funny last name."

"*D'Amico! Da-mee-co!* For Christ's sake, Dakota. *Will you ever get this fucking thing right?*"

Dakota curled his hands into tense fists and looked at our boss, straight in the eye. "I'm trying!" He said, his voice breaking. "But you're just asking us to kiss your ass on camera and that's weird!"

"If that's what you think I want you to do, then you're dead-wrong, Dakota." Franco's voice had quieted in a controlled yet menacing way. "And I feel bad for you. Marco, I think we're done for now. Go ask Jude to get you to do something while I have a little chat with your coworker here."

I looked at the camera. We still had enough time, according to my estimations, to get a decent shot. "Are you sure? We could try again if you want or–"

"*Now.*"

I wanted to help Dakota out and I thought if I stayed in the same room with them, Franco would take it easy, but I also had to look out for myself. Images of an enraged and drunk Franco breaking a bottle on his assistant's head and exploding in hundreds of minute silvery shards, some of them turning a deep red as blood sprayed them, flashed in my mind.

I turned the camera off and left.

19

Dakota did not utter a word for the rest of the day. Him and Franco had yelled at each other loudly enough for everyone to hear, but not clearly enough for us to make out more than a few words here and there. The shouting match lasted for what felt to us like an hour but was closer to fifteen minutes, and when they reemerged, Franco seemed as cool as usual. Dakota's eyes were red, however, and his face was down.

Jude, acting on Franco's instructions, had sent me back to the "office" to get started on editing the fake testimonials and Keesha had talked her way into coming with me to help me out, even though only one laptop had *Adobe Premiere* installed. The rest of the team was in another room going over the details of the Take Your Life Back convention, and Dakota eventually joined them.

"Well, that was something," Keesha said to me while I was importing all of the footage into the computer.

"I know." *Should I tell her about Franco's violent tendencies?* I thought. No. Not yet. I wanted to convince myself that a little bit of shouting didn't mean anything, but deep down I knew better.

"I mean, I get it. We've been doing nothing but bitch work since we started working here," Keesha said, probably trying to get more thoughts about the morning incident out of me. "But Dakota also seems a bit... *off*."

"Yeah, I don't know. He's always a bit off though."

"Yeah, he always looks so serious, I–" Keesha made a pause and cringed. "What's wrong with your hand?"

"What do you mean?" I looked down and saw a few drops of blood dripping on the laptop. They came from my eczema patch, which had been steadily growing over the past couple of weeks. *Thank you, Anxiety.* "Oh, it's a rash," I said, as casually as I could. "I've been scratching it too much I guess."

"Shouldn't you put a band aid on it?"

"No, I just gotta let it breathe and put my cream on. I keep forgetting."

I went to the upstairs restroom, washed the blood off my hand and dried it. The skin of my eczema patch was raw like grocery store ground beef and it almost seemed to have a pulse. It was so ugly and it itched like hell, so I ended up grabbing a band aid from behind the mirror and putting it on, to help myself not to scratch it.

***

At five o'clock Dakota left on his dirty green bike, his cold and blank. "Okay team," Franco said. His mood had improved significantly at this point. I guessed it was because all of the *core team* (and I) had stayed after work to build his stupid deck. "Before we continue where we left off yesterday, let's go to the kitchen. I took the liberty to order some pizza for everyone." That, we found out shortly afterwards, was a lie.

Franco opened the oven and placed three store-bought pepperoni pizzas, the kind that was always on sale because of how plain (and reminiscent of cardboard) they were. Jude served us some generic Cola soda in red plastic cups and we ate our meal mostly in silence, listening to Franco's endless drone about how *alpha* and resilient he'd been over the years. He was so invested in his verbal self-blowjob that he didn't even notice Keesha's (discrete and) occasional sighs.

Ron stopped by the lake house at five-thirty and snatched the last slice of mediocre pizza before I could. "Some of your team members could do without this much, um, junk food, Franco, don't you think?" he said, nodding towards me. My eyes went straight to my belly, where the blue stripes of my shirt curved and distorted, and I suddenly became aware of the warm grease on my hands and around my mouth. I think the comment upset Bailey as well, but I'm not sure. I was too busy remembering how well my shirt had fit me a couple of years before and trying not to cry.

"Come on, Ron, not all of us can be as skinny as you," Franco barked, rubbing his stomach. "But that gives me an idea. We should all join a weight loss challenge."

Of fucking course, I thought. *I bet Cliff would approve that.*

"We should all weigh ourselves tomorrow on an empty stomach, and after going to the potty, and whoever loses the most weight by the end of the summer will get... Hmm..." He made a cartoonish thinking pose, scratching his beard and looking at the ceiling. "If one of you guys wins, I'll give you five hundred dollars."

That snapped Bailey out of her sad moment of introspection. Jude and Keesha moved their attention from their phones to our boss too.

"But if I win," Franco continued, "You guys will have to take me out for supper to a nice restaurant. You can all split my bill, of course. So even if you lose, we will all get to hang out and enjoy some quality time somewhere nice."

"I'm down," Jude said, and then, as it had become the custom that summer, everyone else–including myself–also agreed.

20

Franco and Ron spent most of the evening in the office. The real one, the one with the naked Japanese ladies on the walls and the fancy desk, not the messy tool room we'd just painted. I've always been a work hazard whenever someone gave me tools, so I spent most of the evening being my team's unofficial assistant.

I went around the house, looking for whatever Jude needed– mostly nails and screws–, filling up the water jug and bringing cups out so everyone could stay hydrated and doing other small things to make the construction process a little easier. At seven thirty, when the golden summer sunlight was at its brightest and most melancholic point and the temperature was starting to cool down,

Franco's loud–and snorting–laugh announced his return. Ron wasn't with him anymore. Franco walked around, looking at our progress (and probably judging it) and smiled. "Great job, team," he said and patted Jude on the back. "The deck is looking great. Couldn't ask for a better team-lead."

Jude wiped his sweaty forehead with the back of his hand. "Thank you."

"We're done for the day, team. Next week you can have Monday off, as a token of my appreciation. You can now go back home, or you can stay here and have some wine and cheese with me."

I looked around and saw everyone's faces starting to darken, but they didn't actually grimace until Franco said the next seven cursed words: "I will turn the hot tub on."

***

Jude is a cheese aficionado–a few months before he'd bought me an eight year old block of aged cheddar, along with some nice crackers and chili jelly for my birthday–,so needless to say that he accepted Franco's inappropriate supper party invitation on behalf of all of us, as we depended on him to get a ride home.

The hot tub was located in the backyard, in between the lake and the house, and even though it was fairly large, it could by no means accommodate four summer students and their boss in it. "Sorry, I don't have a change of clothes," I said when I saw the water levels rise as Franco jumped in the tub, squeezing his middle-aged body in between Jude and Bailey. "I think I'll just bring a chair and sit next to you guys."

"Sure," Franco said, spreading his arms on the edge of the tub. Now Jude and Bailey were *really* uncomfortable. "And while you're doing that, do you mind bringing me a cigar? They're in a case on my dresser."

I looked at him, but no words came out of my mouth.

"Oh come on," he said with what looked like a faint scowl on his face. "It's fine. I *trust* you."

I repressed a shiver that went up my spine. "Okay, but, uh, which room is your bedroom?"

"Oh. Just go up the stairs to the second floor and it's the first door to the right. It's the biggest room in the house."

Franco's bedroom was bigger than I expected, and also darker. The bottom third of the walls was covered with black wainscot panels and the top was painted with a uniform dark gray coat of paint. The windows were taller than me and overlooked the steel blue waters of Lake Superior with curtains of pines and rocky shores embracing it. *Looking at it from that height every morning must never get old*, I thought. *Lucky bastard.*

I walked over to the dresser, opposite Franco's bed, and found the cigar box half open. I grabbed one, an *Habanito,* and before I could make my way back downstairs I noticed a framed picture resting near the right edge of the dresser. The photo showed Franco, smiling viciously at the camera, and a kid, no older than twelve or thirteen years old, with an absent look on his face. He was smaller and thinner, but I didn't have to put much effort into figuring out that it was Dakota. *Interesting.*

***

I indulged in cheese and grapes, but not in alcohol, after seeing how tipsy Jude was getting over the course of the night in case I had to drive. The conversations were loud, happy and obnoxious, thanks to the wine. There didn't seem to be an ending in sight for the party, and as time went by I started to regret more and more not having asked Stella to pick me up. But at nine o'clock something happened, and Jude decided it was finally time to go.

"*Come ooooonnnn Jude,*" Franco said, slurring his words. "Don't leave just yeg, the night is young."

"Yeah Jude, stay a little longer," Bailey added, getting back in the hot tub with a new cheese board.

Jude, looking much more sober all of the sudden, said, "I gotta go, I, uh, uh, forgot I had something to do."

Franco slapped the water, splashing everyone. "But you're drunk! You can't drive."

"Oh that's okay though," I said. "Jude asked me to be the designated driver."

"Okay, fine, go home. Bailey and I will keep the party going."

Bailey must have been more drunk than I thought, because she agreed. "*Let's gooooo,*" she yelled after we turned around and left.

Jude insisted that he was capable of driving on his own, but I convinced him to let me do it instead. The *Big Piece of Shit* had automatic transmission, so it was all good. We drove in silence most of the way back home, Keesha snoring in the back seat and jazz playing on the stereo. "So, why did you want to leave, anyway? I thought you were having a good time," I said after we helped Keesha stumble back into her place.

Jude rubbed his face and sighed. "I don't know, dude. Things got weird."

"Weird how?"

"I don't know, all night I thought Bailey was kind of flirting with me."

"Yep, that much I could tell."

Jude wrinkled his brow. "I thought she was playing *footsies* with me but I guess she wasn't because it didn't stop after she left to get more cheese."

"*What?*"

Jude made no comment.

"It could have been Keesha."

"I asked her before we left and she said it wasn't her."

"So... Oof."

"Yeah."

"Franco–"

"Let's not talk about it anymore."

I drove us to Jude's apartment and did not object when he asked me to stay over.

21

Jude appeared like he was back to normal in the morning, and we started the day with the right foot. Jude's phone rang as he was coming out of the shower with a towel wrapped around his waist. He picked up and after a few moments he smiled and hung up. "We won't have to go to work today," he said. "Franco's *sick*."

"Sick or hungover?"

"Who cares? We're off today and that's all that matters. What do you wanna do today?"

"I could do with some breakfast," I said, a growl from my stomach gave my statement more weight. "Then a shower and a nap."

"A nap?"

"Yeah, your couch isn't very comfy. I had a rough night."

"Oh, sorry."

After much deliberation we decided to go to *The Breakfast Queen,* a new restaurant that operated between seven in the morning to four in the afternoon, serving only breakfast food. Jude had a shakshouka and I got an omelette with mushrooms, onions, bacon and feta cheese, with a side of grilled potatoes. The place smelled delicious and their food tasted even better, which made up for the lackluster waitress, who was rude and made a big stink when Jude asked her if they could remove the olives from his dish. "We do *not* accept substitutions," she'd said after snorting at him. "We serve the food as described in the menu. If you have any issues with that I recommend you order something else."

"It's okay. I'll get it as is," Jude replied and the waitress left. "I guess I can just take them out myself."

"What a girl," I said. "I hope our food is better than her attitude."

It was.

***

My fingers instinctively searched for the back of my left hand but I stopped them before they could scratch my eczema patch, from which a clear liquid had started to ooze. I finished the bite of the omelette I had in my mouth, took a deep breath and said, "I know some stuff about Franco."

"Oh?"

I told Jude everything. Everything that Cliff had said about Franco, everything that I had read about him online, and some of the fishy things I had, until then, actively tried to ignore. Jude pushed his steamy cup of hot chocolate with cinnamon and whipped cream away from him.

"That's just sick," he said, putting away his fork. He didn't look hungry anymore. "Do you think he'd do anything to– anything like that again?"

"I'd like to say that he wouldn't, but I don't know. He sometimes gets really pissed about stuff and it scares me."

"Yeah... Like when he yells at Dakota."

Should I tell him about the picture I found in his room? I thought, and decided since I had already opened up about everything else, I might as well tell him about Dakota.

"Don't you think it's a little weird to have a picture like that in his room?" Jude said. "I mean, even if they're related you'd think he would keep it in the living room or something, no?"

"Yeah," I said and stopped myself from scratching my hand again. "Do you feel comfortable enough to keep working for him?"

"Well, it's like four, five of us against one," Jude said and started to push around some chunks of eggs in his bowl. "I'm sure it'll be fine, but maybe we could start looking for another job just in case."

I sighed. "Yep, I guess we could."

None of us finished our meals. We paid our bill, the waitress offered us some to-go containers and we left.

Part VI: Dakota

1

The days leading up to the Take Your Life Back conference were filled with random housekeeping chores, and since the hot tub incident, Jude refused to work on the deck, which in turn caused Franco to lose his little clandestine band of contractors as nobody wanted to stay late after work if they were given a choice (and a ride back home).

One day the following week Franco made Keesha and I watch YouTube videos to learn how to do some landscaping around the house. "We need to beautify the lawn, so that next year when my new clients stay over they feel right at home," he'd said. "If their home was a beautiful waterfront property!" He snorted away, like a spineless pig.

It took us the better part of two days to plant some random, thorn-filled bushes at the front of the house, and to add fresh mulch to make a path in between the half-built deck and down the gradual slope that took you to the artificial beach. When our landscaping work was over, the air was more fragrant and my back hurt terribly. "Great job, guys! Great job," Franco said. He was wearing those tight pink shorts he liked so much and was bare-chested. His hand was fashioned with a large glass of red wine. "Do you want to join me at the beach and have a drink?"

"Sure," Keesha said after she dusted her shirt off.

"Sounds good, and Marco, please call somewhere and order some pizza. I wanna give everyone a little treat before our big trip tomorrow."

I grabbed the fifty dollar bill Franco offered me and took my phone out. Franco interrupted me before I could call *Arturo's*.

"Oh, and remind me to give you the spare keys for the house before you leave. Feel free to invite any of your *friends* over on the weekend if you'd like, as long as you clean after yourself and don't break anything. Understood?"

I nodded. I wasn't in the mood to talk after a long day of doing bitch work, but I was sure once the pig left for his conference I'd start to feel cheerier. Stella was going to be busy on Thursday, Friday and Saturday, having some extended family staying at her house, but we were going to take advantage of having a lake house all for ourselves on Sunday. After all, there weren't any neighbours nearby who'd have a problem with seeing us walking around naked, and that was an opportunity none of us would refuse.

2

Thursday morning Franco and his little fellowship loaded their luggage–of which three suitcases belonged to our boss, who tended to switch outfits at least once a day, even on workdays when his only audience were us–in the trunk of the *Range Rover* I waved them goodbye.

You would think that with a beautiful lake house all to myself I would have had the time of my life, but you'd be wrong. Thursday morning was too cold for swimming, so I instead went to the living room and watched TV until I got hungry at noon and went to the kitchen to see what I could make myself for lunch.

"The fridge and the pantry are all stocked up, the freezer too," Franco had said to me, almost as an afterthought, on his way out. "Feel free to eat whatever you want. I got some snacks in the basement too. And here," at this he handed me a few 20s wrapped up in a rubber band and winked. "Here's some money in case you want to treat yourself sometime. Pizza takes about an hour and a half to get here though."

I put two cheese-stuffed burger patties on the hot and buttered pan–which was a mistake, because the butter got burnt before the meat even had the chance to thaw–, toasted some buns, dressed them with mayochup and prepared my first meal of the weekend. After I took the first bite of my massive double burger I returned to the cupboard and grabbed a bag of plain chips. That was the highlight of my day, because the rain ruined my plans of going out on a nice walk in the woods.

I forgot to bring a book from home, but Franco had that covered. At night I went into his office, which was surprisingly unlocked, and browsed his bookshelves. There were at least ten copies of each one of his books–the ones he'd written himself–, countless essay and poetry collections, and four full rows entirely dedicated to novels. I chose Agatha Christie's *And Then There Were None,* which, fun fact, originally had a questionable and rather racist title when it was first published, and read it all in one sitting. It was a good choice, but Soldier Island was a little too similar to the place where I was going to live for the next three days, so I felt a bit uneasy the rest of the weekend. I knew there weren't any murderers lurking around the lake house, but my paranoid mind didn't care about logic.

I've had tinnitus ever since I can remember, so complete silence is something I have never known. I was worried that the ceiling fan on the guest room where I was staying wouldn't provide me with white noise loud enough to mask the perpetual ringing in my ears, but the nature sounds were somehow augmented at night, and the rain, owls, crickets and the occasional howling wolf eased me into sleep.

3

The next day was bad. The first thing I saw when I woke up and scrolled through Facebook was a face I knew from somewhere, but it wasn't until I read the headline that I figured out who that was. It was Simon Willet, who had just passed. Something in my stomach churned and I put my phone away. *How can someone in Canada just... die like that?* I wondered, but decided not to read the article. I was already in a bad mood and death had always been something that I could not figure out how to handle, but again, I doubt anyone really knows how to. Images of a sterile room, a sickly man in a hospital gown, a syringe with a dark liquid that would go inside his veins and then just end the man's life flashed through my head. I tried to think of something else, but I couldn't. *What did his family think of it? Were they in the room when Simon... Did he even have a family or someone to be there with him during the* procedure? The more I tried to stop thinking about that surreal scene the less those grim images left my mind. In hindsight, that was the first time that I questioned my perception of Canada as a perfect first world country with free healthcare and where there isn't that much suffering. The second time I questioned that perception would be a few weeks after that day. I decided that the best way to get myself distracted would be to stuff myself with junk food, so I headed downstairs to the kitchen.

***

I received a Google drive link at three thirty in the afternoon, and for once I was glad to work on one of Franco's projects. *That will help me forget about Simon.* I downloaded the clips Keesha sent me, imported them into *Premiere* and started to watch them.

Let's see what bullshit Franco tried to pass as life changing advice, I said to myself. Most of the videos Keesha recorded were random bits and pieces of rehashed speeches he'd already given to us over the past couple of weeks, as I expected, but the last one (which was also the longest clip) freaked me out.

The video was shot from the side of the stage and began panning from the audience of middle aged men, most of them balding and holding copies of Franco's newest book tightly in their hands, to Dakota flailing his arms and legs around on the stage to the sound of a classical song. I have no idea what the name of the song was.

Dakota was wearing a black nylon unitard and his hair was drenched in sweat from his passionate yet ungraceful dance. I could almost smell the pungent onion-like scent that was emanating from him. Franco stood at the back of the stage, arms crossed under his leather jacket, bleached teeth bared. After a few more seconds of the performance, Dakota slipped on something–sweat, probably– and fell ass first, but immediately sprung back up as if the floor were on fire, and bowed to the audience, panting. The song hadn't even finished playing. The crowd was silent until Franco started slow-clapping mockingly and the crowd joined him.

"You may be asking yourselves 'What does ballet have to do with personal superation?'" Franco said, pushing Dakota to the side with what looked like a little too much strength, based on Dakota's stumbling. "And the answer is: *everything*. I will explain it all to you, but first let's give my nephew another round of applause."

The audience clapped, this time with more enthusiasm. Some-one whistled ironically. "What you just saw," Franco continued, "is the attitude that I want every single one of you to have when you return home after the conference. Because you see, young Dakota here has a case of *mild* cerebral palsy."

What the fuck?

Some whispers from the audience started, and Dakota stormed out of frame. "I think that's evident from his performance, but my nephew doesn't care about that. What you saw was a young man doing what he *loves*, despite his *mental challenges*. He's always per-severing, you see, and if he can manage to perform his little routine in front of thousands of people without caring about his lack of skills, *then why the fuck can't you do the same and take control of your fucking lives?*"

The audience roared. Keesha zoomed into Franco's face and I could almost see lust in his eyes, as if he was getting off from the attention he was receiving. He let the ovation go on for close to a minute before he asked for silence. "That's the attitude I want you to have from now on," he said and tipped his fedora. "Life will throw punches at you every day, sometimes more than once, but you gotta learn to take them like a man and keep moving forward. You can lose your job, get a divorce, go bankrupt," *–the fuck?–* "but as long as you make the decision to keep your head high and move on, *nothing* will stop you. It also helps if you buy all of my books, of course." Some people chuckled and Franco's toxic smile widened. "Eventually life will see that you're one tough motherfucker and it will get better."

I stopped the video.

I felt gross. I knew I was working for a crook, but seeing how blind and indoctrinated his fans were was a revelation. They all looked like normal, reasonable people–and if I saw them on the street I wouldn't even think that they shared any of Franco's sick beliefs–; that's what worried me. That you really never know how rotten a person can be.

If I hadn't been forty kilometers away from the city I would have walked back to Cliff's. I felt dirty by staying at the place Franco called home.

4

The following day I received even more videos from the conference, but I did not get to edit them until I had applied online for almost every available job in White Peaks I found. At 2 PM I begrudgingly edited a few clips, making sure to only select the parts of Franco's speeches that contained some semblance of actual good advice, which proved to be no easy task. But having a one camera set-up also made editing kind of hard.

For the first time in a very long time, I did not feel hungry all day. After spending four hours watching and listening to the same videos of Franco, I went up to the kitchen and made a bologna sandwich. I took it along with a bag of chips to the living room and forced myself to eat it while I watched *The Disaster Artist* again.

5

I made the decision not to tell Stella about Franco's secrets so that it didn't ruin her mood the same way it had ruined mine. I'd given her detailed directions on how to get to the lake house, and I even shared my location with her on a Facebook message, but I still waited on the side of the road, next to the *D'Amico - 122* sign to make sure Stella wouldn't miss the hidden driveway.

My phone started vibrating in my pocket, and I immediately took it out without taking my eyes away from the road. "Hey, where are you?" I said, squinting to try to see her car in the distance.

"Uh, still in North Bay." It was Jude.

"Oh. Hi."

"We're going to have to stay here for an extra day, maybe two."

"What happened?" I asked, noticing the loud voices in the background.

"We, uh, had a bit of an accident."

"What? Are you okay?"

"Yeah, it wasn't *that* kind of accident. More like an incident I guess. Did you see the video of Dakota and Franco?"

"Of course. What a shitshow."

"Yeah, it was, uh, rough. Well apparently he didn't spend the night at the hotel but nobody realized it until today. Franco got us all separate rooms. Anyway, he was ignoring everyone's calls this morning, so we got worried and someone from the front desk went to his room checked in on him."

"Shit."

"It's all good. He wasn't dead or anything, he was just gone."

"So where is he?" I asked, knowing that if they were extending their stay, it was probably because they still hadn't found Dakota.

"I don't know. Franco got all freaked out and rented a car to look for him in the city. We tried to tell him to give him some space, it's not like he was going to stay in North Bay forever, right?"

"Right." *Except I do think he would do something like that,* I thought. *There's something not right with that guy.*

Jude sighed. "And now Franco is in an even worse mood."

"Is that even possible?" I said and saw a familiar car approaching.

Jude said nothing for a second or two. "He can get really scary, dude. He was speeding all over town, and a policeman eventually stopped him. We were all in the car with him. Bailey kept trying to hold my hand every time Franco sped up. Anyway, when the policeman stopped the car Franco tried to pretend he was like, I don't know, a celebrity or something, but the policeman took his license away from him. He was like thirty kilometers over the speed limit."

"Are you kidding me?"

"No. So we've been at the police station for a while. Franco's been trying to talk to someone to get his license back, and he's really mad. I had to get out of there because I wanted to give you a heads up. He said we'll stay here until we find Dakota, he's his nephew, you know?"

I nodded even though I knew Jude couldn't see me.

"And he booked us all another night at the hotel."

Stella slowed her car and stopped next to me. I waved my free hand in the direction of the long driveway that led to Franco's residence and she drove on. "Do you think you guys will find him soon?" I said and started walking back to the house.

"Oh yeah, he's probably just mad, I'm sure he'll show up at the hotel later."

"Keep me posted my dude, good luck."

Jude thanked me and I hung up.

6

Stella always makes things better. She wasted no time and ran straight to the lake as soon as she exited her car, carelessly tossing away her clothes, leaving a colorful trail for me to follow. I had never skinny dipped before, but that day we spent almost three hours in the cool lake waters until the skin of our hands and feet looked like they belonged to an old couple who had spent many decades together.

After we dried ourselves under the hot sun we put our pants, socks and shoes back on and we wandered into the woods. The needles from the tall firs filled the air with a sweet yet strong smell that somehow managed to both perfume and purify your body as you breathed in and out. We walked until our legs started to ache and only then did we decide to turn around and go back to the lake house. At that moment I didn't even care that Franco owned it.

We ate, made love and ate some more after that. "Yeah," Stella said, laying on my chest and tracing imaginary lines with her fingers on my stomach. "I guess I could live in a place like this."

"I could too," I said, playing with her hair. "But I think I'd prefer a house that's a little smaller than this."

Stella moved her head and looked up at me. "Why?"

"Because it's way too big. I felt pretty lonely this weekend."

Stella breathed in, paused for a second and exhaled. "Yeah, I guess you're right." Her voice had that sleepy, no, dreamy tone that she had whenever she was tired and which I loved.

I tried to reach her forehead to give her a kiss but she moved her head up a little more, letting me find her lips, and soon enough we started *cuddling* again.

***

Stella left the house at midnight, almost dragging her feet out of exhaustion and reluctance, and drove home. I went back to bed and fell asleep immediately. I had a pleasant night.

7

Three short buzzes woke me up. I yawned, turned to my left and grabbed my phone from the nightstand. It was Jude.

We found Dakota at the hotel last night.
We'll fly back today at 5:30.
Are you still staying at Franco's?

Oh good.
Yeah, I am.

Okay, he wanted to make sure you're still watering his plants.

How is his mood now?

8

I made sure to clean after myself during the days I stayed at the lake house, so that by the time Franco and the *dream team* came back I wouldn't have to spend hours making sure every room was organized and every pot and pan was clean, but after their disastrous last part of the trip, I did just that anyway. I wanted to make sure not to stoke the flames of Franco's anger.

I spent all morning sorting out all of the remaining tools from the "office", taking out the garbage, sweeping the floors of every single room–including the ones where I had not stepped a foot on–, and watering his plants.

Sometime after six in the afternoon I finally let myself have a break and I went to the room where I had slept to sit down for a moment, having already packed everything I'd brought, when I saw the copy of *And Then There Were None* laying on the floo. I went to pick it up and my heart sank when I saw that the back cover and a few of the final pages of the book were bent pretty badly. I tried to straighten them as best as I could, but there was still a visible crease mark on it, like an ugly scar. *He'll probably never read it again, if he ever did read it in the first place,* I thought. Franco seemed like the kind of person that isn't much of a reader but likes to buy pretty books for his shelves–something that is a whole different hobby in and of itself than reading.

I walked to his office and squeezed the book in the spot where I had taken it from, in between two other cheesy mystery novels, but the creased corner fought its way outwards and created an irregular gap which was just barely noticeable, but noticeable nonetheless.

The sound of keys unlocking the front door made me panic, but also helped me come up with an idea. While feet shuffled and suitcases rolled on the first floor, I opened one of the drawers from Franco's fancy desk and I looked for some scrap paper. I found a stack of notebooks and when my hands felt the smooth laminated texture of a magazine at the bottom I instinctively grabbed it, not realizing that it was much more possible for Franco to notice that someone looked into his drawers than a little crease in one of his many books.

"Marco?" Franco yelled. He sounded more tired than annoyed. That was good. "Where are you? Did you water my plants?"

"Coming!" I said and rushed to the bookshelf to rip some paper off the magazine to stick between books and flatten the gap. I almost didn't notice the young, androgynous man on the cover, wearing nothing but a police hat, a belt with a fake gun hanging from it and a thong so tight that it showed a clear outline of his... you know what.

"... looks like he cleaned," Franco's voice was growing louder. He was getting closer.

I blinked repeatedly, as if by doing that the magazine would magically disappear, but after a moment I ran back to the desk and replaced July's issue of *Members Only* at the bottom of the drawer.

I made it back to the living room before Franco had the time to see me walking out of his office.

9

Franco was too tired from the trip, so he dismissed us shortly after. Jude drove us all back to our homes, me being last, as usual. I thanked him, said I'd see him later and exited the car. *Oh, that's weird,* I thought when I saw through the window that Cliff's big TV was off for once. I unlocked the door and walked in. The house was indeed quiet. I started to take my shoes off when the silence was broken. "Marco, come here for a moment please," Cliff said from the kitchen table, I assumed.

I could tell something was off, but I didn't know what it was. Cliff was sitting at the head of the table and had an open envelope laying in front of him. "Hey, um, I'm a bit tired, and I think we should chat another—"

"Why did you lie to me?"

My heart sank. "What?" I said, though I already had an idea of what might have been inside the envelope.

"Marco, I'm not stupid. Sit, please," Cliff said and tossed the envelope at me.

I opened it and found a roughly made paystub. *Fuck.*

"I'm sorry that I opened your mail, it was an honest accident, but why should I care if you've been lying to me for weeks now."

"Yeah, why *do* you care?" I said, both to Cliff's and my surprise. "What I do and who I work for is my problem."

"You are not going to talk to me like that while you're living in my own house," Cliff said, his face turning red. His neck tensing. "I told you not to work for a piece of shit like Franco. But did you listen to me? No, you always–"

"Of course I didn't listen to you," I said and sprung to my feet. The chair stumbled but did not fall. "Working at the coffee shop was the worst time I've had in my life and you have no right to tell me what to do."

"*Calm down,*" Cliff said, almost shouting. "*You will not talk to me like that in my own house!*"

"I will talk to you however I please. It's not like I'm not paying you to stay here, but maybe I shouldn't!" I snatched my paystub, turned around and started to make my way to my room.

As I haphazardly packed my phone, some underwear, my computer and other personal belongings. I was already at the door when Cliff slid it open and I found his red, crab-like face inches away from mine. He was incredibly mad, that was obvious. I prepared to get yelled at some more, but, surprisingly, he paused to take a deep breath. When he released it, I smelled a bizarre combination of beer, onions and olives, which only annoyed me further. "Listen," he said to me as I pushed past him and left the room. "I know what I'm doing, that's why I told you to stay away from that son of a bitch."

I said nothing and Cliff followed me to the door. I stopped for a moment to make sure I had enough clothes to last while things cooled down with Cliff–or until I found somewhere else to live. I was sick of Cliff's controlling behaviour and I finally snapped. "I'll see you later, Cliff."

"Well, whatever, do as you please. Just don't come back to me when Franco fucks you up."

I really wish I'd listened to him.

10

Jude let me stay over at his place indefinitely, and the next day that the full team assembled at the D'Amico residence was Wednesday. The decision was made so that Franco could have some time to "recover from a most dreadful weekend" as he had called it. To our surprise, Dakota came back too.

After a quick chat with our boss, in which he spent most of the time sermoning us about the importance of being loyal to your superiors, he sent us down to the "office" with Ron for a *special project.*

"This Sunday is Franco's birthday," Ron said, pacing around the room and inspecting it. Looking for dirt, perhaps. His face looked like he had just smelled or licked something funky. "I borrowed you today so that we can work on organizing a surprise party for him."

"Oh neat. How old?" Keesha asked.

Ron scowled.

"Fifty five," Dakota said from his chair at the end of the table.

"Never mind that," Ron cut in. "We have tons to do and not enough time. We're going to have to make some calls."

***

It turned out that Ron had borrowed us for more than just organizing a surprise party. The first thing he did was dividing us into groups. Jude and I were in charge of the food, Bailey and Dakota had the important task of reaching out to our expected guests and convincing them to stop by the house on Sunday despite the short

239

notice for the *Francofest,* as we had dubbed it, and Ron took Keesha with him.

After Bailey gave Jude and I a list of the eight guests who had nothing better to do on Sunday than to come to the party she joined us to help out with the menu. What sounded like an easy thing to do ended up taking almost an hour of discussion, since Bailey thought pizza was too casual, pasta was too messy, and her idea of hiring a caterer to make us a three course supper was too expensive.

"Why don't we just use the barbecue and cook some burgers and hot dogs?" I suggested after much (pointless) deliberation.

"That's also too low-key," Bailey said. "But I guess that will have to do. Do you know how to use the grill?"

"I do," Jude said and proceeded to write down "Bbq" on the notepad Franco had given him for his *team lead* duties.

Even though I love sugary drinks, I'm not much of a cake person, so I tuned out the discussion after Jude and Bailey started talking about what kind of cheesecake would impress Franco. *They got that covered and I'm not really needed anymore,* I thought and went to see what everyone else was up to.

Ron and Keesha's voices led me to the rec room. I stood in the hallway, listening.

"They don't have it."

Ron scoffed. "Okay, now call the other Walmart."

"Isn't there only one?"

"The one across the river, girl," Ron said, as if it were obvious, and gave her a phone number.

After a few seconds, Keesha said, "Hi there. Do you have the new Britney Spears perfume, it's called–"

"*Prerogative!*"

"Prerogative?" A pause. "Okay, no problem." There was another, longer pause. "Okay, thanks. Nope."

"Ugh, okay. Let's try Target now."

I tried to figure out what was more bizarre, that our work day involved planning a birthday party for our boss and making international phone calls asking about Britney fucking Spear's new perfume or the fact that we were getting paid to do both. I let Keesha's inquiries fade away and I walked upstairs to get a glass of water from the kitchen.

11

I pressed the fridge's dispenser and poured three ice cubes in my glass, then water.

"Marco?"

I turned around and put my glass down. Franco's dead shark eyes were surveying me. "Hi Franco," I said, "I didn't hear you coming."

His grin didn't reach his eyes, as usual. "Are you busy right now?"

I thought about telling him that I was a bit tied up, with all the tasks Ron had given me, but he continued talking before I could give him an answer.

"Come on, let's go to my office. I want to see what you did over the weekend."

*****

The first thing I did when we entered Franco's office was looking over at the spot in his shelf where I'd put *And Then There Were None*. The gap was still there, but it was much less noticeable.

Franco slumped on the chair behind his fancy desk. "Sit," he said.

I did as he said and I put my laptop on his desk, at an angle, so both of us could see it.

"So, let's see what this little Kubrick has to show me."

I cringed, opened my mouth to say something, thought better of it when I saw his smile had disappeared, and closed my mouth again. I played the six clips I'd prepared for his YouTube channel one by one.

Franco remained in silence until the very last one ended. "That's it?" he snapped.

"Uh, yes."

Franco closed his eyes and rubbed his temples, crunching and flattening his wrinkles. It made him look both older and more *real*, for some reason. "Where should I begin?"

I gulped.

"Why are the cuts so jarring?"

"Well, it's because there was only one camera shooting the speeches," I said, no longer containing my urge to scratch the back of my left hand. "So, you see, in order to make the clips more concise and *YouTube friendly* I had to cut some stuff out, because audience spans are shrinking and shrinking."

"Oh, I understand that," Franco said, locking his eyes on mine and leaning over his desk to get a little closer to me. Enough to make me feel more uncomfortable. "What I don't understand is why you didn't think to tell me that we needed two cameras to get my videos to look the way I wanted them."

"I–"

"I even showed you examples of what I wanted the first time we met. Didn't I?"

"Y-yes, but–"

"But what?" Franco barked.

"I thought you were set on bringing Jude, Keesha and Dakota to the trip."

"I was, but I also expect my employees to let me know when I'm not making the right decisions." He shut the laptop close and stood up. "Tell me, did I make a mistake when I hired you?"

"No," It came out sounding almost like a question. "I'm sorry for not speaking up."

"Don't be sorry, just do better next time, for Christ's sake," he said and walked around the desk to stand next to me.

I somehow managed to look up at him. "I will," I said. I tried to sound firm, which I thought Franco would approve of, but I could tell that he knew it was just an act. Sometimes I'm just a coward.

"Good, now go back to the office and keep helping Ron with whatever the fuck he wanted you guys to do."

I got up and went to the door.

"Oh, one more thing," Franco said, sitting on his chair again.

"Yes?"

"Stop scratching your hand, it's gross."

12

Someone (probably Ron) leaked the secret about the *Francofest* and it eventually made it to Franco's ears, so his mood improved over the days leading up to the party. We, however, felt as if we were walking on eggshells, so when Franco asked us to finish building the deck "in case there's any festivities on the horizon", as he had put it, we obliged.

We spent eight hours on Thursday sweating, sawing, whining, hammering, complaining, and sweating again in order to build the stupid deck. I'm fairly sure that if Franco had hired real contractors—or even regular people who, unlike us, knew what they were doing—it would have taken them half the time it took us.

Twice that day Franco took a break from tanning and drinking hard liquor at his little private beach and went into the kitchen to bring us a jar of store-bought lemonade. "Don't want any of you to get a heatstroke," he'd said. It was late July and the temperature didn't get below thirty two degrees celsius until the evening, so it was a miracle that the worst thing that happened to us that day was getting nasty farmer tans.

"Excellent! Great job team!" Franco exclaimed when he saw the finished deck. "I'm honestly surprised, it took you guys forever to build it but it was *so* worth it in the end. Now, as a token of my appreciation, you can use tomorrow to get ahead on any secret projects you may have." He winked at us and Ron let out a girly giggle. "Just check in with me in the morning and again in the evening before you leave."

***

On Friday we accomplished many "important" things, which included buying an obscene amount of hot dogs and frozen burger patties, going to *Dairy Queen* to grab an ice cream cake because Jude and Bailey never ended up agreeing on whatever cheesecake flavor they wanted, and harassing on the phone the guests who hadn't RSVP'd.

By the end of the day we returned to Franco's with his *Range Rover* full of all of the supplies for the party, which he had insisted on letting us borrow because he "had a feeling that we'd need to go to town for some of our tasks." I'd only ever seen him this excited when he was receiving that ovation at the North Bay convention.

"Is your hand okay?" Jude asked when I got out of the car outside of my place, looking at my moist bandage.

"Oh yeah, it's just my rash," I said. "It's nothing."

Jude raised his eyebrows. "Are you sure?"

"Yeah," I lied. "But thanks for worrying."

At the end of the day I excused myself and went to Jude's bathroom to remove the bandage, and winced when I saw what was underneath. My eczema patch had grown another quarter inch in diameter, and there were a few spots on it that were both bleeding and weeping a liquid similar to pus, on the areas where my nails had broken skin. I had forgotten to take my eczema cream with me when I left my room back at Cliff's and I kept forgetting to buy a new one.

I washed my hands with care and re-bandaged my rash. I went back to the couch where I'd slept the past couple of nights and called Stella on the phone while Jude was in his bedroom, probably watching porn.

Stella's voice greeted me after the third beep. "Hey Marco, how was your day?"

"Actually, not too bad, for a change."

"That's good! Have you heard anything back from the jobs where you applied for?"

I sighed. "No, not yet."

"Still? Oh well, just give it some time, I'm sure something will come up."

I wasn't feeling as confident about that as she did, but I also didn't feel like contradicting her. "Hey, um, I don't think I'll be able to skip Franco's birthday party after all, so would you like to come with me?"

"To a nice lake house to have some delicious food and enjoy the nice weather? I don't know," she said in a not very convincing sarcastic tone. "Let me check my schedule."

I chuckled. "Well, I can go on my own if you want–"

Stella made a clicking sound with her mouth. "No, it looks like I'm free that day. Of course I'll go!"

"Okay, it's a date."

13

The sky was gloomy and threatened Franco's party with wind and rain early in the morning, but the weather eventually improved and by the time that I got to Stella's house to help her with her famous macaroni salad. "The secret is to use real mayo, not that cheap *Miracle Whip*," she said, taking out a measuring cup and scooping some *Hellmann's* into it. "You also *have* to get the small shells, not the mini or the baby ones, so that they're relatively small but big enough for the cheese cubes to get in. *That's crucial.*"

At first I was in charge of slicing the pickles and cheese, but my knife skills weren't up to my girlfriend's high standards, so I was demoted from cutting duty to simply boiling the pasta. *I can't mess this up,* I incorrectly thought to myself, because we had to run to the store to buy another package of small shells after I forgot to let them soak in cold water to prevent them from sticking.

When we got back to Stella's house, I decided to just sit at the kitchen table and refresh my emails on my phone every five minutes, hoping that some store manager would be interested in hiring me, but the only emails I received that day were spam.

14

We could hear the soundtrack of the party–Justin Bieber's *Despacito*, a personal non-favorite of mine–as we turned right on the long driveway that would take us to Franco's house. There were ten or twelve cars already parked at the front of the house, but Jude's *Big Piece of Shit* was missing.

We let Justin's awful song lead us to the backyard, where twenty or so people, most of them I didn't have a clue who they were, spread out all around the property. Three old and incredibly obese ladies, each one wearing bright colored tank tops and skirts that enveloped their beefy legs to their ankles, were sitting on white beach chairs at the edge of the deck. They all had a red plastic cup in their hands, the rims adorned with slices of lemon and miniature Hawaiian umbrellas, and they did not seem to notice neither Stella nor I, as they were deep in conversation with each other. Once in a while they would laugh and display their missing teeth at the back of their mouths.

We walked past the happy, colourful ladies and placed our macaroni salad on a flimsy foldable table, in between other summer pasta salads, none of which I found appetizing in the slightest, but that was because I'm more of a hot meal kind of guy. I poured Diet Coke in a cup for us, and Stella smiled when she saw that I didn't forget to add a lemon slice on her drink.

Franco was down at the beach, wearing a pink fedora I'd never seen before and turquoise swimming shorts. He was showing off his jet ski to a couple in their late forties. "Anyone is welcome to try this bad boy out!" I heard him say. He sounded either very merry or slightly tipsy.

"So that's your boss?" Stella whispered, as we walked towards the birthday boy to congratulate him.

"Yep, that's the one."

"He does *not* look the way I imagined him."

"And how was that?" I asked, lowering my voice.

"I don't know, like, manly," she said. "Didn't you say he's all about toxic masculinity?"

"Actually, I gotta tell you something I found out about him when I stayed over–"

"*Marco!*" Franco bellowed. He waved his hand at me, spilling some of his drink in the process. "Come over here!"

I waved back and forced a smile. Stella did the same, but hers looked much more genuine than mine. "Hi Franco, this is my girlfriend Stella," I said and the middle aged couple that Franco was showing his jet ski off to took the opportunity to leave.

"Stella, what a nice name," Franco said, whiffs of alcohol escaping through his mouth. "I had a cat named Stella once. How did you two meet? Couldn't find anything better? *Hwa-ha-haaa.*" His laugh sounded like it had come out of a sickly pig.

"It was through a mutual friend," I said. My fake smile had disappeared. "From school."

"Oh, don't get all touchy, I'm just joking. You know how I am. I was just showing Brad and Maude here–" he said, looking around. "They were here just a minute ago, oh well, I was just showing them my jet ski. Feel free to take it for a ride."

"Thank you," Stella said, looking a little more relaxed now that Franco had changed topics. "You have a beautiful house."

"Yeah, I got my little piece of paradise by the lake, don't I? If you and Marco want to stay over for a weekend you're more than welcome to," Franco said, taking another sip from his cup. Scotch was my guess. "I like taking care of *my people.*"

"Well, I think we will go get some refills," I said despite having most of our cups half full. "But we'll chat some more later."

"Right," Stella said. "And thanks for having us over, I brought some macaroni salad, hope you like it."

But Franco was not listening anymore. Something behind us had claimed his attention"Jude! *My boy!*" he yelled. "What do you have over there?"

And just like Brad and Maude did, we took our opportunity to leave. "That's my boss," I said to Stella once we were far enough from Franco so he wouldn't hear us.

"*Wow.*"

"Yeah."

I waved Jude (and Bailey too I guess, since they were walking together). They were bringing the ice cream cake. Through the plastic cover I could see *Happy 25th Birthday Franco* written with red frosting. "Good luck my dude," I said to Jude. "He's already a little buzzed."

"Isn't it a bit too early to drink?"

"Not for him."

I briefly introduced Stella to Bailey and we continued our way to the flimsy drinks table to get more Diet Coke.

15

After eating a plate full of Stella's macaroni salad–mine with all the tuna, peas and pickle chunks scooped out–, we went inside the house to change into our swimming suits.

The breeze was mild and the sun was strong. My skin was still a bit red from my last sunburn, so Stella covered my body with half a bottle of sunscreen, making me look like Michael Jackson's hispanic (and overweight) doppelganger. We went to the lake but as soon as I dipped my toes in the water I took a step back, goosebumps making the hairs on the back of my neck stand up.

"What are you doing?" Stella asked, already waist-deep into the lake.

"Nothing." I took a deep breath and walked a few steps in. "The water's a bit cold, that's all."

"Are you serious?"

"Yeah."

Stella sank in completely for a couple of seconds and re-emerged, passing her hands through her wet hair, as if she had done it to prove to me that the temperature of the lake was exquisite. "It doesn't get any warmer than this," she said. "At least not in Canada."

I tried easing myself into the lake, little by little, but the farthest I got in was just below my balls, which kept receding with every little step I took. "It's fine, have fun. I'll go back to the house and hang out there," I said after I admitted to myself the futility of trying to dive into the water.

Stella put her fists to either side of her hips and frowned. "Are you sure? I can go with you if you want."

"No, it's okay. I don't want to ruin your fun."

We talked in circles for a few minutes, and when I finally convinced her that I was going to have a good time just sitting on the deck and reading one of Franco's books, I walked out of the lake.

16

This time I chose Truman Capote's *In Cold Blood*. On my way out of Franco's office I looked back, and stood still for a minute. *Should I?* I thought. *Yes, why not.* I went back to the desk and opened the bottom drawer. The gay porn magazine was still at the bottom, underneath a pile of papers. *You're a big ass liar,* I said to myself. I knew from the moment I met Franco that he was full of shit, speaking out of his butt and marketing it expertly to cater to dumb men who still believed in self-help books, but the fact that even his *alpha male* persona (and his sexuality, for that matter) was fake came to me somewhat as a surprise. I turned around and looked through the window. Franco was still at the beach, laying on a chair and sunbathing. A can of beer on a little table next to him. I considered looking over more of his belongings, but I was scared of what I might find, so I left.

Two of the three colorful old ladies were gone, so I sat on one of the empty and warm chairs they left behind. I had just finished reading the first ten or so pages of the novel when the remaining old lady lowered her sunglasses, gave me a quick look and said, "Aren't you a little too young to be hanging out with Franco?"

I put the novel down. "I guess you could say that. I'm Marco, one of his summer students."

The old lady gave me a motherly smile. "Rose, nice to meet you. I'm Franco's big sister."

"Oh, sorry, he never–"

"Yeah, he's a secretive little shit, Franco. It's nice to meet you." She offered me her hand and I shook it. "So tell me Marco, what did the old timer hire you to do? Are you his new personal assistant or something? Maybe his new maid?"

"No, that would probably be Ron."

"Ugh, he's still around?"

I snorted. "Yeah, unfortunately."

Rosemary shook her head. "I never liked that bitch boy, he just encourages Franco when *he* is being a little bitch."

Oh Rosemary, where have you been all this time? "Yep. You got that right."

"And you know why he does it, don't you?" Rosemary said and gave me a little wink. "Money. He's just a parasite, suckling my brother's tit for a pretty penny."

"He's not only doing that, do you know what he did with us, like, uh, me and the rest of the summer students, just a few days ago?"

"Of course, please, do tell."

"He *borrowed* us all day to organize this surprise party–"

Rosemary roared with laughter. "No he didn't."

"That's not all, he also spent like an hour getting one of my friends to call a bunch of stores to see if they got a new perfume."

"You gotta be kidding!"

"Fuck. I wish I was."

"Say, wouldn't you get another drink for a pretty old lady like me?"

I didn't mind. Not at all. I went into the house and refilled Rosemary's cup with another margarita.

"Thank you, son. My knees aren't what they used to be twenty, no, even just ten years ago."

"No problem. Mine are still okay," I said, sipping at my diet coke. "For now, at least."

"Enjoy it while you can. Youth disappears in the blink of an eye," Rosemary said, sounding less cheery and more contemplative now. "You never told me what you do for my brother."

"Oh yeah, right. Well, I was hired to be one of his videographers." I thought about specifying that I was supposed to be his editor, but I doubted she'd know what that meant, and I didn't feel like explaining it to her anyway. Rosemary striked me as one of those people who thought you still needed actual 35mm film to make videos.

"Oh yeah? And what's what you *actually* do for him?" She no doubt knew her brother very well.

I wonder why he's never mentioned her before, I thought. *Or anyone else from his family.* "Do you want the truth?" I asked.

"Always,"

"See this nice deck over here?"

Rosemary opened his mouth to say something but stopped herself after a moment of hesitation. "No!"

"Yep. Again, I wish I was joking, but I'm not. We built his fucking deck. He also got me to paint the basement, do some landscaping, house sit, and a bunch of other shitty things. I didn't mind house sitting, actually."

"I bet. He does have a beautiful place," she said and took another sip of her margarita. "Have you ever made any, what is it you're supposed to do? Videos?"

"Yeah, but I only got to do it once. He didn't like them."

"I wouldn't take that personally. He doesn't like anything but himself."

I didn't know what else to say, so I imitated her and drank from my cup, abstaining from making any more ani-Franco comments. I felt comfortable enough to say bad things about Ron, but although Rosemary sounded like she was almost inviting me to talk shit about Franco, he was still her brother and she must still care a lot about him. Maybe.

"Oh come on, I thought we were having a nice honest chat here. What happened, the mouse ate your tongue? Or was it Ron?"

"It's not that. I had a pretty awful job before this, so I feel like I owe Franco some respect."

"You think?"

I frowned, as if in doing so I could think better. I made no reply.

"I mean, he lied to you about what you'd be doing here all summer, or did he flat out tell you that he was just looking for cheap labor to fix up his house?"

"No."

"Some food for thought. Don't let anyone abuse you like that and convince you that you owe them anything. Not even my brother."

She was right, but my coffee shop, the Toronto trip and Franco had made sure to make me feel, in some strange way, castrated. I was still surprised that I snapped at Cliff. That summer had both turned me into a sad, submissive man while also giving me a lot of anger and resentment that I somehow managed to bottle up, for now.

17

The first unexpected thing that happened that day was when Dakota arrived unexpectedly. He was wearing a straw hat—one that reminded me of the people back home who sold magnets with bright letters spelling *Mazatlan* to American tourists at the beach—, a wife beater vest and black swimming shorts.

Franco must have been in a great mood (and pretty drunk) because he gave Dakota the same speech he'd given all of his guests about how the jet ski was available to anyone who wanted to take it out for a ride. Dakota was the first person to accept Franco's invitation, and Keesha, who had shown up to the party shortly after Dakota, decided to sit behind him on the jet ski and go around the lake.

The *Francofest* continued and at six o'clock Jude and Bailey lit up twenty five individual sparkling candles, and all of the attendants of the party started singing a very uninspiring rendition of *Happy Birthday.* "Oh guys, you *really* shouldn't have!" Franco said when our mediocre chorus was done and blew out the candles after three or four tries. "Now, who wants to volunteer to take a group photo?"

Nobody replied, so I raised my hand.

"No, I'll do it," Stella said, taking her phone out. "I'm here only because Marco brought me anyway."

"Excellent, thank you Stella," Franco replied. He produced his own phone from his pocket and handed it to her. "Take one with mine too, *please and thank you.* By the way, I *loved* your macaroni salad, you'll have to give me the recipe."

Stella smiled the brightest out of everyone else on the other side of the camera. Her salad was her pride and joy, after all. She snapped two or three pictures on each phone and then everyone went back to what they were doing. It would have been an actual good day, had it not been for the *jet ski situation.*

18

I was sitting at the beach with Stella—both of us had bellies full of delicious ice cream cake—when I noticed that something very wrong was going on. Dakota had taken Jude as his passenger after Keesha had decided to stay on the deck to drink in earnest. They, however, had only managed to drive a few meters into the water before the jet ski stopped. I watched them arguing for a few moments before I decided to go see what was going on. "Hey, what's up?" I asked, trying to control my shivering body. The water only reached my knees but it was cold as fuck.

Jude was kneeling with his arm underwater, trying to reach something beneath the jet ski. "Huh? Oh, it's you. The jet ski sucked, uh, a piece of the rope that was attached to the back."

"Now the engine won't start," Dakota said, not sounding worried in the slightest.

I, on the other hand, was already starting to panic. "Crap. And you can't get it out?"

Jude stood up and shook his wet arm. "We've been trying, but I think we need to get some tools–"

"*What the fuck did you do now?*" Franco yelled, startling me and Jude, and walked into the lake towards us. His fedora had slipped from his head and was now bobbing calmly on the water a few meters behind him. After a second or two it got too wet and began to sink.

Jude opened his mouth but Franco pushed him aside before he could say anything. "*Why do you always find a way to fuck things up?*" He was talking directly to Dakota now, spit flying out with every word he said.

"It's okay, we can fix it," Jude managed to say, taking a step back.

"I wasn't talking to you, now, was I?" Franco asked. Rhetorically, of course.

Dakota said nothing, but he had turned his hands into fists and they were trembling slightly at his sides, as if he were containing an urge to punch him, just like he'd done before.

"It wasn't enough for you to make me waste time and money in North Bay, no. *You also had to break my fucking jet ski.*"

"It's okay, I found a video with instructions on how to repair it. It shouldn't take too long," I said in the smallest voice I had, so I wouldn't upset Franco more.

"Well you better get started, then, because if you can't fix it I will deduct the full price of the jet ski from your pay," he said and turned around to return to the party.

***

Jude and I pushed the jet ski towards the dock. We didn't notice that Dakota had left until we were already trying to lift Franco's toy to place it on the wooden boards so we could work on removing the rope.

"No, it won't work," I said after our third attempt. "This piece of shit is too heavy. We need more help."

"I don't know dude, I don't want to go anywhere near Franco until we get this fixed."

"Well, we won't be able to fix it unless we–"

"Hey." It was Stella, walking on the dock towards us.

Jude and I greeted her.

"That was quite a scene."

"Yeah," I said. "Did you hear all of it?"

Stella nodded. "We all did. Your boss is kind of scary. Some old ladies left."

I wonder if Rosemary stuck around, I thought.

"Uh, do you think you could help us lift the jet ski?" Jude said, taking deep breaths out of exhaustion.

"Sure."

Even with three of us we couldn't lift the damn thing, but we were getting close.

"Stella, is Keesha still here?" I said after we were forced to take a break. "I think one more person will do."

"Yeah, she was still around when I came over."

"Could you ask her to come help us?"

She did, and when she returned Bailey had tagged along with them.

***

Franco seemed to have every imaginable tool, so finding the right screwdrivers to remove the lids and cheap plastic parts of the jet ski that we needed gone in order to cut the rope was an easy task. Once that was out of the way, and with the help of a tutorial from a Texas man with a goatee and sports sunglasses, we managed to fix Franco's favorite toy.

We held our breaths for the couple of seconds that it took Jude to turn the engine on and finally exhaled in relief when the jet ski started to move.

I have no idea of how Jude had the balls to take the jet ski for a victory lap after we repaired it, but there are many things about him that I do not understand anyway. I stayed at the dock with Stella for a few minutes, and when I convinced myself that the stupid thing wasn't going to suddenly stop working again we decided it was time to leave. *Way too much excitement for a weekend,* I thought.

Franco, who was staring at Jude, Keesha and Bailey in the water, didn't acknowledge us when we thanked him for having us.

"You really shouldn't let him treat you like that," Rosemary said from her chair after I picked Stella's salad bowl, which was still half full.

"It's easy to say."

"Does that make it any less true?"

Stella and I kept walking. I didn't have the energy to argue with Rosemary, and I have a feeling that Stella didn't either.

19

"I'm so sorry you had to be there for all that," I said to Stella and closed the door of her car.

She had rolled down her window again and the chilly air that had come after the sun fell was blowing on her beach hair. She looked beautiful. Ethereal. "Sorry. What did you say?"

"Uhm, that I'm sorry?"

"Why? You didn't do anything wrong." This was one of the few times that she sounded stern.

"I know, but I brought you here and—"

Stella turned her head to look at me with sad, concerned eyes. "Your boss is not a very nice person."

"No, he's not."

"You still haven't heard anything from any other jobs?"

I shook my head. "No, but maybe I'll still quit. Sometimes I'm scared of him."

"Yeah, I would be too."

Should I tell her about North Bay? No. It won't help. She'll just worry, and I'm doing enough of that for the both of us.

I looked out the window at the trees going by in the twilight, blending together in the night like a deep blue brushstroke as Stella drove us home. "At least he liked your macaroni salad."

"Yeah, right. Didn't you say that he's full of poop?" Stella never swore.

"He is," I said, sticking my hand out of the window to feel the air. It had been a perfectly warm summer day earlier, but now I could almost feel a hint of autumn. "But I did see him serving himself three servings of the salad."

"No way," Stella said, suddenly less worried and half-smiling.

"Yes way. But *someone* was too busy swimming in the lake to notice."

"Well, I do make the best macaroni salad in the land."

"Can't argue with that, even though I don't eat half the stuff you put in it."

Stella shook her head. "If you gave it a chance you'd love it too. You know I'm right."

The rest of the way home felt lighter. Happier, but when I got back to Jude's—he'd given me a key to his place a day after I temporarily moved in—I noticed the thin crusty layer of dry goo and blood that had formed on the back of my left hand. It looked like a yellow, translucent lollipop, dotted with small dark red specks, and a faint acrid smell emanated from it. *Fuck, I might have to get a doctor to get it checked,* I thought. I couldn't even remember scratching it at all that day.

20

There was no trace of autumn in the air the next morning. It was, in fact, the hottest day of that year. We all met at Franco's living room–except for Dakota–at the usual time. "First of all, I would like to thank you all for organizing such a great surprise party," Franco said, not concerned in the slightest about smoking indoors. It was his house, after all, and he didn't seem to give a fuck about courtesy anymore when it came to his employees. "I had a great time... For most of it at least."

Jude and I shared a tense look for just a second before returning our attention to Franco.

Bailey's face was full of color, but not actually blushing. "Thank you for letting us be a part of it," she said. "It was a lot of fun."

Franco bared his teeth in a grin that, as usual, didn't reach his eyes. "Yes it was, wasn't it?"

We all mumbled in agreement.

"Anyhow, the main thing I wanted to talk to you all about was that I'm hosting another seminar in two weeks, this time in Sudbury." Franco put his cigarette butt on a black ashtray on the coffee table, grabbed another smoke and lit it within five seconds. "This time, Keesha, I want both you and Marco to come with me, to make sure we get some good clips for my youtube channel, and that would leave one more spot available. Who wants to volunteer?"

There was nothing but silence and awkward looks.

"Jude? What about you, team lead?"

"Uhh, yeah I guess."

"Excellent! We're going to have *a lot of fun.*"

Not if I quit, I thought and smiled. Franco saw this and his grin morphed into a snare, maybe because he knew what was coming. But none of us did.

***

Ron arrived at the house at noon, while I was doing my task for the day–which was mowing Franco's gigantic lawn–, and went straight to the beach, where Franco was waiting for him with tan lotion and red wine. I could hear them laughing about stupid stuff, the gentle breeze from the lake cooling their saggy middle-aged bodies, while the dark and heavy hair on my head felt like it was melting into my scalp and streams of sweat poured down my face. Even breathing felt hot. The only safety equipment that Franco had provided me with was a pair of rubber boots, which were too large for me.

Jude, Bailey and Keesha were somewhere inside the house, doing more bitch work. I think they may have been cleaning one of the spare rooms so Franco could rent them as B&Bs, but frankly, I don't remember, so for the purposes of this novel, let's say they were indeed doing that. I was incredibly mad at Franco for sending me out to work in the yard while the temperature neared forty degrees celsius and the rest of my friends were at the house, where the AC was always on. To this day, I believe he did that only because Dakota didn't show up to work, and Franco had to make someone else feel miserable to release his frustration from the jet ski incident.

Little by little I marched all over the backyard, pushing the gasoline-stinking lawn mower in front of me like an out of shape mother pushing her baby on a stroller around the neighborhood to make him fall back asleep, except that the thunderous sound of the lawn mower's engine was louder and more savage than the cries of a fussy baby. When I felt like I was halfway done, I saw Ron going inside the house and coming out a few minutes later carrying a tray with a big jar of lemonade. I shut the mower off and followed him across the yard, but when I realized that he had only brought two glasses with him I paused for a moment, disappointed but not surprised. I turned around and headed to the house to drink some cold water instead.

"Are you done?" Franco yelled from his beach chair before I got to the door.

"No," I replied. "I just need to get some water."

He waved a dismissive hand at me and accepted the glass of lemonade that Ron had prepared for him.

Drinking ice-cold water that day felt more satisfying than it ever did in my life. I drank three glasses before I allowed myself to sit on the cool floor for a few minutes to recover. My skin was already turning a few shades more pink and it was emanating heat like a radiator. I leaned my back on the wall and closed my eyes. *I'll just have a little rest,* I thought right before I fell asleep.

"What the fuck are you doing?"

I opened my eyes, sat immediately up and looked around, my heart racing. "W–what?"

"What? What? Why *are you sleeping during work hours? I don't pay you to fucking lay on the floor and snooze like a baby,"* Franco said, shaking my shoulders. I didn't notice at first that he was touching me. His breath smelled strongly of rum.

"I'm sorry, it's just that it's so hot out and I–"

"Oh come on! Don't be a princess, aren't you from Mexico?" He took his hands off me and stood up. "Last I checked, Mexico was *hot."*

"I'm sorry."

"Is that the only thing you know what to say?"

"N–no."

"Then get up and go back to work."

I sprang to my feet and went back outside. I turned on the lawn mower and continued my searing tour of Franco's backyard.

21

I pushed and pushed until my legs throbbed and shook, screaming at, no, begging me to give them a break, but I didn't stop. There were only two things on my mind: fear and anger. There was no room for feeling tired. I had to finish mowing first.

My hands trembled on the lawn mower's handle and my grip on it tightened as I tried to muster enough courage to go to the beach, look at Franco in the eye and quit. But I had to choose the right words, which proved to be harder than I thought. I couldn't just come up with a silly or weak excuse to resign, no, I had to somehow sum up everything I despised about him, his books, seminars and fake persona in a few sentences, because knowing him, he wouldn't let me go on and on shitting on him before he barked back like a mad dog. He loved the image he'd painted of himself as a man that had come from nothing and made a name for himself, and I was sure that anyone who would dare doubt or even question it would bring out the worst out of Franco. *His violent side,* I thought.

That was how the vicious cycle revolved around my head, making me go from fear to anger and back to fear again—because I knew what Franco was capable of doing, and more importantly, what he had actually *done* in the past–, which made it impossible for me to do anything but mow the lawn, soaking my clothes and my boots in hot, sour sweat.

Just keep pushing this shit until you find your missing balls so you stop letting him walk all over you, I said to myself, and that's what I did. I pushed until my head felt like it was going to explode.

Eventually my vision blurred and I lost my balance. I fell on the loose gravel from the path that led down to the beach and my head struck the ground, producing a dull thud. I felt warm blood trickle down my left cheek before everything turned black.

***

Before I regained consciousness, I saw blurry shapes and heard distant, echoey voices saying things I couldn't quite understand. Then, I felt a splash of water on my face and I woke up.

"I think he's okay," one of the voices said. I rubbed my eyes with my filthy hands and saw it was Bailey.

"My goodness, you scared the shit out of me," Keesha said.

Jude crouched, gave Bailey another glass of water and said, "I told you he was fine. It was just, uh, a heat stroke or something."

I licked my wet lips and Bailey handed me the glass. I drank it all in one go. "Can I have some more?"

She took the glass from me and gave it to Jude. "Yes, of course," she said.

"What happened?" My vision was back to normal, and I saw–despite the burning in my eyes–my friends gathered all around me, not hiding the concern on their faces.

"I don't know, we just saw you laying on the ground and went to pick you up," Bailey said, giving me more water. "We don't know how long you were on the floor. Jude picked you up."

I drank, wiped my mouth with the back of my filthy left hand and said, "Did Franco even notice?"

I received no answer, but no answer was all I needed. Of course he didn't notice, and if he did, I'm sure he wouldn't have given a rat's ass about it.

My head was still throbbing, but much less now. I rubbed my temples and finished my last sip of water. I tried to stand up, stumbled, and decided that sitting down would be best, at least for a little longer. "I'm done," I said. "I'll quit as soon as I feel good enough to stand up. Can someone get me something for the pain?"

Bailey left the living room to get me the over the counter drugs I needed while Keesha sat down next to me and said, "Do you have another job or–?"

"No, but being unemployed will be better than this."

"Yeah, I guess so."

Bailey came back with two maroon pills and gave them to me. I dry-swallowed them, and eventually my friends left me to continue their bitch work.

***

The mirror showed me a sunburnt face, soiled with black stuff and swollen. There was a small cut above my eyebrow. I knew it was me, but I was still surprised to see how rough I looked, not only from my fall, but also from the stress I had been under most of the summer: I looked like a fucking mess. *I just can't catch a break, can I?* I thought to myself. I let the water run down the sink, grabbed a bar of soap and started to slowly clean myself up. I winced when the soapy water touched my cuts, and then again when I removed the debris from my face.

When that was taken care of, I opened the mirror, took out a bandaid and covered the deep cut above my eyebrow. My headache was subsiding, but before I exited the bathroom I grabbed another ibuprofen pill for later.

***

Franco was sitting by himself at the beach, opening another bottle of wine when I came out of the house. With each step that took me closer to him my mind felt clearer and the pounding inside my head moved town to my chest, making my heart feel like rudimentary war drums.

Franco turned his fat, ugly head towards me when I was still a few meters away from him, and said, "What do you want? Did you finish mowing the lawn?"

"No."

Franco snarled and drank three long sips of wine straight from the bottle. "Then what are you waiting for? I'm not paying to just stand around looking pretty."

Under different circumstances I would have felt uneasy, but I was too mad at the moment, so I brushed his comment off. "I've never felt more disgusted at myself than since I started working for you." Franco didn't react the way I expected him to. In fact, it seemed like he didn't hear me at all, so I continued. "I was hired to edit videos for you and–"

"I hired you to do whatever the fuck I wanted," he said, dragging his words clumsily and aknowledging me again. "I'm the one that's paying *you* after all."

"Yeah, well, not anymore. I quit."

Franco tried to put the bottle away on the chair next to his but missed and dropped it. Dark red liquid spilling all over the white sand, and the land soaking it. "Ah! Ain't that the drizzling shits!" he said. "You think your Mexican ass is too good to do some good, honest work, don't you? You want to be a movie start or some shit? Well think again, because when you live in White Peaks, you can never leave." He looked inside his pocket for a cigarette, lit it and puffed away. "Trust me, I know what I'm talking about."

"Fuck you."

"Right back at you, princess! Now go home and stop wasting my fucking time."

I turned around and saw the figures of my friends staring at us from one of the big windows on the second floor. I couldn't tell, they were too far away from me to say for sure, but I think they were smiling.

22

"I can't believe you did it," Jude said as I drank more water. My headache had returned and my skin was still burning.

"Me neither. I thought I was going to shit myself, to be honest." Jude had offered me another glass of water, but after my exchange with Franco I felt too proud to accept anything else from him.

"You really should just wait in the car for us to be done though, it's way too hot for you to walk, and I don't know, wouldn't it take you like three hours to get back to town anyway? You might as well just stay here."

Oh, but I was so thirsty. I took the glass of water from Jude, held it above the sink for a moment, thought better of it, and decided to throw it away. It crashed on the floor near the living room.

Jude cringed. "What was that for?"

"I don't know, but it felt good."

"Yeah but now we'll have to clean it."

"Oh yeah," I said. Sorry about that. But anyway, I won't walk all the way back home, I'll ask someone on the road to give me a ride."

Bailey chortled. "Wait, so now you're not only unemployed but also a hitchhiker?"

"I suppose I am."

"I gotta quit too dude," Jude said. "But I can't afford to do it unless I get another job first. I'm scared to even look at how much money I owe in my credit card."

"I'm sure you'll find something soon," I said.

"Yeah, some people from the mall actually called me a while ago to schedule interviews," Jude said, shrugging. "But back then working here didn't feel that bad, so I blew them off."

I sighed and felt heavier all of the sudden. "Lucky bastard, I feel like managers lose interest as soon as they hear my accent. It's not fair."

"No, it isn't. But I'll get you a job wherever I end up if I can."

"Thanks. I'll see you on the weekend though, no?"

"Yeah," he said. "Of course. And good luck hitchhiking."

***

In movies, they make hitchhiking seem a lot easier than it is in real life. I walked for about a kilometer because I felt like the more I physically distanced myself from Franco's, the more likely it would be for me to never see him again, to move on. *You can't get off the hook that easily,* a part of me said, so I kept on going, hoping to leave those thoughts behind too.

I eventually got tired of waiting on the side of the road. The sun was just as unforgiving as it had been when I passed out, so I receded toward the woods to find some shelter under the cool shade of a big tree and sat down with my back on the trunk. After a few minutes went by, I started to feel a bit sleepy, and I closed my eyes. I almost didn't hear a bike approaching. I looked up, squinted, and saw a tall boy with straight, blonde-streaked hair rushing down the road with a gym bag by his side. Dakota.

Why is he biking all the way out here? I tried not to think too much about it, but I couldn't deny that, in thet short instant when I'd seen Dakota's face, his usually absent look was replaced with a chilling coldness I'd never seen before. *He probably just lives around here,* I said to myself, not really believing it. As the sound of his bike kept diminishing in the distance, I began to worry.

You're exhausted, physically and mentally. It would be weird if you didn't feel a little on edge right now. Yet deep down, I knew something wasn't quite right. I looked at the road, saw no cars coming from either way, and decided that I might as well go back to Franco's, just for curiosity's sake. *Plus Jude said he'd give me a ride back to his place if I waited for him,* I thought.

I stretched, stood up and made my way back to Franco's for the last time.

23

Despite my aching legs, I managed to get back to 122 Longview Road in less than five minutes, which was saying a lot for a fat Mexican guy with short legs. Dakota's bike was laying on the ground, next to Jude's car.

I walked to the path beside the house and found Dakota, walking down the slope behind the artificial beach. He was holding something in his hand, but either the sun was too bright or my brain refused to recognize the gun until he lifted his arm and pulled the trigger, blowing a hole in the back of Franco's head. His body fell to the floor, not as dramatically as in the movies, but much more... limply.

The deafening clap of the gun made me flinch and start to hyperventilate. I felt dizzy and hot, and I somehow managed to sit on the ground again. I crawled towards the side of the house, behind the garbage bin, and brought my shaking hands up to cover my mouth, with the hops of holding in the scream that was aching to come out. Time felt like it slowed down and, at the same time, it felt like the seconds stretched into minutes, hours, days. My brain couldn't process what had happened before my eyes.

Dakota proceeded to shoot Franco's dead body three more times. He turned around and I felt as if someone else had entered my body and taken control of it, because from one moment to the next, I found myself running into the woods, no longer feeling tired at all.

I stopped about two hundred meters deep, panting with burning lungs. "*What the fuck what the fuck what the fuck.*" Tears started to drip down my cheeks. Tears of anger and confusion. *Jude, Keesha, Bailey. Oh no.* I dialed 911 and sprinted towards the house while the phone rang.

"911 what's your emergency?"

I had to repeat myself twice for the operator to get everything I was trying to say. "I'm outside of White Peaks, at 112 Longview Road. There was a murder and me and my friends are in danger. Please send help."

I hung up the phone and crouched behind Jude's car, hiding from the big glass windows that overlooked the front yard. I hadn't heard any more gunshots since I ran away, but if Dakota had shot someone inside the house I could have missed it.

A few moments later, almost as an answer to my thoughts, I heard a crash followed by a scream, but I couldn't tell from whose mouth it had come from. I knew I couldn't just wait there until the police came, because even speeding it would take them at least twenty minutes or so to arrive at Franco's, but I felt like I wasn't really in control of my body. Most of my actions seemed alien and automatic to me.

You gotta go in and sneak up on him, try to disarm him before it's too late, a voice in my head said, and it was right. I owed it to my friends. I closed my eyes, said a little prayer: *Please, don't let us die.*

***

I turned my head around when I saw the dark red–almost black–puddle of coagulated blood on the sand when I got to the backyard. I threw up. The wind had blown Franco's fedora away, and it was gently floating in the lake, not unlike it had done at his birthday party, indifferent to the horror that was happening. The stillness of the lake seemed like it was mocking us.

More crashes and thuds came from inside the house and made me cringe, but at least I knew that Dakota hadn't finished everyone off. *At least not yet,* I thought.

I dropped to the ground and crawled towards the back door, past the stupid deck we'd built for a dead man. The noises from within the house had subsided. I closed my eyes, took a deep breath that did nothing to calm me down, and went in.

***

I walked across the "office" and stopped at the door which led to the hallway. Footsteps above me let me know that I was safe for the time being. I looked around, as if the answer to my problems were somewhere hidden, and this time, it was.

I opened a big red toolbox and grabbed a large hammer. I had also seen a box cutter, but I didn't mean to kill Dakota–I couldn't even picture myself doing it in self defense–, and decided to leave it in the box.

Muffled grunts, perhaps coming from the gagged mouths of my friends, paved the way for the slow, heavy sound of Dakota's footsteps going down the stairs. All at once I stopped hearing the booming beats of my heart. I slipped my feet out of my sneakers to make less noise on the hardwood floor and headed to the rec room, where I could find a better place to hide.

That ended up being the right move to make, because after I crouched behind one of the La–Z–Boys I saw Dakota's dark shape moving in the direction of the "office". I stayed low, not knowing what to do until I heard the back door open. *What the fuck is he doing?* There was no time to come up with a hypothesis. I had to act quick. Improvise. Just do *something*.

I walked upstairs and found Keesha and Bailey–the latter with a wet, dark circle on her crotch area–, their arms and legs tied up, duck tape wrapped around their mouths, but no Jude. They yelped when they saw me, and I put my index finger in front of my lips. "*Be quiet!*" I whispered and walked to the big windows that overlooked the beach. I saw Dakota coming out of the shed with a red gas container. *Fuck.* I returned to my friends and said, "I gotta hide now, he's coming back and the only thing I can do is wait until he gets distracted so I can hit him with this." I showed them the hammer, which made their bloodshot and teary eyes widen. "The police are on their way."

I left Keesha and Bailey behind, wishing I would have taken the box cutter so I could have given it to them, and went into the bathroom, leaving the sliding door open just a crack so that I could peek into the living room. It didn't take long for Dakota to make it back upstairs. He disregarded the screams from my friends as if they were merely a source of white noise, like the waves of the ocean, and started to dump a thick, transparent liquid out of the red container. I heard my heartbeats thumping in my chest again when he started to pour the trail of gasoline down the hallway, towards my hiding spot.

This is it, I thought. *When he turns around, if he turns around after he soaks the entrance with gas, I'll get out and knock him out.* My tight grip on the hammer was surprisingly firm and steady, turning the palm of my hand white from the pressure, but when he walked past the sliding door my bladder gave in and I wet myself. *Still a coward. Will I be able to do this?* Dakota opened the front door, dumped the last little bit of gasoline on the steps that led up to the house and tossed the red container away.

Dakota walked back into the house, and when he passed the slit I left open to look through, I froze. Cold sweat on my face, hands shaking, smell of urine filling my nostrils. *Do something!* I said to myself, but my body refused to listen. *Your friends are there, in danger. Do something!* My stomach twisted and contorted, and I felt something warm and rumbling on my chest wanting to come out. *Do something!*

Keesha—or maybe it had been Bailey—let out another dull scream, a plea for help that I knew was directed to me, and I finally regained control of my body. I slid the bathroom door open and walked as quickly and quietly as I could. I was just two or three meters behind Dakota, with the hammer secured in my hands, no longer feeling scared, when I heard a grunt coming from our right. Jude smashed a knock-off Japanese vase on Dakota's head, and both dropped on the floor.

I stopped on my tracks and watched my best friend overpowering Dakota, who was trying to reach for something in his pocket. The gun. They were both laying on their sides, Jude wrapping his long, skinny arms around Dakota. I ran and threw myself at them, dropping my hammer in the process. I reached inside the pocket where the gun was waiting, and I took it.

I immediately got back up and unloaded it, and saw that the cartridge was empty.

"Dude, a little help!" Jude cried, still wrestling with Dakota.

I found the hammer on the floor, felt my stomach revolt again, and picked it up. I walked to Dakota and hit him on his forehead, staining the hammer with a couple drops of blood.

24

"Dude what the fuck!" Jude yelled.

"I don't know," I said, looking for a small knife in one of the kitchen drawers. I picked one with a white handle.

"Did you—"

"No, he's still alive. I checked."

Jude opened his mouth to say something, but instead threw up on the floor even though the sink was next to him.

We went back into the living room and I sliced the ropes around our friends' arms and legs. Jude removed the duck tape from their mouths. Bailey and Keesha screamed and stopped him from trying to take the tape off their long hair.

When they were both free, Keesha said, "I fucking quit, man."

"Me too," Bailey replied.

Jude said he'd do the same.

We walked to the front door and stopped when we heard a metallic click. Then another ear-piercing shot followed, and we turned around to Jude sway, and then fall.

Keesha and Bailey let out a blood-curdling scream that, to this day, still haunts my dreams. I somehow managed to take a step forward, and Dakota shot me in the right shoulder. I tackled him before he could shoot me again. I gripped his wrist with both of my hands and slammed his hand against the floor three times, but the bastard wouldn't let go of the gun. I saw Dakota straining and I bit his ear. That's when he finally dropped the gun, letting out a cry of pain, but it was interrupted by something. I turned my head back and saw Bailey, sticking the small knife I'd used to set them free in and out of Dakota's stomach. She was sobbing.

I put the gun in my back pocket and walked over to where Jude lay, not even five feet away from the door. I wanted to lie to him and say that everything would be okay, that the police must be almost here and that they'd take him to the hospital, but I thought that he'd appreciate honesty, and the truth was that I didn't know what was going to happen. I simply sat next on the floor and held him in my arms.

***

Flies had started to swarm around Franco's body at the beach while we waited for... I don't even know what for .

Jude groaned and I let go of him. "No," he said to me, softly. "Don't– don't leave me alone."

"Never."

The police car sirens rang in the distance and Jude smiled. "Maybe I'll be able to make it?"

Keesha and Bailey were a mess, and couldn't articulate a single word, so I spoke. "Of course you'll make it," I said and my voice cracked. I finally started weeping. The sound of cars on the driveway got louder, and, suddenly, the distinct siren of an ambulance reached our ears. "Just hold on a bit longer, Jude."

273

ABOUT THE AUTHOR

Jesús Ernesto Beltran-Ruiz is a Mexican writer based in Sault Ste. Marie, Ontario, where he lives with his wife and his cat. He is happy.

The Lying Tongue